ISBN 978-0-483-77977-8
PIBN 10494212

This book is a reproduction of an important historical work. Forgotten Books uses state-of-the-art technology to digitally reconstruct the work, preserving the original format whilst repairing imperfections present in the aged copy. In rare cases, an imperfection in the original, such as a blemish or missing page, may be replicated in our edition. We do, however, repair the vast majority of imperfections successfully; any imperfections that remain are intentionally left to preserve the state of such historical works.

A DAUGHTER OF MUSIC

NEW NOVELS.

———◆◆◆———

THE SURRENDER OF MARGARET BELLAR-MINE. By ADELINE SERGEANT, Author of 'The Story of a Penitent Soul,' etc. In 2 vols.

BENEFITS FORGOT. By WOLCOTT BALESTIER, Author of 'The Average Woman,' etc. In 3 vols.

A SUPERFLUOUS WOMAN. In 3 vols.
' Uncommonly well worth reading.'—*National Observer.*

THE KING OF SCHNORRERS. Grotesques and Fantasies. By I. ZANGWILL, Author of 'Children of the Ghetto.' etc. With Ninety-eight Illustrations by Phil May, George Hutchinson, and others. In 1 vol. 6s.

OUR MANIFOLD NATURE. By SARAH GRAND, Author of 'The Heavenly Twins,' 'Ideala,' etc. In 1 vol., with portrait of the Author. 6s.

THE RECIPE FOR DIAMONDS. By C. J. CUTCLIFFE HYNE. In 1 vol. 6s.

————————

LONDON :
WM. HEINEMANN, 21, BEDFORD STREET, W C.

DAUGHTER OF MUSIC

BY

G. COLMORE

AUTHOR OF
'A CONSPIRACY OF SILENCE,' 'CONCERNING OLIVER KNOX,'
ETC.

IN THREE VOLUMES
VOL. II.

SECOND EDITION

LONDON
WILLIAM HEINEMANN
1894

.

CONTENTS OF VOL. II.

BOOK II. (*continued*).

A DAUGHTER OF MUSIC

BOOK II.

(Continued).

PAUL GARNET'S MARRIAGE.

CHAPTER III.

Each hath his fortune in his brest.
SPENSER.

THE winter drew on. At Heather Den old
Boniface Wichelow, crouching over the fire
that brought him a shilling every day, found
the long, lonely evenings full of dreariness.
He missed the companionship he had been
used to for so many years ; he missed all that
Rhoda had done for him, and her help in
the management of the farm ; and he
suffered also a more positive trouble, the
discomfort of an unquiet spirit when it is left
alone with itself.

It was very cold at Heather Den ; the
winds blew over and about the house with

all the force gathered in an unchecked rush across the heath ; the frost froze the pipes on the outside walls, and entered the rooms and turned the water in the ewers into ice. Sally shivered in her bed at night, and cursed—though the curse remained unformulated in her heart—her master's 'closeness.' Old Wichelow shivered, too, but with the inward satisfaction that by the shaking of his worn old frame he was saving wood and coals.

At Fanelands Hall the cold was less intense : the wind strove angrily in the woods, crying out with moaning voice against the trees that checked its course ; yet the trees stood bravely, like a guard around the house, and gave it partial shelter ; and when the still frost came, it could not force its way through the thick old walls and bite into the rooms, as it did in the lonely, unprotected house upon the heath. And at Fanelands big fires were always blazing ; in Rhoda's bedroom, with its windows facing north and west ; in her sitting-room down-stairs, where the firelight, dancing and glowing on the white-panelled walls, made winter seem a joyful and lovely thing ; in the great wide fireplace in the hall, where the sparks rushed up in streams from the logs, and the light of the flames fell upon and mocked the organ's dark, mute bulk. Often Rhoda, sitting alone beside the hearth, waiting for Paul to come in from his day's shooting, with no light but the firelight to battle with the early winter darkness, looked at the organ with half-curious, half-fearful eyes, and wondered if it would ever speak again ; for Paul had not touched it since his marriage, and it stood in silence and neglect. Sometimes, looking round from the ruddy brightness of the fire into the moving lights and shades that hung about the pipes and the frame, she almost seemed to see the face of the musician who had given it a brief, wild space of life ; and once she rose up and moved a few steps across the hall, with the feeling strong upon her that if she uncovered the keys, somehow the notes would be pressed down and the pipes would breathe forth sound.

She lived softly now compared with her former rough, hard life at Heather Den. There were not many servants at Fanelands, but enough to let her live at ease, and Paul Garnet liked to give his wife as many luxuries as his straitened means could afford ; she wore more costly and beautiful clothes than she had ever seen before ; there was a refinement and grace in her surroundings which were new to her. She enjoyed the novelty ; the sensuous part of her grasped eagerly at the gratification of those desires, the existence of which in her own nature she had not hitherto suspected. It was pleasant to sit in a room where at every turn her eyes rested on something that pleased them ; it was even more pleasant to exchange the short, scanty frocks of her girlhood for gowns of soft texture and skilful make, that made her seem to herself, when she looked at her likeness in the glass, like some beautiful creature whom she had never known truly till now, familiar yet strange. Yet, as the days went by, time began to lie heavy on her hands, and she longed sometimes for her old rough life at the farm, free in the midst of bondage, full of interest, though narrow and hard. Almost every day she went up to Heather Den to see her grandfather and take him the shilling, the getting of which came to be the chief enjoyment of his life; and often she would go into the farmyard and through the fields, talking to the hard-working men and women amongst whom the greater number of her days had been passed.

'It's harder than ever now you be gone,' old Micah Yates said to her one day. 'It do be like the song says:

'Sorrow and toil, and neither let nor stay.'

'I am sorry, Micah,' she answered; 'and all the more because I cannot come back.'

'For sure not, ma'am.   When a woman takes a man, by her man she must bide, let come what will in the way.'   The old man paused in his digging, and resting one hand on his spade, raised the other to his head, and slowly scratched it.   'And besides,' he said, 'you never could come back—not to what you was—not if it was ever so.'

'Why not?' Rhoda spoke almost sharply; there was something in the old man's words and voice that gave her a sense of being shut out of the world she knew best.

'You're different,' said Micah, 'and none goes back to what they was, when once they is what they wasn't   You're different dressed, for one thing; you're like the ladies I used to see when I was young enough to go to Breybridge of a market day.'

'Clothes don't alter me,' Rhoda said.

The old man shook his head.   'It's as it should be,' he said.   'We allus knew it, all of us, that you was a lady and above the

likes of we—as I hope we behaved to show
it in a proper way ; a born lady, the same as
in the singing, fit to teach and us to learn.'

'When the days get long, I will come and
sing again,' Rhoda said.

'It's a comfort, for sure,' said Micah, 'and
I don't speak alone when I say it. You was
allus a sort of angel to us ; we all looked up
to you—and does still, though being raised
higher gives us further to look.'

'A sort of angel !' The words rang in
Rhoda's ears as she took her way home
through the woods. She had been used to
feel sometimes in these old days at the farm
that as life went on she might rise above the
trials and temptations of the world as she
knew it then, and become, not an angel,
indeed, but a veritable servant of the Lord,
leading a life according to the teachings of
Jeremy Taylor and Henry Law. But Paul
had told her that she would sin easily, and
that goodness was far away from her ; and

she knew now that in what had formerly been
her great spiritual outlet, in the music which
had seemed to raise and purify her, there
lurked a spirit of evil, which had already
shown itself in temptation. What would
become of her? As she entered Fanelands
she heard the report of Paul's gun in the
covert below the house. She took heart;
with Paul she was safe, and the great temptation lay behind her.

That evening Rhoda did not glance back
at the organ as she waited in the hall for her
husband to come in.

CHAPTER IV.

When all sins grow old, covetousness is young.
GEORGE HERBERT.

IT was Christmas Day. In the room at Heather Den old Boniface Wichelow sat huddled over the fire; he had had his Christmas dinner—a lean hen which had ceased to lay—and he now sat down to digest it, and to enjoy the one luxury which he allowed himself on occasions of unusual festivity, a pipe.

It was a still, frosty day, with a wintry sun shining cold on the bare heath and the brown branches of the woods. Everything was very quiet, for Sally had gone to dine and spend the afternoon with friends in the village below, and there was no sound in the bare, cold house but the faint ticking of the kitchen clock and the crackling of the wood on the hearth.

Old Wichelow smoked slowly, lengthening out the enjoyment as far as possible, and getting the utmost that was to be got out of every whiff; but at length the pipe went out. He drew and drew, but there was nothing more to burn in it, and at last, with a sigh, he got up and put it back in its place on the mantelpiece.

When he had done this he stood for several minutes looking into the fire, glancing round the room out of the window, and back at the fire again. After awhile he went into the passage and lifted the bar across the outer door; he entered the kitchen and saw that the back-door was locked and the windows both securely fastened; then he returned to the room. He went over to the windows and drew the curtains across them, leaving in each window a small uncovered space, sufficient to let a scanty stream of light enter the room, but not wide enough to allow anyone outside to see in. Having satisfied himself that he could not be overlooked, he walked slowly across the floor to the opposite wall, stopping now and again to listen for sounds that never broke the stillness, and at last he drew the red curtain aside and entered the room that had been Rhoda's.

Here, too, his first care was to screen the window; then he shut the door; and then he went over to the corner where Rhoda's table had formerly stood. There was a loose stone in the flooring; it was easily detached, but it was heavy, and the old man struggled with it for a minute or two before he could lift it from its place. Beneath it was a hole hollowed out in the earth, damp and irregularly shaped; in the hole was an old tobacco-pouch and many little packets of varying size, wrapped in paper that was mildewed and rotten; a worm wriggled in and out amongst the packets and slid against the old man's hand as he put it cautiously into the hole. He drew out all the contents one by one, first the paper packets, and at the last the old pouch; he spread his handkerchief on the floor and put everything into it. Then he replaced the stone, and, carrying the loaded handkerchief carefully with both hands, returned to the room.

He placed his burden on the settle and left it there a minute while he went across to one of the windows and looked out. There was no sign of life visible on the broad heath; no moving thing broke the expanse of loneliness; old Wichelow replaced the curtain and returned to the settle. Then he knelt down and worshipped; with the full undivided worship which a man gives only when the god of his devotions is a reality to him, and not a tradition.

Boniface Wichelow's god was money: he served it faithfully; when he had an opportunity of coming into the presence of his deity, of entering into communion with it, his heart grew warm with fervour.

Kneeling before the settle, he undid the packets one by one ; the paper tore away in many of them and let the sovereigns roll out before he could unfold it. In little heaps of varying height he ranged them side by side along the seat ; last of all he opened the tobacco-pouch and took out a roll of bank notes, yellow, and slightly damp, but pro-tected from positive harm by their indiarubber covering.

He counted them all, the notes first, and then the little piles of gold, slowly, his fingers touching them with a lingering touch that showed they loved their task. When each sovereign had passed separately through his hands, he began to brighten them, rubbing them against the sleeve of his coat to remove the film of damp that had dimmed their sur-face.

'Still, it doesn't hurt them,' he muttered.

'It's the only thing the damp can't touch is gold. The notes—well——'

He took the notes and spread them one by one on the extreme edge of the circle of firelight ; he felt them every now and again with his hand to see if the damp were drawn out of them ; he watched the sparks anxiously, lest one should chance to find its way so far from the hearth.

Kneeling thus in the half-darkness that covered most of the room, his clean-cut, eager old face catching the moving light of the fire, the moments, as they passed silently by, held each for him a curious, half-fearful delight, the keenness of his pleasure being held in check by a latent terror, lest by some untoward and unlooked-for chance his solitude should be broken in upon.

By-and-by he collected the notes together again and laid them carefully on the settle ; then he took from one of the drawers of the dresser a sheet of newspaper, and, returning to his first place, kneeled down once more and began to tear the paper into many pieces, and to wrap up the sovereigns anew. He forgot his surroundings as he became more and more absorbed in counting and arranging his wealth ; he forgot his fear of interruption ; he forgot everything but himself and his god. There were words running in his mind that he had heard or read somewhere—he did not remember nor consider where or when : 'Where neither moth nor rust doth corrupt, and where thieves do not break through nor steal.' Those were the words ; he chuckled to himself as he said them again and again, thinking of that hole in the ground where moth and rust could do but little harm, and which thieves would never discover. The words took a sort of rhythm as they re-peated themselves ; he began to count the sovereigns to its flow, a sovereign to each word : ' Where—neither—moth—nor—rust —doth—corrupt—and—where—thieves——'

In the midst of the silence, broken only
by the whispering, pausing voice, came a
loud, sudden sound, a knocking at the outer
door. The old man started, and a look of
confused terror destroyed the rapt delight
that had possessed his face. Still kneeling,
his head half turned towards the door, his
hands stretched out over the settle as though
to cover and protect the treasure that lay
there, the light of the fire, burnt low now,
shining faintly on his pallid, frightened face,
he listened anxiously, making no sound or
movement.

The knocking was repeated, and again
repeated, and then went on in a long, continuous rapping. After a minute the old
man's power of thought came back to him;
quickly, and with hands that trembled, he
took a flat basket that lay in the chimney-
corner and swept into it all the sovereigns,
loose or in packets, the paper, new and old,
and the tobacco-pouch with the notes. With

a shambling run he made his way to the dresser, opened a drawer, and emptied the contents of the basket into it. The sovereigns clinked and rang as they fell, and the sound was terrible to him. He covered them with a sheet or two of paper; then he closed the drawer, and went back to the fireside.

He slipped off his shoes, and in his stocking feet went noiselessly along the passage to the outer door. He stood a few paces away from the little grating, and looked through; he could see a portion of a man's cap, and he knew the cap. The knocking became louder. The old man waited for half a minute, hesitating; then he hurried back to the room again, and put on his shoes; and in the same moment that he glanced round him and gave a quick, anxious look towards the dresser, came a tapping on the window-panes.

Boniface crossed over to the window, and drew aside the curtain. He saw, as he expected to see, the face of Paul Garnet looking in upon him ; but he gave a little start as though he were surprised, and, nodding his head with a trembling, deprecating smile, signed to Paul to go to the door. He hurried across the room, and, as quickly as his strength would allow him, unfastened the bolts and let down the bar.

'What the devil's the matter ?' said Paul Garnet.

Boniface rubbed his eyes.

'I had fallen asleep,' he said. 'I did not expect anyone ; and Sally being out and the place so quiet—I hope you have not been here long ?'

'I don't know what you call long. I have stood here for fifteen infernal minutes !'

Paul spoke calmly, almost carelessly, but his face was ugly with anger. Old Wichelow followed him silently into the room. Paul went over to the window that was still darkened, and drew the curtain aside, thus letting into the room all the light remaining to the short day. Boniface Wichelow took a log from a pile of wood in the chimney-corner, and laid it on the sunken fire.

'Come and warm yourself,' he said; 'you must be cold if you waited so long. The fire got low while I was asleep, but it will soon burn up—very soon.'

Paul Garnet came over to the fireside.

'I expected to find Rhoda here,' he said.

'She has not been here; I am sure she has not. I have heard nothing—nothing, all the afternoon.'

'She started to come here half an hour before I did.'

'She has not been—cannot have been; if she had, I should have—awaked.'

Paul Garnet sat down in the chimney-corner and looked across at old Boniface as he knelt before the fire, blowing it with the bellows, gently, so as not to make the flames too fierce.

'What devilry have you been up to?' he asked.

'None.' The air came from the bellows with such force that the flames rose high with a crackling sound. 'By Jehovah! none.'

'What have you been doing?'

'I have told you.' Boniface laid down the bellows, and retreated to his usual place on the settle. 'I was asleep.'

'Likely.'

'And why not?' The old man, his face shaded by the settle's high back, looked across the blazing logs at the dark face on which the firelight cast a ruddy glow. 'Holidays don't come often,' he said; 'and when you're as old as I am, you'll find perhaps a quiet nap's as great a treat as you can have.'

'Shall I draw the curtains, do you think, and bar the door before I begin?'

'I think you will, if you sleep as sound as I do.' Something like a smile flitted across old Wichelow's frightened, malicious face;

then he added, 'It's a lonely place up here, to live all alone. Who's to know who might come prying at the windows, or stealing in at the door?'

'Yes, there are thieves everywhere,' said Paul—'everywhere, that is to say, where there's anything to steal.'

'I keep no money in the house,' said Boniface quickly, 'nothing but just enough to pay the little odds and ends. But there are some would murder you for the sake of the few shillings you might have in your pocket.'

'Yes,' said Paul; 'there are people, I know, who would kill, or help to kill, for the sake of a very little gain.'

There was a pause.

'Do you know any such?' Paul asked.

'No, I never—I have lived so much out of the world, as you know; I have never known—seen——'

The voice died away into silence,

' Come here,' said Paul Garnet.

' I will not come,' the old man breathed.

' You shall, though.' Paul's voice took on a great and pitiless scorn. ' Do you think I don't know,' he said, ' that Rhoda's mother owed her death to you ?'

' She did not ; it is not true. She pined away bit by bit. Am I almighty that I could have saved her ? By Jehovah ! I was not near her the night she died.'

The old man's eyes, screwed up under quivering lids, were full of mingled malignity and terror as he looked from his shadowed seat at the face in the chimney-corner.

' Come here,' said Paul again.

' I will not come,' Boniface repeated ; but he rose from his seat and came with dragging steps a few paces towards the fire.

Paul rose too ; he stretched up and took a candle from the mantelpiece, thrust it into the flames, and then held it, lighted, close to the old man's face.

'Did you stint her,' he said, 'in the things she ought to have had? Did you give her half-quantities for whole ones? Did you grudge her firing, so that the cold nipped and starved her? I know you did, but you must answer me.' The old man's face, malicious and obstinate, quivered visibly, but he did not speak. 'Answer,' said Paul, 'or I will ask you no more till Rhoda comes. Am I right?'

Boniface Wichelow's pursed-up mouth relaxed.

'Ay,' he said.

'When Rhoda was taken ill,' Paul went on, 'and could not go to her mother's room, did you screw and stint still more, knowing that there was nobody to mark or check you?'

Again the wrinkled face quivered, and the old trembling voice gave the same answer as before.

'Ay,' it said.

'Did you, on the night on which she died, leave her with no fire to temper the fierceness of the cold?'

'I did not know the frost would be so strong,' the old man cried. 'I was warm, quite warm. How could I know by the morning she would be dead?'

'Did you leave her with no fire?' asked Paul again.

The answer came as before:

'Ay.'

'And it killed her.'

'No, it did not—it could not; and, besides, it was not my fault. I did not dream, could not tell.—Why should you say it is my fault? How can you tell what I did? and why?'

'I know you,' Paul answered. 'I knew you then, and I knew what you would be likely to do. When I came that morning, and went into the room where she lay, I knew just what had happened and why.

You knew at the time that I knew : all these years you have known it.'

The old man repeated Paul's words :

' All these years.'

' For which cause you have hated me,' said Paul.

For a little while old Boniface did not answer ; then he cast a furtive glance at his questioner's face, and said again :

' Ay.'

Paul threw the candle into the fire ; the flames swallowed it eagerly, rising high about the logs. Old Wichelow gave a lurch forward, his hands outstretched as though to save it from the blaze.

' Never mind,' Paul said ; ' it has been well paid for out of what you kept back from your son's wife.'

He sat down again. The still cold outside had grown harder and blacker ; the frosty red had faded from the sky, and left it a dull cold gray ; the room was almost dark.

'It was none of my business,' Paul said presently, 'and the woman was an ailing, miserable creature, who must have died soon in any case; but I could have made it awkward for you if I had liked.'

'I almost wonder,' old Wichelow's high, unsteady voice answered back out of the darkness, 'that you did not like.'

'I meant to marry Rhoda,' said Paul, 'and I did not care to set all the country-side gossiping over her relations. Did you think it was out of regard for you?'

A step sounded in the passage, and in a minute the door of the room opened, and Rhoda came in.

'Are you there, grandfather?' she said. 'It is so dark I cannot see.'

'I am here,' answered Boniface, 'and Paul is here.'

'Where have you been?' asked Paul, coming out of the chimney corner. 'What has kept you?'

'I went in to see old Micah, and he said that Molly Burns was ill and wanted to see me. Have you been waiting long?'

'Some time,' Paul answered, 'but it has passed quickly. Your grandfather and I have had an interesting conversation, although, as it appears, I disturbed him, awoke him, from a very deep sleep.'

'I had gone to sleep, Rhody,' said the old man hurriedly. 'I did not think you would come to-day. You told me that Paul's friends from the other side of Breybridge were to drive over to see you.'

'They wrote to say they could not come,' Rhoda answered, 'so I thought I would come and see if you had a good fire, and Paul said he would bring me home.'

'The fire is good—very good. You can see how many logs there are, and how it blazes.'

'Candle grease makes a fine blaze,' said Paul. 'The fire was poor till I mended it.

Come, Rhoda, we should be going home; the cold is getting more bitter every minute. It will be almost as cold a night as the night your mother died.'

'Why do you speak of that, Paul?' Rhoda asked, a tremor in her voice.

'Your grandfather and I have been grieving over her death. Are you ready?'

'Yes; in a minute.' Rhoda drew her grandfather aside. 'Here are the shillings,' she said, 'from Tuesday till to-day.'

Paul Garnet's sharp ears caught the words.

'What shillings? What are you giving him, Rhoda?'

'Do not tell him,' the old man whispered, clutching the girl's arm.

'You are giving him money,' said Paul.

'I am giving him nothing that I have not the right to give,' Rhoda answered.

'He shall have no more money—least of all yours.'

Rhoda did not speak.

'Come here,' said Paul.   He was standing in the light of the fire.   'Come here, my wife, where I can see you.'

Rhoda went forward, and stood where the light of the flames showed her face plainly.

'Do you intend to obey me?' Paul asked.

'I am not sure.'   Rhoda waited a moment, and then added: 'It depends.'

'On what?'

'On your commands.'

'And yet,' he said, 'you must do my will.'

'Quite certainly?'

There was a smile in her eyes, though her voice was grave.

'Quite certainly.'

'Then let your will be mine,' she said, the smile spreading over all her face.

Paul shook his head.

'Not in this thing.'

She looked at him, and as she looked, gradually the smile died away.

'I will obey you,' she said.

'What is this money?' he asked.

'Come out into the passage,' said Rhoda. 'I do not like to see your eyes.'

Paul answered her by leading the way out of the room, and she followed him. In the darkness she stood by his side, and said :

'It is only that I give him a shilling for every day that he will keep a good fire burning. He would save the firing and starve himself now I am not here, and I do not like the thought of him sitting in the cold alone.'

'In other words, you give him back, bit by bit, the money he had robbed you of. And to keep him warm!' Paul laughed. 'Wait here a minute,' he said, 'and I will put this right.'

He went back into the room. Old Wichelow still stood in the dark corner, holding tightly clasped in his hand the shillings that Rhoda had given him.

'My wife gives you no money,' Paul said. 'That you know now and for always. If you take so much as a penny from her again, you shall repeat to me, and she shall stand by and hear it, the tale that you told me this afternoon.'

'No, no ; don't tell Rhody !'

'You understand me ?'

'Ay.'

Paul went out into the passage again.

'Rhoda !' he called.

There was no answer. Rhoda had gone.

CHAPTER V.

Could I only stand
Between gray moor and gray sky
Where the wind and the plovers cry,
    And no man is at hand.
And feel the free wind blow
On my rain-wet face, and know
    I am free—not yours—but my own.
    Free—and alone !

E. NESBIT.

WHEN Paul went back into the room, Rhoda moved down the passage to the outer door and opened it. The passage was very dark, and the darkness seemed weighted with Paul's scorn and anger : she longed to get away from it.

Outside it was almost light, for the snow that covered the heath caught and held the last gleams of daylight; the frosty sky was strewn with trembling stars; a crescent moon was rising over the woods.

·The air was very still and very cold; the young night held a calm purity that was in sweet contrast with Paul's dark wrath and old Wichelow's tremulous greed; and a sudden longing came upon Rhoda to escape from the unquiet darkness within the house, and to flee out alone into the dim white peace of the heath and the woods.

She yielded to the longing; she drew the door gently to behind her, and went forth with swift steps across the rough, frozen ground and in amongst the trees. She did not wait to consider whether Paul would be angry with her for her flight; the desire to be alone with herself, to be free from the influence of any spirit but her own, was so strongly upon her that it overpowered all other feelings; and she went on quickly, almost running, the keen air and her own impulse towards flight alike exciting her to rapid motion.

But after awhile the gaunt trees, holding their bare white arms above her head, calmed her mood; their stillness was in reproachful contrast with her unrest, and worked upon her bit by bit, till, hardly knowing why, she slackened her pace, and at last stood still.

It was perfectly silent, with the clear silence of frost, upon which any slightest sound breaks with keen precision; the sky was growing darker, the stars brighter; through the network of bare white twigs and boughs Rhoda could see the shining space undimmed by any cloud: and it seemed to her that the beauty of holiness was vivid in the glistening sky, and covered the quiet trees, and possessed the calm air. Her old longing after a higher, finer life awoke once more within her; the strength of it annulled for the time all the subtler instincts and tendencies of her many-sided nature; once more her girlish ideal of saintliness seemed a reality, the attainment of it possible. And the ideal music that she had dreamed of before she had known Anthony Dexter, that held heights and no depths, that had remained faint and undefined in her imagination, became possible too: it seemed to her that the stars sang it above her, that the trees held it prisoned, that the keen air was full of it. If she could but hear the notes! She felt sure that the music was about her as she stood. If only her ears could be opened to the sound of it, the memory of the sound would stay with her, she knew, all through her life, and become a shield, invisible but strong, between her and evil.

She waited: the silence was so beautiful in the growing darkness; the darkness, with the stars looking down upon it, was so beautiful in the silence: the music perhaps would breathe through the stillness at last.

Then, far off, she heard the sound of footsteps; it grew more distinct, and she knew the tread, and that Paul was coming towards her. For the first time in her life she shrank from the influence of his presence; the strength she had trusted in so far had some hardness in it to-night; the look in his eyes when he had commanded her obedience was still present to her mind, and impelled her anew to flight. For a moment she hesitated, then moved on quickly, in and out amongst the trees, her blood tingling, her spirits rising with the rapid motion through the frosty air. But all at once her flight came to an end; a root that twisted across the path, and rose here and there above the ground, caught her foot and caused her to trip; she stumbled forward, and her head came with strong force against the trunk of a tree. The blow stunned her, and she fell helpless, the sky and the woods and the sense of pursuit fading in one moment into a blank darkness.

Paul Garnet came striding through the woods. He did not look up at the splendid sky, or pause to observe the naked, patient trees, or take any delight in the pure cold air. He was half angry with Rhoda, half pleased that she had in a certain sense defied him; placid, implicit obedience he did not desire; he liked to compel his wife's submission, not caring for victory without a sense of contest. He began to think as he went along that she could not have taken the path to Fanelands; he was nearly through the wood, and he had not overtaken her. Then, all at once, his quick eyes saw something dark lying on the white ground at the side of the path some yards ahead of him. He started forward, and, reaching it, kneeled down in the frozen snow.

'Rhoda!' he said, 'Rhoda!'

There was no answer. He could not see distinctly the pale face with the closed eyes and parted lips; the one hand lying outside the folds of the cloak was icy cold. For an instant Paul thought that she was dead, and the thought gripped his heart with a passion of terror, making him sway and tremble as he knelt : then he raised her in his arms, and, holding her tightly to him, set out towards Fanelands Hall.

He walked quickly ; he was strong and big, and the fear and pain within him made Rhoda's weight seem as nothing in his arms. She could not be dead ; it could not be that she had passed away from him ; yet the dread was constant in his heart, and his face was white and drawn with fear. On the borders of the wood, in the space between the gardens and the trees, Rhoda's head stirred slightly, and a little moan came from her lips. Paul stopped and bent his head.

' Rhoda !' he said again, ' can you hear me, Rhoda ?'

' Where am I ?' she said.

'You are with me, quite safe. We are almost home.'

She did not speak again, and he hurried on. He reached the side-door, and, passing along the passage into the hall, laid her on the sofa by the fire. Then he saw that her forehead was bruised, and that above the left temple there was a little cut from which the blood oozed slowly; her eyes were open now.

'What is it?' said Paul; 'what happened?'

'I fell—against a tree; I remember now. It must have stunned me.'

Paul rang the bell, and sent the servants hunting all over the house for different remedies; then he came back to the sofa and kneeled down beside it. His eyes had a hungry look; his face was still pale and drawn.

'I thought you were dead,' he said in a whisper.

Rhoda smiled.

'Would you have been sorry?'

He bent over her and covered her with fierce kisses.

'I should have cursed God and died,' he said, 'if He had dared to take you from me.'

'Ah, Paul!' she said; 'take care.'

'Of what?'

'Of His anger—if He should mark your words——'

Paul laughed.

'You are still here. I care for nothing else.'

All the evening he kept her lying on the sofa. He brought her her supper with his own hands, and watched her while she ate it, standing with his back to the huge fire, his dark eyes fixed upon her face.

'Don't you think,' said Rhoda, half laughing, and passing her hand across her brow, 'that you had better go away for a time—till my face comes back to the face you know?'

'How do I know I should find you here when I came back?'

'Why not?' she asked.

'I left you for two minutes this evening,' he said, 'and when I came back, you were gone. I called to you, and there was nothing but darkness.'

Rhoda said nothing.

'Why did you go?' Paul asked.

'I hardly know; and yet—yes, I will tell you. Your eyes were almost cruel when you spoke to me, and while I waited alone, the darkness seemed filled with the power of your will. I wanted to get away from it, to be by myself; and outside it seemed all peace and freedom.'

Paul came close to her, and once more kneeled down by her side.

'I told you,' he said, 'that when we were always together, you and I, we should come to have but one mind, one will.'

'Yes,' she said in a low voice, 'but must that mind, that will, be always yours?'

Paul laughed.

'Nay,' he said; 'by-and-by, as our life goes on and we grow in our thoughts closer and closer together, we shall not care or know whose the will may be.'

'My will has no power to influence yours,' she said.

He answered her with a sort of a cry.

'You do not know.'

'Have I any power?'

She smiled with something both of pleasure and sadness in her eyes.

'When I saw you lying there to-night——'

Paul paused and drew in his breath.

'Surely I love you, Paul,' she said.

There was a question in her voice.

'If you did not,' he answered, 'I almost think I could kill you. And yet,' he went on after a pause, 'how can I tell whether you love me; or whether, if you did not love me, I should have strength to cut you off altogether and for ever from my life? Your face is a mystery and a charm. Can I be sure that I read it aright, or that if it deceives me I could withstand its charm?

No, I cannot; I can be sure of nothing with which you have to do.'

'Yet you were hard with me this evening. Your will was more to you than my desire.'

'Can I dare to let you go free?' Paul said, 'to let you escape from my will? No, I must keep and hold you for my own. If once you should go forth, I doubt—— I cannot tell if you would ever return, submit to me again.'

'I am not likely to go forth.'

Paul's eyes grew stern again, and his voice took on its ordinary tone as he answered her:

'You shall not.

CHAPTER VI.

Yet to be loved makes not to love again.
                    TENNYSON.

In the new year Paul and Rhoda were much together. There were not many neighbours near Fanelands Hall; none who lived quite close; and the husband and wife saw very little of any world but their own. In February, when the days began to lengthen, they spent much of their time in rambles through the fine country that stretched for miles on every side of their home. Beyond the wide heath the character of the country changed: the desolate wildness of it disappeared, and it became soft and rich, with shady lanes winding between the sheltered fields and up and down the gentle slopes. Rhoda had never before been more than a mile or two away from Heather Den, and the thick hedges, the well-to-do villages, the snug homesteads, were all new to her.

'If I had been born and had grown up here,' she said one day to Paul as they were passing through a little village, clustered about an ivy-covered church, 'instead of at Heather Den, I should have been quite different from what I am now.'

' How ?'

' I should have been better, and—sleepier.'

' I prefer the mould of Heather Den,' said Paul.

' I know you do ; but you are wrong.'

' How ?' he asked again.

' If I had been better than I am, why, of course '—she paused, and ended with a laugh —' of course I should have been better than I am.'

' I doubt it,' he said.

'Have you no hope of me ?'

'All hope ; but the bad and the good is in you, not in where you chance to live.'

'But the things that happen to one,' she said, 'that is what makes the difference ; and if I had lived here——'

She hesitated and stopped speaking.

'The things that happen to one depend quite as much upon one's nature, as one's nature depends upon the things that happen to one.'

'Do you think so, really ?'

'I know it.'

Rhoda thought for a minute.

'Perhaps it is true,' she said.

There was a short space of silence.

'Why do you never try to play the organ now ?' asked Paul abruptly.

'I dare not !'

The words were said involuntarily, almost before Rhoda knew that she had spoken.

'You need not be afraid.'   Paul laughed

a curious laugh, and turned his eyes upon her. 'You mean, of course, that you fear you would never attain perfection?'

She hesitated.

'No. I mean,' she answered, 'that music does not belong to my life; and it is not wise to bring into one's life things that have nothing to do with it.'

'But music,' he said, 'is a great part of your life.'

'Of my nature,' she answered, 'it is a part; of my life, no.'

'Why thwart your nature by putting it in opposition to your life?'

'You said just now that one's nature is responsible for the things that happen to one. I almost think it is so. Then has one any choice but to hold one's nature fast, and see that it works no harm upon one's life?'

'Yet there was a time,' Paul said, still looking into her face, 'in which through music you saw what you thought was heaven.'

'Did I tell you that ?' she said quickly.

'No ; but I knew.'

'How could you know ?'

'You never spoke to me about your music,' Paul said ; 'you never let me come into the room in which, in a sense, you lived with it alone ; but I knew how large a part of you it was.'

'You never said — spoke of it,' Rhoda breathed.

'No. Why should I ? I thought I would wait until you were my wife.'

She was silent, thinking of a time when it had seemed as if she might never be his wife. He almost seemed to read her thoughts.

'Your lodger,' he said presently, 'showed you a strange music that was as new to your imagination as to your ears.'

She glanced at him with startled eyes, but he kept his face turned away from her, look-ing straight ahead along the road.

'It stirred in you feelings that you did not understand,' Paul went on; 'it revealed to you parts of yourself that you had not known or suspected.'

'It is true,' Rhoda said, but in so low a voice that he could not catch her words.

He walked on for a few paces, then he turned to her.

'Did you think I did not know?' he asked suddenly.

'Know what?' she said in the same low voice; but Paul, looking at her, saw the movement of her lips and answered her words.

'That the man, with his strange music, had gained a sort of influence over you; that the things he played affected you in a way that was new to you; that in the beginning you thought all the power lay in the music; and that afterwards you began to think some of it was due to the man? Did you think I didn't know?'

There was a quiver in Paul's voice. He stopped short and faced his wife; and she, too, stopped; and they stood and looked at one another.

'I knew,' said Rhoda at last, 'that you knew, must see, that day in the hall at Fanelands, that the music — some of the music—told upon me in a way that made me forget the things about me. It was new to me, and it stirred me strangely; and being new, and I unused to—— Now it would be different; by-and-by, if I heard it often, or if I had known it all my life——'

A great scorn sprang up in Paul's eyes.

'Do you think I was afraid?' he said— 'am afraid now? I am not afraid.' He waited a moment. 'Which was the stronger,' he asked, 'the musician with his music, or I?'

'You.'

'If I had left you to him then,' Paul went

on, 'if I had let you go, you would have come to think you loved him.'

She looked at him with a look he could not read ; she did not speak.

'Now,' he said, 'you must, you shall love *me*.'

'I know.'

'You belong to me.'

'Yes.'

He stood with his eyes upon her face.

'Why don't you speak to me?' he said suddenly.

'I have spoken.'

Rhoda's voice sounded monotonous and cold.

'Why don't you say you love me?' he asked ; 'or that you don't,' he added, with a bitter laugh, 'if that be so?'

She answered him very gently.

'I thought you knew.'

The harsh voice in which he had spoken

grew suddenly soft and pleading ; he grasped her hands and held them tightly.

'Say it,' he said. 'Tell me, if it be so, that you love me.'

'Surely I love you,' she answered. 'As far back as I remember, you have been the centre of my life ; and it must—I know it will be so always.'

'Yes,' he said, 'I am sure, I know it will be so.'

Then he dropped her hands and walked on ; and they went down the road, side by side, but in silence.

CHAPTER VII.

I would look
Liker my nature's truth : and both are frail.
R. BROWNING.

THAT evening after supper Rhoda asked
Paul to have the organ made fit to play
upon, after its months of silence. From
time to time during her girlhood she had
pleased herself by spelling out upon its keys
the airs she knew; but she had been very
seldom at Fanelands Hall before her
marriage, and she understood little about the
instrument or the way to play it. Paul was
able to help her; his knowledge of music
was greater than Rhoda's, in the same proportion that his musical sense and feeling

were less; and he set himself now to teach her all he knew.

Evening after evening she worked on under his guidance. At first the lessons held a sort of nightmare pain for her; she shrank from the sound of the notes, and touched the keys with trembling hands; by-and-by, as she became aware of the difficulties in her way and had to grapple with them, the drudgery of her task made it in a sense easier; the music was hidden from her as she learned to make it; later on, when she began to gain some command over the instrument, and to make it obey her will, some of the troubled feeling of the first few days came back to her; but with the trouble was mingled a consciousness of power and a delight in the sounds she was able to bring forth; and soon delight gained the victory, and the organ-playing became a keen pleasure.

But before this time had fully arrived, Paul said to her one day:

'You have learned all I can teach you. Now you must go on alone, so far as learning goes.'

'You have taught me a great deal,' she answered. 'I should have learned nothing but for you.'

'You must go on alone,' Paul repeated, 'but only as far as concerns the learning. You must no longer keep your music apart— shut away from me ; the whole of you must be mine.'

'It shall be so,' she said ; but even while she spoke, she knew that the promise was one she could not keep.

Very often after this, Paul made her play to him ; but while she was conscious of his presence, she played mechanically ; and if the music became a reality to her, it carried her into a region of thought and fancy in which Paul had no place, of which he had no knowledge, which was closed to him, not by her will, but by his own nature.

The winter passed into spring, and the spring went by, and the year reached its longest days. Rhoda had kept her promise to old Micah. About once a week, during the long evenings, she took her way to the clearing in the woods, and again led the songs that she had taught old Wichelow's labourers in her girlhood. Sometimes Paul followed her there and watched her while she sang. He never showed himself; he stood back amongst the sheltering trees, and looked at her from behind the screen of leaves, as Anthony Dexter had looked a year ago. Yet he never saw her as Anthony had seen her. The self-forgetfulness, the exaltation that had come of her belief that she was chosen by the Lord to be His servant, the confidence in her own mission to teach the people about her, the sense that she had power to rise herself, had passed away with the past year; the simplicity of her girlhood was gone ; her nature had been stirred, and

could no longer ignore its own complexity.
And the people felt the doubt in her, knowing her to be changed, though they did not
define, or seek to define, wherein the change
might lie ; it seemed to them only natural
that marriage should alter her, and they
sought no other explanation. Yet, as the
summer went on, and Rhoda lived much of
her life out of doors in the fields and the
woods, and on the heath, as something of the
character of her old life repeated itself in the
way she passed her days, something of the
spirit of that life seemed to touch her too ; and
the monotony of the uneventful weeks brought
her a certain semblance of her former self.

The summer had reached and passed its
prime ; August had come ; the days were
shorter, but the heat of the sun was fierce,
and autumn still seemed far off. Paul
Garnet had gone away for a few days, and
Rhoda was left alone at Fanelands Hall.
She spent a good deal of her time at

Heather Den ; her grandfather had become much feebler lately, and begged her each time she left him to come back again soon and break his solitude ; and the pure fresh air of the heath was inspiriting after the heavier atmosphere of the low land about the Hall.   In   the   evenings   she   bribed Rufus Stockbridge with sixpences and sweet-meats to blow the organ for her ; and play-ing on and on in the twilight or after the darkness was fully come, the time passed swiftly by, and she had no thought of loneli-ness.

The organ had lost in a great measure the impalpable mystery which had enwrapped it when she first came to live at Fanelands. The silence which had stricken it then was broken now, and by her own will and hands ; the seal that Anthony Dexter's personality had impressed upon it was partly destroyed ; the prosaic touch of her own learning fingers had swept away the charm

that had been worked by his. Yet the
charm was not wholly gone, nor the sense
that the organ waited till he should come
and rouse its full power again; and sometimes when she had ceased to play, and
sat facing the great mass that rose up dumb
before her, Rhoda found herself wondering
involuntarily when that time would be.
With her full consciousness she very rarely
thought of Anthony Dexter; when she did,
it was to tell herself that she was glad he
had passed so entirely out of her life; that
the emotions he had awakened in her were
unrealities that never could be conjured up
again; and that it would not have been
possible to love him as she loved Paul.
She chose very carefully the music that
she played, avoiding all that could stir that
part of her being which Anthony's playing
had revealed; and by-and-by she thought,
or said in her thoughts, that music had no
longer any power to excite or very much to

move her; and hiding from herself, she thought she was at peace.

It was at the close of a sultry day that Paul came back to Fanelands.

Rhoda went a mile or so towards Brey-bridge to meet him. The evening had brought a little coolness, and she was glad to get up on to the higher ground, and to catch the slight breeze that was stirring on the heath.

Far off she saw him coming, a black speck on the verge of the horizon, just as she had seen him many and many a time when he had been her lover. He walked rapidly; he was soon near enough for her to know that it was surely he; she recognised his strong figure and the peculiar stride that indi-vidualized his walk.

He did not nod or smile to her as he drew near; he came on, almost as though he did not see that she was there, till he was within a few yards of her. Then he stopped and

looked into her face and smiled ; a smile
that changed his dark face utterly, and gave
it for a moment a look of perfect tenderness
and love.

'So you are there ?' he said.

'You did not expect I would come to
meet you ?'

'I expected nothing. How could I be
sure that I should find you again at all ?'

'Where should I have gone ?' she asked.

'That is not for me to consider ; only I
could not know that if I left you even for
a day I should be sure of finding you
again.'

'I saw you a long way off,' she said.

'Yes, and I saw—what I thought was
you.'

'You seemed as if you did not see me
at all.'

'I could not be sure, till I was quite close,
that it was really you. Do you think I
was going to waste my gestures on a

mocking phantom that might have taken your form ?'

'And it is only I,' she said, 'after all; it is altogether I. Your goblin myth has ended in this prose.'

She touched her breast with her hand as she spoke. She stood looking at him with laughter in her eyes, her face shaded by the broad frill of her cotton bonnet.

' The prose will do,' said Paul.

Then at last he came forward and kissed her; and they walked back to Fanelands Hall together.

CHAPTER VIII.

Our present is and is not,
Our future's a sealed seed plot,
And what betwixt them are we?
D. G. ROSSETTI.

'I HAVE to go away again for a few days this week,' said Paul in the evening after supper, 'on Wednesday.'

'Not to the same place?'

'Yes.'

'All that way so soon again?'

'Yes; there was some business I could not finish to-day.'

'It is a pity you could not have done without the two journeys.'

'I could if I had not come home to-day.'

Rhoda looked up at him.

'Why did you come?'

'Don't you know? I had to-day and to-morrow free; I could not get on with my business till Thursday. Don't you know why I came?'

'To see if I were still here?' she asked with a smile.

He answered her gravely:

'Precisely. To-morrow,' Paul went on presently, 'if the day is fine, I am going to take you over to Wrexholme. It is a beautiful place, and it will be looking its best just now.'

'Wrexholme? where is it?'

'It is some way from here, about ten miles—a sort of hamlet on the farther side of the Kingswold Hills. We must start early, so as to catch the coach at the Fern-lake cross-roads. We will have a long holiday, now I have found my way home, before I leave you again.'

'I think it will be fine,' Rhoda said; 'the moon is clear.' She crossed the room to the window, drew the curtains aside, and looked out. 'Yes,' she said; 'it is a fair weather sky.'

Paul followed her, and stood looking over her shoulder.

'It is wonderfully still,' he said.

'Not stiller than it often is down here in the hollow.'

'Yet it seems to me that it is,' answered Paul; 'more positively still, with the sort of waiting stillness that comes before a storm.'

'But the sky gives no sign of a storm.'

'No; the sky, as you say, is a fair weather sky.' Paul turned back into the room. 'Perhaps the storm is in me,' Rhoda heard him say, 'or in you.'

She looked round. He was standing before Leonardo's picture.

'Did you speak to me?' she asked.

'Hardly; rather to her.'

He pointed to the face on the canvas. Rhoda came and stood beside him.

'Am I still like her?'

'A minute ago, no.   Now'—he turned and looked at her—'now, yes.'

'Once you were glad of the likeness,' Rhoda said; 'but now I think it is no longer so.'

He did not answer her; he turned abruptly from the picture and went back to his seat. He knew that much as he had loved her before she had been his wife, he loved her now with a tenfold strength; and the knowledge made him fearful: the possibilities of her nature appealed to him in a different way; for as his love deepened, his ideal grew higher.

The next day opened gently, with a gray, quiet dawn that grew into a morning of perfect loveliness. Rhoda was out in the garden early. There was a light dew on the grass, on the half-wild roses, on all the early autumn flowers that were already beginning to bud and bloom. The air was full of sweet freshness; the sun shone

generously; only above the trees the whirling, circling rooks struck a melancholy note
in the midst of the brilliant beauty.

The morning was still fresh, when Rhoda
and Paul set out for the cross-roads; on the
hedges thin, gauzy webs glistened here and
there as the sun just touched them; a slight
haze dimmed the horizon, and wrapped the
outskirts of the heath in mystery. They
crossed a corner of the heath, passing within
a few hundred yards of Heather Den, and
reached the cross-roads about ten minutes
before the coach came in sight. Rhoda sat
down on a shaded bank to rest; she was
warm with the walk, and she took off her
hat and fanned herself; Paul sauntered up
and down the road. Sitting there in the
shadow of the hedge, the silent brightness of
the place, Paul's moving figure as he crossed
her line of vision every now and again, the
strong blue of the sky against the little mound
of green that faced her, made a sort of

picture in her mind, vague and unnoted
then, but which remained clear through
many years ; a brilliant picture in a black
frame.

The silence did not last very long ; soon
the sound of wheels and of horses' feet broke
into the stillness, and a minute or two more
showed the coach as it rounded the corner of
the lane. There were empty seats ; Rhoda
and Paul mounted behind the driver; and the
coach went swaying and rattling along the
undulating road. The rapid motion made a
seeming wind ; the sensation of rushing air
was a delight to Rhoda after the sultry stillness
of the last few days ; and the whole drive,
past yellow corn-fields, through shady lanes,
across gorse-decked commons, was a continual,
increasing pleasure. Her spirits rose ; her
heart grew light ; there was happiness in
her eyes.

It was still early when the coach reached
Wrexholme, not more than eleven o'clock.

The village was small and quaint : it stood all huddled up together round the church, disproportionately large for the number of the inhabitants. It was very quiet just now ; the children were in school, and all the men and most of the women were out harvesting in the fields hard by ; here and there an old woman or man sat at a cottage door, or a child with staggering wide-apart legs gave itself a lesson in walking. Rhoda and Paul strolled about for a little while, and then returned to the inn at which the coach had stopped, to order lunch. The inn stood back from the road ; there was a square of grass before it, on which was a tall post with the sign swinging at the top, The Good Intent ; on the narrow sanded path between the grass and the house were wooden benches set close against the wall, so that drinkers out-side could have their liquor handed out to them through the low lattice windows.

Rhoda sat down in the little inn parlour,

while Paul went to speak to the landlady in
the bar. The parlour smelt of beer and stale
tobacco smoke : the walls were decorated with
a print of the Prince of Wales over the
mantelpiece, one of Lord Beaconsfield over
the door, and, opposite the window, a repre-
sentation of a dying mother with her children
kneeling by her side, and an angel poised
between the bed-head and the ceiling. In a
corner was a rickety little table with one leg
shorter than the other, and on it lay a
crocheted woollen mat under a glass vase, a
man's glove, a pipe, and a newspaper of the
day before.

Near the table a door led out at the back
of the inn ; it stood open, and showed a strip
of garden gay with a profusion of tangled
flowers. A little stream bounded it at the
further end, and beyond the stream was a
copse. At lunch Rhoda faced the door, and
looked down the path that divided the mass
of brilliant colour, into the cool green shade

that lay beyond. After the meal she strolled out into the garden for a few minutes.

It was intensely hot; the sun beat down upon the gaudy flowers and made their rich hues hard and glaring; the green of the copse was like a promise of rest. Rhoda moved on down the path to the little stream : a plank reached from one bank to the other : she crossed it, and stood in the shade of the trees looking back into the brightness she had left. The air was alive with the buzz of insects; far off there was a sound of whistling that seemed to come from the other side of the little wood. After awhile it came nearer, and Rhoda turned her head ; she could see nobody, though the sound became more and more distinct; and just then she heard Paul's voice calling to her, and she crossed the stream again, and went back along the garden path to join him.

They set out at once for the place they had come to see, an upland plain, a few

miles from Wrexholme village. The way
lay at first along a straight, dusty road; but
soon they left the road and followed a path
that led up a wooded hill. The path was
narrow and very steep, and the air was heavy
in amongst the close-growing trees. Paul
and Rhoda paused often to rest, and the top
of the hill seemed a long way off. But at
last the narrow path branched out into a
wide grass road; the ascent was no longer
very steep, and there was a freshness in the
air. The road ran on for half a mile or
so between the trees, then it reached the
borders of the wood and led on over the
open ground.

It was a wide plain that Rhoda saw stretching on two sides of her, in a gentle upward
slope: to the left and behind were the woods;
in front, and far away to the right, great
spreading undulating fields, with wide spaces
of grass land, led on and on; and there was
no human dwelling in sight, and no human

being; only in a far-off cornfield a loaded waggon made a moving object, tiny in the distance. Paul still went on, and presently reached a mound that rose in a gentle slope.

'Now,' he said, 'you can see all that is to be seen.'

Behind were the Kingswold Hills, beyond which lay the country that Rhoda knew; in front was a rich country of wood and valley that stretched away and away till the sky came down and made a boundary for the eye. The full afternoon light was upon it; here and there a lake or a river flashed back the sunlight that flooded its surface; in the far distance the earth had borrowed the blue tone of the sky.

'It is very beautiful!' Rhoda said.

'You are glad you came?'

'Yes; it was worth the climb.'

'To-morrow,' said Paul, 'at this time, I shall be back in Mercheston. It will be grimy, hideous, close.'

'And I,' said Rhoda, 'I shall be alone at Fanelands with the rooks.'

' Rooks are better than smoke.'

' I can't judge.   I have never been to a town.'

' Some day, you shall go to London.'
She shook her head.

' I don't feel as if I ever should.'

' Do you dislike the rooks?' Paul asked.

' Not altogether ; they are melancholy, that is all.'

' It is unlucky to kill them.'

' Do not kill them—for the luck's sake and their own.   You will not be away more than two days?'

' Or three, or four ; not one day longer, you may be sure, than I can help.'

She looked at him with a half-pitying, half-smiling look.

' Poor Paul !'

' Will you meet me again ?' he asked.

' If I know when you will come.'

'You will still be there?'

'Where else should I be?'

'Come,' he said, 'it is time to be going back.'

The fierce heat of the day was over when Paul and Rhoda reached the inn again; the garden was shaded now; through the open door the scent of the flowers came and filled the little parlour as the husband and wife sat at tea. A little later on Paul went out on to the road in front to smoke a pipe, and to watch for the coach; Rhoda lingered by the garden door, looking along the path, as she had looked when the noonday glare had added a brilliant glory to the tangled mass of bloom. In the softer light the flowers had a slightly drooping look, as though they thirsted for the dew of the coming night; the shade of the copse was almost like darkness; the bubbling flow of the little stream could be faintly heard in the stillness.

Then, as Rhoda stood looking dreamily

before her, the murmur of the stream became mingled with the sound of the whistling she had heard amongst the trees earlier in the day. She was sure it was the same whistling ; her quick ear recognised something in the tone of it ; she began to hope that Paul would not call her again before she had time to see who it was that made the sound. There was no sign from Paul : she waited while the whistling grew louder, and as she heard it more and more distinctly, it seemed to her that she knew, yet did not know, the air that came towards her in the soft floating notes : a curious feeling was upon her, as though she dreamed, knowing herself to be awake.

Then all at once the whistling ceased, and at the opening of the copse beyond the stream a man stood silent and looked at her. Rhoda did not stir ; she stood gazing down the path ; and Anthony Dexter looked back across the flowers. After a minute he moved forward, crossed the little plank bridge, and came on, without hesitating, but slowly, towards her. Still Rhoda did not move ; but her eyes never left his face ; and it seemed to her that suddenly the bright, strong light of noon-day was shining again in the garden.

Anthony Dexter stopped a few paces away from her, and he spoke the same words that Paul had spoken when he had met her on the heath the evening before.

' So you are there ?' he said.

She did not answer, and he went on speaking.

' I did not know if you were real, or a phantom that mocked me.'

Still she did not speak, and he added :

' I have seen you so often ; and it has always been a phantom till now.'

' Till now,' she repeated.

Her lips said the words very softly ; her silent eyes cried aloud with joy.

' Rhoda !'

It was Paul's voice calling to her from the door of the inn. Her face changed suddenly ; without a word she turned back into the little parlour, crossed it, and went out to the road in front.

Anthony Dexter stood alone in the garden, and felt with his hands towards the place where she had been.

CHAPTER IX.

Out flew the web and floated wide;
The mirror crack'd from side to side;
'The curse is come upon me,' cried
The Lady of Shalott.

TENNYSON.

THE next morning Paul went back to Mercheston. Rhoda walked with him as far as
the place where she had met him on his
return home two days before: he would not
let her go any further.

'This is our meeting-place,' he said; 'it
shall be our parting-place too. Good-bye.'

Rhoda stood and looked after him till he
had disappeared in the distance: he never
looked back. When she could no longer see
him, she walked slowly towards Heather Den.

Old Wichelow was sitting outside under the fir-tree, basking in the heat of the sun. Rhoda went and stood by him.

'So Paul has gone?' the old man said.

'Yes, he has gone.'

Boniface waited a minute.

'Are you glad?' he asked, peering up into her face with his penetrating eyes.

'Oh no, oh no!'

The answer was like a cry, of fear or of helplessness. Old Wichelow screwed up his eyes.

'Are you fond of him?' he asked; 'really?'

'Why should I have married him if I had not loved him?' Rhoda said.

'There are many fools in the world; one of the ways they show their folly is to think themselves in love.'

Rhoda turned to the old man.

'Were you ever in love?' she asked.

'With a woman?' Old Wichelow shook his head.

'Did you ever care much for anybody?'

He looked at her curiously.

'I believe I care for you, Rhody, more than any of the others I have had to do with. But even you—I should be a fool if I were to care for you much.'

'Why?'

'You are human—more, you are a woman. If I were to trust my happiness to you I should deserve to lose it.'

'Oh no——' Rhoda began and stopped. 'Perhaps you are right,' she said.

'You always had some sense about you,' the old man said approvingly. 'I have sometimes thought,' he added presently, 'that I would leave you all I have. It is little, very little, but—— If I were to leave you my money would you care for it—grow to love it, eh, Rhoda?'

The girl shook her head.

'I do not know. I hope not,' she answered absently.

'It is the only thing,' the old man said, 'that it is worth while to care for, that does not deceive you. It is yours for always; it stays with you, always the same, if you take a little care to keep it.'

Rhoda stood looking across the heath.

'I think I will go back,' she said; 'it will be so hot by-and-by.'

'Well, well, and I must go round the farm,' said old Wichelow.

. He got up and hobbled away without further farewell. Rhoda walked back towards Fanelands. On the border of the woods she met old Micah Yates.

'There'll be the singing to-night, I suppose, ma'am,' he said, 'as usual?'

Rhoda answered him quickly:

'No, not to-night, Micah; I cannot come to-night. To-morrow — or Friday. Will you tell them all it will be Friday instead?'

'I'll tell them, ma'am. We'll all be there.'

Rhoda walked on. She was in a restless

mood, created by the conflict of many feelings. The sight of Anthony Dexter had shattered the calm happiness that had grown into her life; she hardly knew what the strange feeling was that had taken its place. She told herself that she was sorry he should have come in her way, that she had seen him once more; in reality she knew that it was joy that had risen up triumphant at the sight of his face; and deep in her heart was a strong, unacknowledged desire to see him yet again.

The weather was still sultry and close; in the shut-in, low-lying grounds of Fanelands Hall the stagnant air seemed weighted with a languid unrest. Rhoda would not go into the house : she wandered about the garden, plucking the overblown roses from the straggling bushes, setting herself, in an aimless, desultory way, to what had become her daily task, the care of the long untended plants and flowers. She worked on till dinner-time, and afterwards, in the afternoon, went back into the garden with a book, thinking she was tired enough to be able to rest. But her thoughts would not follow her eyes along the page : soon she rose and walked to and fro in the shade of the trees, the cawing rooks calling around her with harsh voices : and after a while she returned to the house again.

The great hall was cooler than the heated air outside. She sat for a while on the cushioned seat beneath the stained window with her book open upon her knee ; then, as the day began to wane, she sent to the lodge for little Rufus Stockbridge, and seated herself before the organ, feeling that with its voice she might be able to unburden herself of some of the restless emotion that worked within her.

She waited ; but the little boy did not come ; and presently the maid she had sent for him returned, and said that he was out gleaning in a field some distance away. Still Rhoda sat before the organ : she had already opened it,. and she let her hands rest on the keys, striking now and again one of the dumb notes. The big outer door was open ; the golden light of early evening lay over the lawn outside, and entered the doorway, lingering about the further end of the hall.

Rhoda sat with her eyes on the tall pipes that rose up high above her head, and seemed to reproach her with their silence : everywhere was the oppressive, sultry hush, broken only by the monotonous, constant cawing of the rooks. It seemed to her as she sat there in the shaded gray beyond the yellow haze about the door, that she and the organ were growing each into the other, becoming one, and that if she still sat on with her hands upon the voiceless keys, she would soon have no power to move or speak, until the organ, too, was released from its bond of silence.

Then her ear caught faintly the sound of footsteps on the drive; but she did not turn: the footsteps seemed to mount the steps leading up to the door; and still she did not turn: though her ear heard, her consciousness only half accepted her hearing's message; and she still sat without moving, her hands pressing down the waiting keys.

Then at last the clock struck out six vibrating notes. The sound roused her from her dreaminess, and she turned and saw a man standing in the doorway. She could not see his face because of the stronger light behind him; but she knew at once that it was Anthony Dexter; and in the first moment it seemed neither strange nor startling that he should be standing there.

'May I come in?' he said; and advanced without waiting for an answer.

Rhoda rose to her feet, but she did not come forward.

'I have come,' said Anthony, 'to pay my

bridal call, to offer my congratulations on your marriage. I ought to have rung the bell, I know, but it seemed superfluous when the door was so wide open.'

'When did you come?' said Rhoda.

'A few minutes ago.'

'From Wrexholme, where we were yesterday?'

'Yes. I found out at the inn that you really had been there. At first I—well, never mind. I did not know that Wrexholme was so near this country.'

'You are staying there?'

'I was; for a couple of days. I am going on to Weyminster to play at a concert, and I thought I would take Fanelands on my way.'

'It must be out of your way.'

'It is—a little; but I wanted to pay my bridal call.'

Rhoda was standing by the organ, her hand resting on the lower key-board. She crushed down the notes as she said:

' My husband is not here.'

' Then I can only do half my duty ; I can only congratulate *you*.'

' It is a pity,' Rhoda said, ' that you came out of your way for such a small duty.'

' Is it a pity ?' He looked round the hall, and back at Rhoda's face. ' I don't know.'

He touched the organ.

' Do you play this ?' he said.

' I have been learning.' She hesitated. ' Paul has taught me.'

' Your husband ? Ah yes, I remember ; he has a knowledge of music. Will you let me hear his pupil ?'

' I play badly.'

' Let me give you a lesson.'

She shook her head.

' Do you go on to Weyminster to-night ?' she asked.

' No ; to-morrow.'

A maid came round the corner of the hall.

'Little Stockbridge is back now, ma'am,' she said, 'and he would like to see you.'

'He can come in,' Rhoda said.

The maid stepped back a few paces and made a beckoning sign, and Rufus Stockbridge came forward, panting and hot.

'I have just got back, ma'am,' he said, 'and mother, she told me as how you'd sent; and I am very sorry, and I will blow now, ma'am, as soon as you please.'

'I don't think——' Rhoda began, and paused: in the pause Anthony Dexter, standing close to the organ, passed his hands over the soundless keys.

She turned to him with a sudden movement; there was an eager, half-fearful look on her face.

'Will you play?' she said.

He did not answer; for a moment his eyes met hers; then he sat down and began to pull out the stops.

Rhoda moved over to the fireplace. It

was bare and desolate now; but she sat down and looked into its cold emptiness, her back to the organ, as often, in the winter evenings, she had sat and watched the flames, and half expected to hear the dumb notes sound. The stillness seemed to last a long time; she heard and yet did not hear the cawing of the rooks outside; she waited with a sort of trembling terror, and yet with passionate longing, for the music to begin. The pipes were filled now; the organ was alive; and once more Anthony Dexter bent forward and touched the keys, and made it speak.

CHAPTER X.

O Mother, Mary Mother,
Three days, three nights between Hell and Heaven !
D. G. ROSSETTI.

IT was twilight when the music ceased; all
the gold had gone out of the light ; the gray
ghost of the dead day walked in the hall and
in the lonely garden outside.

Anthony Dexter ceased his playing, and
turned and looked round.   Rhoda was standing a few yards away from him : her face
was dim, and he could not see the quiver of
her lips ; but it seemed to him that the light
of the faded sunset had passed into her eyes.

'You must go,' she said after a minute.

He did not answer.   She waited a little
while with her shining eyes looking into the

shadow in which he stood; then suddenly she turned away from him; and before he could touch or speak to her she was gone.

Half an hour passed away, and then, very slowly, and pausing every now and again, Rhoda came down the staircase and stole, with wary eyes and tread, into the hall. It was empty; the dim twilight held a vacant loneliness; she waited awhile, standing in the darkness made by the organ's shadow; then she 'moved on through the open door out into the quiet garden.

At the back of the house was an avenue of copper beeches : it had once been a carriage-way up to the house, but it had not been used for many years, and the grass had covered the space between the rows of trees. Rhoda took her way to this avenue, and paced up and down beneath the dusky branches. The brown, dark leaves looked weird in the waning light; there was a sense of disquiet in the still air, a weight of fore-

boding in the heavy sky. To Rhoda everything looked unreal and strange ; a glamour
lay over the eyes of her mind, a fever of
excitement made her blood run hot and fast.
She walked from end to end of the avenue,
her hands clasped together at the back of
her head, her face looking up through the
sad-coloured branches to the sullen sky
beyond. There was no clear thought in her
mind ; emotions, impulses, dormant for many
months, were awake and strong once more,
and swept away the power to think.

It was quite dark when she came back to
the house. She paused in the hall to tell
the servants that she wanted nothing more
that evening, then went on up to her room.
It was not late, but she shut herself in for the
night, and locked the door. She did not
undress, and she did not strike a light : she
went over to the window and threw it open
as wide as it would go ; then, leaning her
elbows on the sill outside, she rested her

chin upon her hands, and looked out into the darkness.

The sky was clouded, and there were no stars; the air was motionless and sultry; there was no sound. The girl's face was flushed, and her eyes still shone; there was a whirling in her brain, and in the silence she could hear the loud, fast beating of her heart. Later on, a little thin breeze stirred the heavy air and made a light rustling in the trees; and by-and-by it increased in strength and came in long sweeps through the trembling leaves.

The time went on : the servants had gone to bed now, and all the house was in darkness. Rhoda still stood by the window, leaning out, and looking through the blankness that met her outward sight into a strange world, wherein good and evil masqueraded in perplexing guise, and the soul of one took on the form of the other.

It was very early the next morning when

she unlocked her door and went down into the garden. In her pocket was the pencil-case ˉshe had found at Heather Den, and which she had taken from the drawer where it had been locked out of sight for nine months. Anthony had said he was to leave Fanelands in the morning; yet she felt sure he would come again; and as she wandered about the garden in the freshness of the early day, as she sat in the hall and toyed with the breakfast that had been prepared for her, she had no thought but of his coming. She awaited him with a feeling that was almost dread, but with a certainty of expectation.

It was still early when he came. Rhoda met him on the threshold of the big door. She made no pretence of surprise at seeing him.

'I knew you would come,' she said.

He followed her back into the hall.

'How did you know?'

She did not answer the question.   She put her hand into her pocket and drew out the pencil-case.

'This is yours,' she said.   'I found it at Heather Den.   I am glad to be able to give it back to you.'

Anthony Dexter took the pencil-case and stood for a little while silent before her.

'You do not ask me to sit down,' he said at last.

'I am going up to Heather Den—almost directly.'

'I may go with you?'

'But you are going to Weyminster—to the concert.'

'I have altered my plans.   I have written to say I cannot play.'

'You are not going away to-day?'

There was a sharp, frightened intonation in Rhoda's voice.

'I don't know.'

She turned and walked a few paces down

the hall, and stood looking away from
him.

'Come out into the garden,' he said.

She shook her head.

'I must speak to you,' he said, 'before
I go.'

'What have you to say?'

'Only good-bye.'

'That can be said here—and quickly.'

'I know, and yet—— It is gloomy
here; I would rather say it in the sunshine.'

She did not speak, and after a pause he
went on:

'Give me only ten minutes. It is not
likely that we shall ever meet again.'

She stood with her face still turned away
from him.

'I suppose not.'

'Can't you spare me ten minutes,' he
said, 'out of the whole of your married
life?'

She turned and walked past him to the open door, and he followed her out into the sunshine.

An ·hour later Rhoda Garnet came back into the hall alone. She sat down before the organ, and leaned her head upon the uncovered keys; and she sat almost in the same position for a long time, moving very slightly now and again.

The day passed heavily; a great listlessness followed upon the excitement of the morning: now that Rhoda believed temptation to be over, the thought of it became perilously sweet; now that she had found strength to send away the man whose music, whose presence even, influenced her so strangely, a half-conscious desire awoke in her to see him again. As the afternoon wore away, the weight of depression grew heavier; she felt very lonely and miserable when, towards dusk, she strolled out of the quiet house, and went to walk again in the avenue of copper beeches.

It was half an hour later, and when she was about to go back to the empty rooms, that Anthony Dexter came out of the village inn. He had not kept his promise of the morning; he had not gone away. He had waited in the inn all the afternoon; now, in the evening, he went back once more to Fanelands Hall. He found Rhoda in the garden, and he found her worn out and lonely.

That night there was a great storm of rain; it beat against the side of the house where Rhoda watched. She drew her chair close to the open window, and, sitting down, let the rain drive in upon her face and breast. The storm was welcome to her; the fierce, dashing rain answered to something in herself that clamoured for release, development, dominion; her heart leaped with a wild exhilaration that grew and grew as the night went on.

She sat on by the window till the gray of the dawn was lost in the clearer light of the sunrise; then she rose, and began to move about the room, and presently went downstairs and out of the house.

The rain had cleared the heavy air, and made it fresh and sweet; the day was one of quiet beauty; a little breeze blew lightly in the woods and the garden, and swept with bolder force across the heath.

Rhoda felt no fatigue after her sleepless watching; the fever of the night was upon her still, and with it the same sense of expectation that had filled her the morning before. Yet to-day was not as yesterday; for whereas then the knowledge of Paul's absence had caused her heart to tremble, now the thought that he was far away gave her a delirious sense of freedom: yesterday she had looked to him as a saviour; to-day the strange spirit that possessed her showed him as a gaoler to her eyes. She said to herself that she would see Anthony Dexter once more this morning, and then never again ; but the once more was near, and the never again seemed a very long way off.

In old Wichelow's cornfields the men and women were hard at work : a good deal of the corn had been carried, but there was a field that must be cleared by the morrow evening before the Sunday's rest, and the workers knew that they must labour hard to finish their task. They worked steadily. In the evening Rhoda would come to the clearing in the wood, and break with her singing the hard monotony of their life, and they shortened the time set apart for dinner and tea in order to be free to meet her at the usual hour.

The sun dipped down towards the edge of the heath ; the shadows of the harvesters

stretched far across the field ; the breeze that
had blown all day died away as the sky grew
red with the sunset.   Then gradually the
colour faded from the sky and earth, and the
twilight came softly.

'This'll be the last load,' said one of the
men, pausing for a minute to wipe his brow.
'To-morrer 'll finish it well.'

'It will so,' said another.

'We'll be in time for she,' said a woman.

'Ay, and she'll wait a bit for us if we're
late,' said Micah Yates.

In the corner of the field old Wichelow
stood looking on.   He advanced when he
saw the people preparing to leave off work.

'It must all be in by to-morrow evening,'
he said ; 'mind that.   I'll have no lazy
workers in my hire.   I know what a day's
work ought to be, and those that take my
wages must earn them.'

'It'll be done for sure, master,' said old
Micah.

Boniface Wichelow stood for a minute, measuring with his keen eyes the space that yet remained to be cleared; then with a grunt he turned and hobbled away.

When he had gone, the people trooped off in a straggling line towards the woods. It was a little past the usual hour of meeting, they knew, and they hurried along as fast as their tired bodies would allow them to move. With their weary, shuffling feet they followed the path through the wood; some of the faces took on a faint brightness of expectation as they neared the open space; the lagging footsteps became brisker. But when at last they reached the clearing, the first man stopped short.

'She's not come,' he said.

There was incredulity on the people's faces as they came out from amongst the trees into the open space; it changed to blank disappointment, mingled with a dull wonder, when they saw that their leader had spoken the truth. Rhoda was not there.

'She'll come presently,' said one.

They waited, leaning on their pitchforks or against the trunks of the trees.

'Maybe she's ill,' somebody said at last.

'Nay, she's not weakly, and she 'ld have sent to tell us.'

'Or she's forgot,' hazarded another.

'Have you ever knowed her to forget us?' old Micah Yates said, turning with a sort of anger to the last speaker.

'She'll come yet,' said a woman.

'Ay, she'll come,' Micah repeated.

The twilight grew deeper. It was strange to be in this place, associated in the minds of all who waited with the singing that had arisen thence for so many years, and to meet only silence. The silence awed them as they stood; by-and-by the voices ceased to speak, and they waited in dumb patience.

They waited till the twilight had faded

and passed away ; they waited, fearing to go, lest she for whom they looked should come at last ; they waited till the air grew chill and the night was close at hand. But Rhoda did not come.

CHAPTER XI.

Hope led me all the way,
With eyes of promise fair,
And waving golden hair ;
But at the threshold paused and would not stay.
Within, grim-eyed and gray,
In Love's own kingdom lay
Despair.

PAUL GARNET walked with long, even strides
across the heather. The cool breeze met
him as he went, and blew with refreshing
softness on his brow ; he carried his hat in
his hand. There was a gentle upward slope
of the ground till he had reached the top ;
he could not see across the wide expanse of
heath that stretched away to the wooded
descent leading down to Fanelands Hall.
He was soon at the brow of the slope, and

the bare, flat space lay clear before him ; but he would not let his eyes run on ahead with his heart ; he looked down at the ground ; there was so much that might deceive his sight, and give false confirmation to the waiting hope within him.

He went on steadily, rather slackening than hurrying his pace ; he glanced sometimes to the right or to the left, but never straight ahead ; he knew every yard of the heath, and he could tell exactly where he was without looking about him. He reached and passed the little hollow, from which, concealed by the heather, he had seen and spoken to Anthony Dexter for the first time. The incident came back to him as he passed the spot : he turned his mind away from it with a feeling of triumph that yet held a touch of jealous disquietude.

He went on ; a little space of sand lay yellow amidst the purple of the heather ; further on a gorse-bush broke the sameness

of the colouring. Paul knew them both;
they were landmarks to his watching eyes;
a few yards ahead, he would pass a little
heap of stones, then another clump of gorse,
and then—— He strode on, still looking
on the ground, as he had done when he had
followed the same path six nights ago; he
reached the point where on that other evening he had paused; and he paused again,
and looked up, straight before him, at last.

The heather stretched away, its solitude
unbroken, to where, half a mile ahead, the
trees rose up, barring the view; and between
him and them was nothing, except the rough,
broken ground, and the fading yellow sunlight. Paul stood quite still, looking with
fixed eyes into the emptiness that lay before
him. A slight flush rose to his cheeks, and
his lips pressed each other more closely; but
he showed no other sign of disappointment
or of anger. He did not wait long. Soon
he moved on again, with the same measured

step with which he had crossed the heath ;
but now he looked forward instead of on the
ground, and though his mouth was set firmly,
his eyes had a strained, searching look.

He reached the edge of the open ground,
and entered the sloping wood that led down
to Fanelands. He crossed a corner of the
village and entered his own grounds by the
lodge-gate. In the drive, about half-way up
to the house, little Rufus Stockbridge, on his
hands and knees, was crawling slowly from
side to side.

'What the devil are you doing here?' said
Paul.

The boy got up hurriedly, and made a
snatch at a lock of his front hair.

'Beg pardon, sir,' he said, with a catching
of the breath that was caused partly by his
own private distress, and partly by fear of
the questioner, 'I've lost the half-a-crown.'

There were traces of tears on his freckled
face ; his under-lip trembled.

'What half-crown? What do you mean?'

'What the gentleman give me.'

The tears broke forth again, and two grimy sets of knuckles were stuffed into the eyes from which they flowed.

'What gentleman? Speak out at once, and tell me what you mean.'

There was something in Paul Garnet's voice that stopped the boy's tears.

'Him what plays the organ,' he said, shrinking away as he spoke; 'what was here last year, the first time ever I blowed.'

'He has been here again?'

The words were rather an assertion than a question.

'Yes, sir.'

'And he played?'

'Yes, sir.'

Paul Garnet went on up the drive. He entered the house by the side-door, and found his way into the hall. It was empty; the organ stood open. He called: 'Rhoda!'

There was no answer. He went to the foot of the stairs and called again : 'Rhoda!' Still the silence.

As he waited before mounting the stairs, the door into the servants' wing opened, and Mrs. Shand, the housekeeper he had had for many years, came into the hall.

'Where is your mistress?' Paul asked.

'She didn't write, then, sir?'

'Write? N— Answer my question.'

'She went, sir, yesterday.'

'Yes ; go on.'

'I was to say, if you should ask, that she had gone away.'

'If I should——' Paul laughed. 'Was that all?'

'That was all, sir.'

'Ah! it's all right.'

Mrs. Shand still stood hesitating, while Paul looked at her with sightless eyes. At last his set face quivered, and he spoke.

'What are you waiting for?' he said.

' I thought, sir——' the woman began.

' What have you to do with thinking ?' Suddenly Paul's voice strengthened and broke out fierce and loud. ' Damn you, don't think !' he cried. ' It's perdition to think !'

The woman turned, but before she had reached the door, he called after her.

' Mrs. Garnet was to have joined me at Mercheston,' he said, in a calm voice. ' There has been some mistake, and I have missed her. I shall follow her to London to-morrow.'

CHAPTER XII.

The man, my lover, with whom I rode sublime
On Fortune's neck.

TENNYSON.

ANTHONY DEXTER lived in a house facing
Hyde Park. It was occupied by a little
colony of artists ; a writer, two painters, and
Anthony Dexter, who had a room on the
first floor, whence his music could not reach
and disturb the writer, who lived at the top
of the house. Anthony's room had four
windows ; two looking across the busy road
into the London half-quiet of the Park ; two
at the back, facing a large, still graveyard, a
silent space in the midst of the stir of life.
An organ came from the back wall far out

into the room, leaving a deep recess on either side of it. In one recess the window was wide and low, and through it could be seen the branches of the trees that rose above and covered the tombstones ; in the other the window was of a high, narrow shape, and it showed no glimpse of what lay beyond it, being filled with stained glass.

The colours of the glass were of a wonderful richness ; the subject was the awakening of the Sleeping Beauty. In the lower half of the window a gray, mailed knight, amidst a mass of rich green and flowers of brilliant red, bent forward and touched the shoulder and the golden hair of the princess, who slept, leaning her head upon her hand, her blue robe falling in quaint, lead-divided sections to her red-shoed feet. In the upper part, the figure of Love stood, a halo round his head, one hand uplifted, the other holding a branch of green, with three roses in a full red bloom ; red, feathered wings stretched

out behind him across the flowing blue of the
background, and others, furled about his
white garment, added a touch of passion to
his purity. Between the knight and the
princess, hidden here and there by her hair
and his outstretched arm, a scroll ran, bear-
ing the words from the song of Solomon:
'Surge, amica mea, speciosa mea, et veni:'
across the sky behind the figure the motto
showed: 'Fortis ut mors dilectio': and both
the upper and lower parts of the window
were bordered with a space of vivid green,
in which, in glowing letters of red, the
triumphant words repeated themselves again
and again: 'Omnia vincit amor.'

The window, the work of an artist little
known at the time he had designed and
carried it out, had been left to Anthony
Dexter by an uncle who had discerned in
him a certain artistic sympathy which his own
children had failed to inherit. At first Anthony
was not much pleased with the bequest;

he cared little for any art but music, and the
stained window was a sort of white elephant
that he did not know what to do with.   But
he did not like to part with it ; and when he
arranged to take his rooms in St. George's
Terrace for a term of years, he had one of
the windows altered in such a way that the
stained glass could be fitted into it.   Since
then the beauty, the marvellous colour of
the window, had become associated with all
that he thought out and did in his own art,
until the two became almost unconsciously,
and quite indivisibly, blended in his mind ;
and in his music he found the vivid colours of
the glass, and in the glass found harmonies.

It was before this window that Rhoda
stood, gazing at it intently, while Anthony
Dexter, moving about the room, collected
various papers and note-books together.
After a time he came and stood behind her.
She turned suddenly.

'What does it mean ?' she said, 'the words

that run all round the frame? They are the same words over and over again, but I cannot read them.'

'Love conquers all.'

'It is true,' she said, with a flashing smile; 'it is the very truth, the only truth a woman needs to know.' She looked at Anthony with the smile still lingering. 'Play me again,' she said, 'the music that taught me the truth.'

He sat down at the organ and played the air that had been born amidst the solitude and the sighing winds of Heather Den. Rhoda listened, still standing with her eyes upon the rich beauty of the window. Her breath came faster as she listened, but her face no longer wore the look of doubt and fear that had troubled it when first Anthony had touched her with his music: now there was a smile upon her lips, half exulting, half defiant, and a look of determination in her eyes. When the music ceased,

she turned and came a few steps towards the
player; as she did so, her eyes met the view
of the Park through the front window, and
she stopped to look at it. The afternoon
was gray; it was not raining, but rain-clouds,
borne onwards by a slow, persistent wind,
covered all the sky; the dusty leaves moved
lazily; the brown, worn grass was spotted
with poorly-clad children, gathered in little
groups or running hither and thither in their
play. The scene had a prosaic sadness about
it; the glory of the summer seemed to have
passed away, leaving only dust and weariness
to the drooping trees; there was no beauty
of light and shade on the sunless, even-toned
tract of grass; the poetry of childhood found
no place amidst the romping, squalid children
and the uncomfortable babies in the peram-
bulators.

After a minute's gaze, Rhoda turned to
the vivid colours of the window again.

' Beauty and music and love,' she said half

aloud; 'those shall be the whole of my life. I have—will have—nothing more to do with the cold and gray.'

'What is that you say?' Anthony asked, coming close to her.

'Love conquers all!' she said, 'and having conquered, reigns. I give myself to it—and you.'

They stood side by side, a reckless self-abandonment in their faces, while in the front part of the room the cold, stern light of the real world outside came in and fell upon the print in which Anthony had first seen her face.

A few hours later they were far away from the stained window, the dusty Park, the heavy air of the streets, carried by a rapid, onward - rushing train, further and further towards the sunlight and the poetry of Italy.

CHAPTER XIII.

At this grief my heart was utterly darkened ; and what
ever I beheld was death.—*Confessions of St. Augustin.*

IT was evening. Old Boniface Wichelow
sat on the settle in the room, where the last
gleams of daylight struggled feebly with the
advancing night. He did not like to waste
even a ray of light, and he waited to go to
bed till the darkness should be fully come.

The outer door was locked and barred as
usual; in the kitchen, Sally, not daring to
light a candle till her master should have
gone upstairs, sat dozing with her head and
arms on the table. Then, all at once, both
Sally and old Wichelow were roused, the one
from her slumbers, the other from the silent

heart-worship of his god, by a knocking at the door. Sally woke up with a start and a little scream, and came running out of the kitchen; old Wichelow came with slow, cautious steps into the passage.

'Are you there, master?' Sally called in a loud, piercing whisper.

'Ay.'

'Shall I open the door, master?'

'No.'

'Shall I fetch a candle, master?'

'No.'

'What shall I do, master?'

'Be quiet.'

Sally withdrew to the door of the kitchen, and stood on the threshold, her stupid, frightened face looking out into the darkness of the passage. Boniface Wichelow went along to the little grating and called through it, 'Who's there?' but he almost knew whose voice would answer.

'It is I, Paul.'

The words were said in calm, measured tones ; there was none of the impatience and anger at being kept waiting that the old man had expected.   He withdrew the bolts and bar and opened the door, and Paul entered.

'I will get a light,' said old Wichelow. 'Sally, bring a light. I do not care for light,' he went on, following Paul into the room, 'not when I am alone ; it hurts my eyes. But now that I have company——'

'I want no light,' Paul broke in ; 'I have only to speak to you, and I can speak in the darkness.'

'No light?' The old man hobbled quickly across the room. 'Sally, do not bring a light.   Mr. Garnet does not care for light this evening.'

When he turned, Paul was standing by one of the windows, a tall, dimly-outlined figure against the dull gray of the sky outside.   Old Wichelow went back to his settle.

'How's Rhody?' he said.   'I haven't seen

her since Thursday, and this is Monday; quite a long time.'

'She is away from home,' said Paul; 'that is why you have not seen her.'

'Away? Rhody away? Dear me! I hope there's nothing the matter?'

'What should be the matter?'

'Oh, nothing; only I thought—— But it is so sudden, you see; and she never told me anything about it.'

'She did not tell you that she was to join me at Mercheston, and that we were going on to London together?'

'No, she did not tell me—no, nothing.'

'The plans were not quite settled when she was here,' said Paul, 'and the letter I wrote to her from Mercheston did not reach her.'

'Did not reach her? You should inquire into it. The postal arrangements about here are not too good at the best of times. You should certainly inquire into it.'

'Damn you!' The words were spoken under Paul's breath ; out loud he said : ' Did not reach her in time, I mean.'

' For what ?'

' To tell her where she was to meet me. I missed her, and she went on to London alone.'

' Alone ?'

Paul did not notice the question nor the faintly sarcastic tone of the voice that asked it.

' I followed her yesterday,' he said.

'And you are back to-day ! You did not stay long. And Rhody—why did she not come with you this evening ?'

' I thought I told you ; because she is still away.'

'Ah, yes, I remember. She is away, and you came back ?'

' Precisely.'

' Each of you left alone.'

' She will be away some months,' Paul said.

'I cannot leave Fanelands for so long. I shall go to London only for a day now and again.'

'It will be lonely for Rhody all alone.'

'I have many friends in London; she will not be lonely.'

'And she has a friend—our lodger of last year; he lives in London, I believe. By the way, he was here last week, while you were away.'

'So I heard.'

'Ah! Rhody would tell you. He spent most of his time at the Hall, I was told.'

'You were told rightly.'

'He should have taken charge of Rhody on her way to London—if he went back to London, of course, I mean.'

'He did.'

Paul's voice, that had been so strong and firm hitherto, said the last words with a slight falter. Old Wichelow did not appear o notice him.

'I thought perhaps he would,' the old man said, with a sort of snigger; 'I thought as much.'

The latent sneer in Boniface Wichelow's tone, the half-laugh with which he ended his speech, made a sudden change in Paul's attitude and voice. In two bounds he was beside the settle.

'Tell me what you mean,' he said.

The old man cowered down into his dark corner.

'Nothing, Paul. Paul, I mean nothing,' he cried, in a jerky, frightened voice.

Without speaking, Paul left the room, and returned presently with a lighted candle. He came back to the settle, and held the candle close to the old man's face.

'Now,' he said, 'tell me what you mean, and tell me at once.'

Old Wichelow shrank from his gaze, but he could not withdraw his eyes from the fierce eyes before him.

' I thought——' he began.

There was no sarcasm in his voice now, only a trembling fear.

' Go on.'

' That Rhody——'

' Go on.'

' Might have left you.'

For half a minute there was intense, dead silence in the room ; the two faces, the old, white, wrinkled one, and the other, dark, set, with a world of fierce, crushed-back pain in it, were close together, vivid in the light of the candle that flared and flickered between them. Then suddenly Paul rose up and threw the candle away from him, and in the darkness that closed over the space of light where it had burned, gave a sharp cry.

' You have spoken the truth,' he said.

He stood there, silent again, motionless, while old Wichelow, crouching on the settle, and hidden by the darkness, let his frightened face relax in strange contortions. Presently Paul came back to the settle ; he kneeled down, and seized one of the old man's hands in his, crushing it in the strength of his grasp. Boniface winced and writhed, but made no sound.

'What you have said is the truth,' Paul said, with low, suppressed utterance. 'She has left me.'

'With——'

'With Anthony Dexter.' Paul's voice rose in a groaning laugh ; then sank immediately to its low, concentrated tone again. 'You and I know,' he said, 'you and I and the devil, we three. But nobody else. You remember what I said when I came here to-night ?'

'Ay !' the old man said softly.

'*That* is the truth, for everybody else ; and for you—after to-night.'

'But how—if she never comes back ?'

'She will come back.'

As Paul said the words, the old man shuddered, hardly knowing why.

'You—but you will not forgive her, Paul?'

'No.'

'And he?' old Wichelow asked, in the whisper to which his voice had sunk. 'Shall you kill him?'

'If I had found him yesterday, I should have killed him.'

'You did not find him?'

'No; but sooner or later he must bring her back to London again.'

'Till then——'

'I can wait.'

Paul was quiet a minute; then, with a sudden movement, he threw the old man's hand away from him and rose to his feet.

'You know now what has happened,' he said. 'If you ever tell as truth anything other than what I have willed to be the truth, I shall know how to reckon with you.'

He crossed the room and went down the

passage, and old Wichelow heard the door
bang to. He sat for a long time crouched
up on the settle without moving : Paul's
presence, his words and manner, something
in the tone of his voice, had created in the
old man a nervous dread, which continued
long after Paul had left the house. But
gradually he recovered from the impression
which had been made upon him, and at last
he got down from his seat and moved slowly
across the room.

'Poor Rhody!' he muttered ; 'a fool, like
all the rest—a doting, blind fool!' All at
once he began to chuckle. 'And Paul?' he
said ; 'he is down at last! Anyhow, she has
paid my debt to Paul.'

Paul Garnet went out on to the heath.
The unheeding stars shone faintly, with a
mild, benignant light, between the slow clouds
that trailed across the sky; the stretch of
heather lay blank and dark before him. He
walked on at a slow, even pace, till he was

about a mile away from Heather Den; then, when the loneliness around him was complete, he sat down upon the ground. He drew his knees up nearly to his chin; his head bent over them; his hands clasped them round. And so he sat without moving for two long hours.

The night grew thick about him; the breeze brushed him coldly; the dew lay damp upon his unshielded head. He still sat on, his body rigid and motionless as death, his heart wrung with a living agony of passionate despair and pain that, by its very intensity, destroyed at last the capacity to suffer. Worn to exhaustion, Paul's figure bent and swayed; he sank upon his side; and lying in the heather, in the place where Anthony Dexter had seen him first, he fell into a deep and heavy sleep.

CHAPTER XIV.

I, if I sin, sin with my mind and will,
And if the price of sinning be my soul,
Then let it perish quickly.

IT was drawing on towards sunset. The broad lagoon lay still, offering its quiet breast as a mirror for the fairy colouring that clothes the sky and floats in the atmosphere of Venice in September. Stretches of motionless opal were broken here and there by rippling lines, wherein the magic light took life and moved and danced; far off the sky, in love with the image of itself, dipped down to reach the sea; from out the water rose the palaces and towers of the floating town.

On the lagoon the gloomy gondolas, like

realities of death in a dream of life, moved over the smooth water; in one of them sat Rhoda Garnet and Anthony Dexter. Rhoda leaned back on the soft cushions. There was a languorous grace in her attitude; one hand, hanging over the side of the gondola, touched the water now and again; the light cloak she wore was unfastened, and had slipped from her shoulders, leaving her throat bare. As the sun sank, the sky grew glorious with shaded reds and pinks, violet and palest blue, and the wonderful Venice green, which, finding no grass wherein to lay down its beauty, will yet not quite desert the favoured fairy town, but shows itself at sunset in the sky; and the water, drinking in the colours glowing and brightening above, painted them afresh with a transparent touch that made their richness a marvel; till the whole world seemed a magic globe, with Venice and the black gondolas in the midst, glory divided from glory by the life of men and the floating shadows of death.

Rhoda, looking from sky to sea, spoke after a space of silence.

'I never knew,' she said, 'what beauty was till now.'

'Nor I.' Anthony's eyes were on her face. 'You are much more beautiful than you have ever been.'

She smiled.

'Yes; I know it. I am very glad. It proves to me that I have found myself.'

'Give me the credit. You would never have found yourself if it had not been for me.'

'I wonder,' she said.

'When I first saw you——'

'Oh yes,' she broke in quickly; 'when you first saw me, I thought the world was a wilderness and I myself a pilgrim.'

'And now?'

'Now I know that the world was made for life, and that I was meant to live.'

He looked at her a little pensively.

'Yet,' he said slowly, 'you were very beautiful all that time; there was a charm——'

Her laugh had a discordant note in it.

'The charm of mystery. Now that you know me for what I am, the charm is gone; there is nothing more to discover.'

'I am not so sure.'

'No,' she said quickly; 'I shall never change from what I am now. I shall go on'—her voice sank and died away into a whisper that he could not hear—'further and further away from what I was, until I die.'

'What is that you say?' Anthony asked.

'I was prophesying,' she said lightly, 'but prophecies are futile. It is as foolish to look forward as it is fatal to look back.' She paused a moment, and drew her cloak up about her. 'We will go on,' she said, 'without thought or doubt, to the very end.'

The sunset was still gorgeous when the

gondola touched the stone edge of the Piazzetta. As Rhoda and Anthony walked down the wide Piazza of St. Mark, the rich front of the great cathedral was shining and brilliant in the evening light. They reached their hotel by narrow streets and little bridges over side canals, and entered it from the back.

When Rhoda went up to her room, the sky was still pink over Santa Maria della Salute and beyond San Georgio, and the beauty of the colouring seemed twofold after the sober light of the shadowed side streets.

At *table d'hôte* she sat next to a stolid, prosperous Englishman. After a time he passed her the salt, and began to talk to her.

'Have you been long in Venice?' he asked.

'Only a week.'

'A week is not long for Venice.'

'No,' she answered; 'it has passed very quickly.'

'There is so much to see,' said her neighbour, looking at the *menu*.

'Yes; or one wants to go on seeing the same things over and over again.'

'St. Mark's is very fine.'

'Very.'

'I don't know which is the finest, the outside or the interior.'

'I have not been inside.'

'Not been inside, and you have been a week in Venice?'

'I never go inside anything,' Rhoda said.

'But—don't you think you ought to?'

Her companion looked at her with a grave, half-puzzled face. He knew exactly what he ought to admire, and was prepared to do it cheerfully; to refuse deliberately even to look at the beauties which everybody discussed on their return home seemed to him almost morally wrong.

Rhoda looked at him and smiled.

'I do the things that I like,' she said; 'there is no *ought* in my life.'

Her neighbour's face relaxed; she was very pleasant to look upon.

'Well, of course, when one is abroad,' he said, 'one is not quite so strict. The Sundays, for instance. When one is at Rome, you know——'

'But I am at home,' the girl broke in, with a backward twist of her head, and a thrill of enjoyment in her voice.

'At home?'

'Yes; this place and I belong to one another; the atmosphere of it is my native atmosphere. I lived here once—long ago—when Venice was in her prime; and in those days I went to Florence, and Leonardo da Vinci painted me.' She looked with a curious, half-amused smile into the puzzled face beside her. 'Have you never seen my portrait?' she said.

'I—yes; I begin to see. You really have a look of the faces in his pictures.' The man began to suspect a joke, and made an effort to carry it on. 'It was clever of him,' he said, 'to paint your face so long before it existed.'

'Oh no,' she said quickly; 'any painter can paint a face—whether it exists or not. The cleverness lies in this, that he painted my heart—three centuries before it began to beat.'

Her neighbour laughed, still on the track of the joke, but unable to see wherein it lay.

Rhoda turned to Anthony.

'Let us go,' she said; 'I have had enough dinner, and the room is so hot.'

They went out into the garden of the hotel; it overlooked the Grand Canal, and there were seats and little tables here and there along the low wall by the water's edge. A gondola, gay with coloured lights, lay in

front of the hotel; it was filled with people
playing guitars and mandolins, and singing
Venetian and Neapolitan songs.

'This is better than the dining-room,' said
Anthony.

'Much better.' Rhoda leaned her arms
upon the wall, and looked down into the
water. 'How dull and stupid people are!'
she said. She gave a little laugh. 'All but
you and me.'

'What are you thinking of?'

'That man that sat next me to-night. He
seemed to think that I should spend these
glorious days in the dark insides of things.'

'Most people do.'

'To come to Venice, and miss all the light
and life of it! Give me some money,
Anthony. These people are not quite in
tune, but they are part of the careless Venice
of pleasure and beauty, and they and I are
friends.'

The gondola drew close under the wall,

and Rhoda threw down some coins to the singers. They looked up with white-teethed Italian smiles, showing faintly in the pale moonlight ; then, with slow, deft strokes, they moved on down the canal.

'I am going to get a light,' said Anthony, taking his cigarette-case from his pocket.

'Very well.'

His footsteps crossed the garden. Rhoda still gazed down into the water ; motionless, the moonlight shining on her white dress, she looked like a carved statue as she leaned upon the wall. The singing had died away ; but gondolas, some black and weird, some gay with Chinese lanterns, still moved silently by ; the impalpable charm of Venice, the ghost of her past splendour, was abroad and ruled the scene. The lawless self-abandonment that dominated Rhoda spoke out loud in answer to the subtle influences about her.

'I want — will have only the beautiful part of life,' she said in an audible voice.

As she- spoke, out of the darkness below
a face looked up at her. Close to the wall
of the garden a gondola was drifting by ; it
bore no lights, and the dark dresses of the
gondolier and of the solitary figure that
leaned back against the cushions had hidden
it from her notice ; but when the face was
raised, the moonlight fell upon it, and
showed it to her plainly. It was a woman's
face, worn and pale, yet with a singular
beauty, partly of feature, partly of expression ; a strange face, strangely interesting.
The eyes met Rhoda's as she gazed down
towards the water ; the lips seemed to move
and form the word ' No,' repeated twice,
as though in answer to her speech. Then
the drifting gondola bore the face away.

CHAPTER XV.

I had great beauty : ask thou not my name ;
No one can be more wise than destiny.

TENNYSON.

A FEW minutes later, Rhoda, still leaning
upon the wall, was talking to Anthony and
another man, who were seated near her.
The latter sometimes sat next Anthony at
table d'hôte and had once before joined
them in the garden.

'It must have been Lady Mary Shadwell,' he said, when Rhoda had tried to
laugh herself out of the startled uneasiness
that had seized upon her, by relating in
flippant terms the incident that had caused
it. 'It could have been nobody else.'

'Who is she?' Rhoda asked.

'A rather interesting person.'

'She had an interesting face. I should like to know something about her. Can you tell me anything?'

'I can, if you really care to hear it.'

'I want above all things to hear it. You have made me curious.'

'She is a woman—You don't mind smoke?'

'Oh no!'

'A woman,' Mr. Soames continued, 'with a history.' He stopped a minute to blow at his cigar, then went on. 'She was married when she was quite young to a man more than double her age, with a tremendous fortune; or I should rather say, perhaps, that she married a large fortune, with an elderly man attached to it.'

'You mean,' Rhoda said, looking down at the passing gondolas, 'that she had no love for her husband.'

'Yes; the love came later on—for another man.'

' Ah !'

The sound was so low that neither of the men heard it. Mr. Soames went on speaking in his leisurely way :

' These things will happen sometimes, as you know ; and sometimes people are wise, or crafty, or both, and they blow over without an open scandal. But Lady Mary was neither the one nor the other, and she did about the most foolish thing a woman can do—she ran away.'

' I don't know——'

Rhoda turned suddenly and stood upright, facing the story-teller.

' Don't know what ?' he asked as she paused.

' Nothing ; go on.'

She turned round to the water again.

' Well, after a time the inevitable came to pass : the man got tired of her. Old Shadwell took no notice ; he didn't go after her, and he didn't get a divorce, which, I suppose,

was what she expected.   The man could not
marry her, of course.   I never heard that he
very much wanted to ; but however that may
be, Providence, in the shape of old Shadwell, would have none of it ; and after a
time he got tired of her and the sort of
life they had to live, and—he left her.'

'There is not much chivalry in your tale.'

Anthony Dexter forced a laugh as he
spoke.

The stranger shrugged his shoulders.

'He was an ordinary man.'

'But she '—Rhoda moved a little as she
spoke, and the moonlight showed her white
profile—'she was not an ordinary woman ?'

'I don't know ; women are more extra-
ordinary than men at all times.'

'What became of her afterwards ?'

'Oh, well, nothing very much out of the
way ; she was not particularly original.   She
did what a lot of women do who muddle
their earthly concerns, she turned to heaven.

She became violently religious—a sort of reaction, I suppose.'

'She has a wonderful face,' Rhoda said.

'She was very beautiful as a girl; I saw her before she was married.'

'She is almost beautiful still. Let us talk of something else.'

'By all means. Have you been to Torcello yet?'

'No. Why is she here in Venice?'

'Lady Mary do you mean?'

'Yes.'

'It is a fancy: it was here in Venice that the man she ran away with left her. She comes here every autumn; she has become one of the features of the place; everyone who knows Venice knows Lady Mary too.'

There was a little pause; then Rhoda turned to Anthony.

'Is it too late to go out in a gondola?' she said.

'I don't know,' Anthony began.

' Don't let me keep you,' Mr. Soames said, rising.

' Won't you come too ?' asked Anthony.

' Thank you, no. I have an engagement a little later on.'

When Anthony and Rhoda were left alone, neither of them spoke for a minute or two.

' Would you like to go on the water ?' Anthony asked presently.

' No, not now ; it is melancholy to-night, the water. We will go and walk on the Piazza.'

The Piazza was crowded with people. In the middle a band was playing : by the colonnades, walled with gaily-decked shops and brilliantly lighted, the clusters of chairs and tables were all occupied by eaters of ices and drinkers of coffee : at the further end, the façade of St. Mark's showed its beauty dimly in the moonlight ; and, like a silent guardian, the belfry tower rose near it, tall and dark, above the noise and the crowd, upwards to the still, clear sky.

'Would you like to sit down?' Anthony asked.

'No, we will walk.'

Rhoda moved on to where the crowd was thickest. As she mixed with it, as the life and movement of the scene swept past her, the colour flushed into her cheeks, and her eyes grew bright. People turned and looked at her. Her brilliant face was alight with a strange beauty, not so much of the flesh as of the spirit; a spirit neither divine nor lofty, but wild, self-glorious, triumphant, and strong with the indefinable strength with which spirit asserts itself over any mere quality of body.

When Anthony and Rhoda went back to the hotel, Rhoda went straight up to her room, while Anthony wandered out into the garden again to finish his cigar.

On the table was a vase of flowers of a

deep pink shade of red. Rhoda took them out of the water and twisted them into a wreath; she lighted all the candles in the room, and standing before the long glass in the soft, bright light, twined the wreath into her hair; then waited, looking at the image of herself, a tall, white figure, crowned with the red, delicate flowers, till Anthony came up. She turned when he entered and faced him: there was hardly a touch of doubt in the confident exultation of her voice.

'Am I beautiful?' she said.

His eyes answered her, and she smiled.

'You can never tire of me.'

Her confident voice took on a tone of more passionate assertion.

'You will never be able to leave me; not even your music can ever hold you again with so strong a strength as I. What do I care what other women have been, or done, or suffered? It is all nothing; I can hold my own.'

The man in Anthony Dexter told her that what she said was true; but faintly the artist voice that had been silent so long whispered that by-and-by the music in him would rise up and claim its right again, the chief place in his life.

CHAPTER XVI.

Beauty and anguish walking hand in hand
The downward slope to death.

TENNYSON.

ANOTHER week passed by. Anthony Dexter and Rhoda were still at Venice, and the warm cloudless weather still lasted day after day. They spent the greater number of their careless hours on the water, visiting Torcello and all the islands within easy distance of Venice. Once they went to the theatre to see an Italian play; Rhoda would not go when an opera was performed.

'I do not want music,' she said.

'Why not?' Anthony asked.

'I have done with it; it can do nothing for me now. It cannot rouse what is already roused; and for the rest——'

'For the rest, yes, for its own sake? You used long ago——'

Rhoda broke in upon him.

'I know,' she said quickly; 'that is what I could not bear. I dare not listen to what I heard in it long ago.'

Then, with an abrupt change of manner, she began to talk of some people she had seen at the Lido that morning. Anthony Dexter listened to and answered her, but his face wore a slightly absent look; and she knew, much better and more surely than he did, that the longing after music was awake in him again.

She had spoken the truth when she said that she did not want music; but besides the dread of hearing in it that appeal to the higher part of her nature, stronger and more constant than the strange sound influences that called into activity her more lawless impulses, she feared, though she would hardly own to herself the fear, that the

charm of his art, the only passion which, as
she felt instinctively, had power to compel
the sure and lasting devotion of Anthony's
uncertain artist nature, would break in upon
and devastate his love for herself; and the
fear made her shrink from that which might
tend to its development. And with the un-
owned dread upon her, she grew each day
more reckless, more extravagantly careless
of her own shame; denying her better self;
seeking to forget that she had ever been
other than she was; the more eager to forget, the more inexorably driven forward into
the life which she had chosen, by a doubt,
lying deep below the surface of her mood, a
doubt so bitter that she fought against the
very shadow of its existence, but which
existed nevertheless, and gnawed and bit
into her consciousness. The doubt was this,
that the feeling with which Anthony had
inspired her, and which was inseparably con
nected with his personality, was hardly love

for him, but rather an impetuous desire to understand and to set free the long latent, mysterious energies of her own nature. She had been in love, not so much with the man who had stirred these energies, as with a world richer in possibilities, in sensations, in beauty, than the narrow world of her up-bringing : Anthony Dexter had opened the door from one world to the other, and the mask of the magician had seemed to her curious, wondering eyes as the face of the god of love. The unacknowledged anguish of the thought she would not think, made her dread of a failure in Anthony's allegiance all the more terrible ; if she had mistaken both herself and him, the conditions of their present life must inevitably change ; and change would mean for herself only more complete disaster. For Anthony the few weeks of madness would be but an interlude in that man-life into which the world takes care to look no deeper than the surface ; but

for her they meant moral and social destruc-
tion. She could never return to what she
was before ; she must sink below her sin or
rise above her innocence ; and there was no
ladder by which she might rise, no platform
on which she could stand and look towards
heaven ; she felt that for her, separation from
Anthony meant a sinking to the lowest.

So, as the days went by, she grasped each
minute eagerly ; she would not acknowledge
the half-formed fears that tormented her ; and
shutting her eyes, lived on in defiant joyful-
ness.

It was a sweet, still afternoon. Rhoda
had been down to the flower-market, and
came back with a profusion of flowers heaped
on the seat beside her. The hot glory of
the day was lapsing into the gentler beauty
of evening ; the full blue of the sky declined
to a softer tint ; the perfume of the flowers
floated around Rhoda, as the gondola moved
slowly along in the deep shade of the wind-

ing side canals. Presently it shot into the brighter light of the Grand Canal ; and then a few strokes brought it to the steps of the hotel, where the water, restless with the motion and pressure of the many burdens it bore, lapped ceaselessly against the stone.

Rhoda passed through the cool, marble-floored hall, and up the staircase, carrying the flowers in a great straggling bundle in her two hands. She had some difficulty in opening the door of her room.

'Look !' she cried, when at last she had turned the handle and could push the door open with her arms. 'See what I have got !'

Anthony was sitting bending over the table, which was covered with sheets of paper. He turned, almost impatiently, as Rhoda spoke.

'Yes,' he said, 'they are beautiful ; I will look directly.'

'What are you doing ?' she asked.

She put the flowers down and advanced to the table. The sheets of paper were music paper ; some of them were covered with notes.

' You are writing ?'

' Yes, something I want to put down. Don't speak to me for a minute.'

Rhoda obeyed him literally ; she did not speak again. She stood for a minute or two quite still, the brilliant flowers lying forgotten beside her ; then, slowly, she retreated to the door. When at last Anthony looked up and turned to speak to her, she was gone. His eyes fell upon the mass of flowers ; their rich colours reminded him vaguely of the stained window in his room in London ; the subtile connection that had grown up in his mind between sound and colour appealed to him in a way of which he was hardly conscious ; after a minute he turned back to the table and went on with his writing.

Rhoda, meanwhile, walked quickly through

the narrow streets at the back of the hotel. The gnawing fear which had been gradually growing in her mind, had stirred at last ; she would not allow it to have a positive existence ; but it had quickened, and she knew, even while she would not admit the knowledge, that it would soon struggle forth and confront her in a definite form. Even as she walked, the fear began to cry aloud and speak in articulate voice, to tell her that the rival, put aside and forgotten for awhile, had come forward again, and that Anthony had already begun to own its power.

She walked on, not heeding whither she went, turning to the right or to the left as the canals barred her onward progress, until at last she found herself on the narrow ledge of pavement which divides the water from the church of San Giorgio degli Schiavoni. She went in, without thinking, through the narrow door that faced her. It was nearly closing time, and in the afternoon light the

frescoes on the walls were dim : she stood
looking with half-seeing eyes at Carpaccio's
realistic allegories, indistinct with the age
of centuries and the failing strength of the
passing day.

- It was wonderfully still : there were only
herself, the old sacristan, and one other
person in the place. The sacristan moved
about noiselessly, hovering around her, eager
to give information about the frescoes and
the building, if she would allow him a chance
to begin ; but there was something in her
face that checked his speech. He watched
her, but she did not stir, nor did her face
change ; and at last he moved away ; it
might be that she was one of those people
who came again and again to look at the
pictures, and knew as much about them as
he did.

At last Rhoda turned and went out again.
She had only looked at one picture ; the

fight with the dragon. She carried away a vague impression of it, but she could never remember afterwards when or where the impression had been made.

As she went out, the other person in the church rose from a bench and followed her. It was a woman, and as she came out into the fuller light outside, Rhoda, standing irresolute, not knowing which way to take, recognised her face with a start of quickened consciousness. It was the same strange face she had seen in the moonlight a week before; and it almost seemed as if Lady Mary Shadwell remembered and knew her too. Rhoda was moved with a curious impulse to go forward and put out her hand. The two women's eyes met; for an instant it seemed as if they would speak; then, with a little abrupt movement, Lady Mary turned away, and in another minute she had disappeared round an angle of the street. All the rest

of the time she was in Venice Rhoda never
saw her again ; but the strange face haunted
her, and it seemed to her that she knew and
understood the heart that looked forth
through the sorrowful eyes.

CHAPTER XVII.

'Tis God's voice calls : how could I stay ? Farewell !
R. BROWNING.

WHEN Rhoda got back to the hotel, Anthony had finished writing and was waiting for her.

'Where have you been ?' he asked. 'I was beginning to think you had gone away altogether.'

She answered him with a laugh, and in the very words she had used to her husband when he had said something of the same kind some weeks before ; but there was a bitterness in her heart now which had had no existence when she had answered Paul.

'Where should I go to ?' she said. 'You

seemed busy,' she went on lightly, 'so I thought I would do some sight-seeing. I have seen a church.'

'A church?'

'Yes; I have been inside something at last.'

'Not St. Mark's?'

'Oh no. I don't know what it was; it was a long way off, and it was small and silent and dreary.'

'I thought afterwards that perhaps you had been—well, offended, affronted, annoyed that I had kept you waiting.'

Rhoda laughed again.

'Why should I be? Did you think I was ealous of the music? Oh no, I was not afraid, either of it or of you.'

'You need not be,' Anthony said.

But Rhoda knew, though he himself did not, that he had not spoken the truth.

All through the evening she talked and laughed with extravagant gaiety. Later on, when the moon rose, Anthony suggested going on the water, and they drifted about the silvery lagoon for over an hour. There was a mystery of sadness in the still night; the beauty of it was too real to escape melancholy; the spirit of it almost impelled silence : yet Rhoda would not be silent. The restless determination of her mood would allow her heart no pause in which to feel, her brain no interval in which to think ; she talked persistently, with an almost aggressive gaiety, in passionate revolt against a dull sense of misery that would not be entirely quelled.

The next day she was much alone. Anthony settled down to his music soon after breakfast, and she would not seek to draw him away from it; she went out by herself and spent the greater part of the morning on the Lido, where she could walk freely, without the turns and twists of the narrow, canal-hemmed streets. In the afternoon Anthony went with her to Murano, and the next day they spent together in an excursion to Chioggia.

All through these days and the days that followed them, Rhoda lived in a sort of nightmare - dream.   She would not look forward; she would not think; her only effort was to stifle thought, to forget the precipice ahead until she should reach its very edge.   Yet, with all her efforts, thought would not be annihilated; though she locked the skeleton out of sight, she was conscious that it was still there; and insensibly a determination formed itself in her mind : it was full-grown before she knew that it had begun to exist.   It made its presence known to her suddenly one afternoon, when, as on many former afternoons, she and Anthony were on the lagoon at sunset.   It was a sunset of equal glory and beauty with the one that had glowed and faded on the day on which she had first seen Lady Mary Shadwell; again the varied tints of green and blue and purple covered the sky and repeated themselves in the water, again the whole scene seemed a vision of enchantment and no part of the tangible world.

'I wonder how much longer this will last?' Anthony said.

'What?'

Rhoda had sunk into a rare silence; she answered now as though she were glad to break it.

'The weather that makes such sunsets as these.'

'Oh, it will last,' Rhoda said, 'it must—till I have left you.'

Anthony turned to her quickly.

'What do you mean?'

Her face had grown suddenly pale. The words she had said had been said involuntarily, had spoken themselves out of that inner consciousness, the workings of which she had wilfully ignored: now that they had been formed in language, she knew that

through the turmoil of the last few days the
current of her being had set immutably
towards a sure decision ; the decision to part
from the man who had been to her the
embodiment of freedom and of love.   As
she sat with Anthony's eyes upon her, it
seemed to her that the turmoil had suddenly
ceased ; there was only a great blankness
before her.

' I mean,' she said after a moment, ' that I
am going away from you.'   She turned her
calm eyes upon him.   ' You must have known
that it would come.'

' Oh no—oh no !   Why should it come ?'

She gave a little bitter laugh.

' You should not have given me Byron to
read.   " Man's love is of man's life a thing
apart," he says, and——'

' Is it Byron,' he asked, ' who has put this
insane notion into your head ?'

' No,' she said, ' not Byron.'

' What then, or who ?'

'I hardly know. I did not know it was there till five minutes ago.'

'Do you know how the words go on?' he said, 'Byron's words?

> " Man's love is of man's life a thing apart ;
> 'Tis woman's whole existence."

What are you going to do?'

'I do not know. Byron gives no advice.'

'I might have known,' he said, ' that you would never care long.'

'Yes, you might have known.'

'Why is it?' he asked.

She waited a minute. 'I don't know, except that it is better that the end should be of my making, rather than of yours.'

'Why should there be an end?'

'Why?' She turned on him, her face alive with a sort of pitiful scorn. 'Do you think this kind of thing could last?'

Anthony Dexter hesitated.

'Oh, don't answer me,' Rhoda went on. 'You know—we both know—that it could not last. You will go back to your music; and I——' She did not finish her sentence.

Anthony's anger, the instinctive knowledge that she spoke the truth, made him cruel. 'To your husband?' he asked with a half smile.

'Ah,' she said, 'it is surely time we parted.'

They had reached the mouth of the canal; the gondolier piloted them with unerring skill through a little crowd of gondolas to the steps of the hotel.

They went upstairs without further speech; and throughout the *table d'hôte* dinner neither of them referred to the talk in the gondola. Anthony was irritable, restless, ill at ease; Rhoda was possessed by a calm which had in it the elements of despair, but bore the outward form of peace.

In the evening, when they had come back from their walk in the Piazza, Anthony spoke out of his troubled mind.

'What did you mean this afternoon?' he asked.

Rhoda was sitting in an arm-chair by the window; there were lines of weariness on her face; her hands lay listlessly in her lap.

'Simply what I said,' she answered, 'that I am going to leave you, now, while there is still a little merit in the going, and before you cast me off.'

'So you think me an unmitigated scoundrel?'

She shook her head. 'No; only that it is the natural, inevitable end of madness like ours.' She rose, and raising her arms with a despairing gesture above her head, let them drop again heavily to her side. 'Oh! to think,' she said, 'that I should ever have thought it possible!'

'Thought what possible?'

'To sin easily; to cast away all the past years and the effort of them; to taste only the evil and forget the good; to float over the surface of life, and refuse the bondage and the pain of it. To think I could ever have thought—dreamed—imagined it could be possible ; and to a woman made like me !'

'What are you made of, pray ? Since I first saw you I have wondered ; I had begun to think I knew.'

' I don't know—I don't know. I only know that it is almost as hard to sink as it is to rise, that it is almost as hard to kill the little good in one as to stamp out the much evil, that hell is not in abandonment to the lowest, but in the hopeless, passionate longing after the highest. Oh ! how have I suffered all these weeks ! How I have mangled my soul ! How I have courted the devil and everywhere found God ! You ask me what I am made of ? I do not know ; but I know this, that in the last few weeks I have lived through years and years, and I have learned much of myself, of you, of the great, horrible, sinful, suffering world that I must know for now and always. I know, I see, by intuition, by instinct—I don't know what you would call it ; to me it seems that the force of pure suffering gives the insight of a God to see both good and evil.'

The strong emotion in her face died out as she finished speaking ; she stood quite quiet and still, with a blank inscrutability of aspect that Anthony could not fathom. As he looked at her, he felt that he had not understood her after all ; the mystery which had clothed her when he had seen her first was a mystery still ; he had been mistaken in his reading of her, or he had not read deep enough. The thought that there was still something to find out revived the waning passion that was partly love and partly a fascinated curiosity, and he cried out vehemently :

'You shall not leave me ; I will not let you go !'

She answered him only with a sigh, that
was neither very long nor very deep, but
that trembled as if the burden of sadness it
carried were greater than it could bear.

'Rhoda!' Anthony came forward and
touched her hand. 'You cannot leave me, if
I will not let you go!'

'I can.'

She answered without moving, her face
half turned away from him. He waited a
minute; there was something in the passive
determination of her mood that he could
neither understand nor grapple with.

'What are you going to do?' he said at
last. 'Where are you going to? What
does it all mean?'

She moved away from him and sat down
in the arm-chair again.

'It means,' she said, turning her face to
him and looking at him while she spoke,
'that my eyes have been opened. For many
days I would not look at what they saw; but

to-night at last, I have seen plainly. It came quite suddenly, when I first spoke to you on the water ; the words were said before I knew I was going to say them or what they meant. Afterwards there was no more hiding, and I am humbled into the very dust —mud—filthiness—of misery.'

' You are behaving absurdly,' said Anthony. ' You are hysterical—nervous—something that you will not be to-morrow morning. Let us put this subject away from us : by the morning you will look back with laughter at yourself of to-night.'

She shook her head. ' By the morning you will know that I mean all I say.'

' But where can you go to?' he asked half angrily.

' Back to London.'

' And then ?'

' And then ? I can tell you nothing. I do not know.'

' What can you do?' he said brutally.

'You have no choice except to take up with somebody else instead of me. If there is virtue in change, well, then——' He shrugged his shoulders. 'I see nothing,' he said, 'except to sink lower and lower.'

Rhoda's eyes widened, and she caught her breath, but she did not speak.

'Paul Garnet will not take you back,' Anthony went on.

Still she did not answer.

'And how are you going to get to London?' he asked, his angry mortification making every word a sneer. 'Are you going to beg your way? or '—he hesitated a moment, and then let the words come forth—'or have you arranged with a new travelling companion?'

A slight flush rose to Rhoda's pale face, but she did not answer the sneer.

'I have some money,' she said; 'I brought it away with me; it is more than enough to take me back to London.'

Suddenly Anthony was on his knees by her side.

'Forgive me,' he said; 'forgive me, Rhoda! I did not mean—did not know what I said. I love you so that I cannot let you go, and the thought of your going makes me mad.'

She laid her hand for an instant on his head. 'By-and-by,' she said, 'you will be very glad that I left you.'

Then she rose and passed into the neighbouring room, and Anthony Dexter felt that he must not follow her.

CHAPTER XVIII.

Faint and blind as a wasted wind
That beats its life out trying to find
Its lost way over a moor.

ROBERT LORD LYTTON.

PAUL GARNET had settled down in London. The third time that he made the journey up from Fanelands and called at Anthony Dexter's rooms to ask if there were any news of his return, the landlady told him that she did not expect Anthony back for some months. His sister, she said, who went abroad with him, had called the week before to leave a book which was his, and in answer to her inquiries had said that she believed he would not be back before Christmas; and since then, the woman added, he had written to her, desiring her to forward his letters to the Poste Restante at Rome. Would the gentleman like to write down the address, or——

Paul Garnet interrupted her. No, he did not want the address ; his business could wait. If she could tell him where the lady, Mr. Dexter's sister, was living, he would be obliged to her. But she could not tell him ; and he went away to hire a lodging and to begin the task he had set himself, the finding of his wife.

Day after day passed by, and the days ran into weeks, and still the agents he had set to trace her had found no clue to her hiding-place ; and still Paul lived on in the belief that she was in London, and that in the end he must find her again. All day long he trod the pavements, dividing the wilderness of streets into sections, and thoroughly exploring one, visiting the different parts of it at different hours, before he moved on to another ; and in the evenings he haunted the places where misery in the guise of pleasure most openly and pitifully flaunts itself, and sought among the many faces for the face that was hidden from him still. Sometimes he was very near to his wife; it happened more than once that as he passed out of a street she entered it, or that a block of houses divided them the one from the other.

Rhoda Garnet lived a life of extreme privation. After drifting from lodging to lodging, and always from a better to a worse one, she had hired a room in one of the wretched streets that run like a network of squalor behind and about the prosperous quarters and thoroughfares of the town; and she lived there more sparely, more grudgingly, more careful of every farthing than her grandfather had ever lived. She lived on the little store of money that remained to her after she had paid the expenses of coming back to England. In the end Anthony had prayed her to take

from him at least a sum sufficient to pay
the journey; but she would take nothing.
Now she hoarded what was left with a
desperate dread of coming to her last
shilling, counting each day the sovereigns
that were left to her, and shrinking from
the inexorable necessity of changing them
one by one into silver; for when they were
all gone she would have to find some new
way of living, and her heart sank trembling
at the thought. The London that in her
girlhood she had desired so much to see,
inspired her, now that she was swallowed
up in it, with a sort of terror. The wretchedness amidst which she lived, oppressed her
with its sordid ugliness; and the miles and
miles of streets, the multitude of people, the
noise and rush of the town, were like a
nightmare after the idle beauty of Venice
and the still, stern peace of the moor. She
learned to know vice and misery well; and
became familiar with sin, not clad in the

brilliant garments that had tempted her surface eyes, but hideously naked. She saw it not only in the glare of gas-lamps, with a gloss of splendour smeared upon its wretchedness and a voice of laughter that mocked at mirth, but in the hard gray light of day; she saw it walk hand in hand with disease; she saw it clasped in the arms of death; she saw it with the glamour of freedom swept from its brow, and the weight of servitude upon its crawling head: and the sight of it, the sight of the vice and the suffering, the despair, and the slow strength of it, created in her a horror of the place she was in, of the terrible un-ending streets, of the struggling masses of humanity around her, that grew and grew, and must have risen into madness had it not crushed her into an apathy that deadened the power to realize what she endured.

When November came, and the fogs wrapped themselves about the houses, the nightmare of her daily life became still more terrible. She could not look forward at all at this time to what she was to do when all her money should be spent; amidst the confused pain which made up the greater part of her consciousness she clung stedfastly to only two ideas; the one how to live so that the sovereigns should dwindle as slowly as possible, the other a half-formed, yet passionate, resolve not to sink in the flood of misery about her.

One day when she was coming in, a girl who lived in the room next to hers spoke to her.

'You don't ever go out of a night?' she said.

'No.'

'How do you live? What do you do?'

'Nothing.'

'You are starving yourself,' the girl said, half curiously, yet with a sort of rough pity.

'No, I have enough.'

'Tell that to them as 'll believe it—not to
me.   It's a pity : with a face like yours, you 'ld
make it pay ; and you soon get used to it.'

'Ah !' Rhoda said between her teeth, 'that
is the worst—to get used to it.'

'Well, it's easier,' the girl said doggedly,
'than sewing button-holes, as I used to do ;
and the drink helps you if you feel mopy.
It's a easy, lively life, take it all round.'

'Is it easy ?'

There was a strength of passionate denial
in the question.

'Mostly,' the girl answered with a touch of
defiance, 'and more particular if you keeps
your looks.   And I'll tell you what it is,' she
added, in a lower tone of warning; 'they
won't keep you here long, if you don't do like
the rest.   It's not their ticket.'

'But if I pay my rent ?'

'What's the rent ?' the girl asked.   'It's
nothing to them, the rent ain't.'

She laughed and went on down the stairs ;

and the words : 'Won't keep you,' haunted Rhoda all night. The room she lived in was small, noisy, close ; but it was a refuge and a shelter, a hiding-place ; to be driven forth from it into the crowded, desolate streets ; to have to seek another lodging ; to face again the curious glances and questions that had frightened her before, was a thought of horror. After that night she went out every evening and wandered for hours about the street trying to appear to the people in the house to be of a class to which she did not belong, but which, as she told herself bitterly, was truly hers. Yet nevertheless, at the end of another week, the landlady told her that she should want her room ; and Rhoda found herself face to face with the dread she had tried so hard to escape from.

It was at this time that hope drifted away from her, that endeavour almost failed, that she leaned towards despair.

CHAPTER XIX.

A game to play, a love to clasp, a hate to wreak.

D. G. ROSSETTI.

IT was a damp, gloomy evening; the yellow fog, thin but persistent, spread itself over London like a double night; the lights in the streets were blurred; the pavements were covered with a layer of slimy mud. Paul Garnet ate his dinner in a little cheap restaurant near the Tottenham Court Road. He had not much money to spend, and he lived frugally, passing his restless, monotonous days in an unceasing search that left him but little time to feel the need of rest or food. He had grown thin and worn in the weeks since he had left Fanelands; his face was haggard; his features were sharper; his

skin, always pale, had that tinge of darkness
which is worse than pallor. But suffering
had in no wise subdued him; his lips were
more firmly set, his face sterner than of old;
from his eyes a spirit fierce with pain looked
forth with unquenchable determination.

He finished his dinner, and went out
of the eating-house into the greasy streets.
The dampness hung about him, chilling him
as he walked; the lamp-flames were like
dreary ghosts of light; the newspaper boys,
in shrill, demoniacal voices, were calling:
''Orrible murder of a elderly gentleman!'

Paul walked on, along the Tottenham
Court Road, up Oxford Street to Oxford
Circus, and down Regent Street. Then,
keeping in the neighbourhood of Piccadilly
and Regent Street, he walked for hours,
looking into the faces of the crowd with an
unwearying gaze of eager hopelessness, going
on and on, turning and going over the same
ground again, never allowing his attention or
his vigilance to relax for an instant. He was

hardly conscious of fatigue; he had trained himself now to his daily and nightly watches, and his unflinching purpose made him strong. Night after night had passed in wanderings such as this, and night after night had ended without a single ray of hope, a remotest promise of success. To-night his heart grew hard with its own soreness; his soul cried out in blasphemy; his hurt, angry spirit beat itself against the power—fate, chance, God, that was stronger than his will. Almost the inward turmoil relaxed the continual watching of his outward eyes, the fixed attitude of his mind; yet not quite. Instinctively, of habit, his attention remained on the alert; and in an instant it leapt up into a force of concentrated strength that engaged the fulness of his consciousness.

From a side street, a few yards ahead of him, a woman turned into the main thoroughfare. He knew the pose of her figure; he knew the grace of her walk; he had no single moment of doubt that it was his wife.

For a moment his heart stopped beating, and the misty, dimly-lighted street swayed and whirled before his eyes. The strength of self-control, which had held his emotions in check for many weeks, was suddenly re-laxed; and the wild force of these emotions surged upwards from his heart to his brain in a quick spasm of madness that for one flash-ing moment set the whole world aflame. Then his will gripped his senses and his passion again, and he was master of himself, knowing what he would do, and calm enough to do it. The thing he had waited for was almost within his grasp; it should not escape him.

He did not quicken his pace; but he fol-lowed the woman, gaining slightly upon her yard by yard. When he was near her, a man passing by, turned, stopped, and spoke to her. Paul could hear her answer in a

low, hurried tone : ' I am not what you think.'
She did not pause, and the man, after an
instant's hesitation, went on his way.   Paul
was close behind her ; he spoke in a strong
whisper.

' Are you not ?' he said.

She started, but did not answer, and
walked on more rapidly, turning presently
into a side street, and hurrying still more
when she heard his pursuing footsteps, though
she did not once turn her head.

And now began a terrible pursuit ; terrible
in the frenzied, pitiful agony of the woman
who fled ; terrible in the fierce, unswerving
pitilessness of the man who followed her.
The woman went on with hurrying, unfalter-
ing step.   She seemed to be familiar with
the many turns and windings of the intricate
streets : she branched off into narrow alleys ;
she fled down dark, close-walled passages ;
she doubled back into the thoroughfare she
had left, and tried to screen herself amidst

the crowd. And all the time Paul Garnet followed her; and all the time she never looked back, and tried to hope she had escaped his vigilance, yet knew that he pursued her still.

On and on: the woman's face grew whiter and her limbs began to tremble; she was weak from insufficiency of food, and suffering and loneliness; only the terror in her heart supplied her with a fictitious strength that carried her onwards; and the terror grew as her bodily forces failed. Now and again she was jostled by the passers-by; once in a blind, helpless sort of way she struck against a lamp-post; she began to sway and stagger as she went, and the people in the streets jeered at her for a drunkard as she struggled on. At last, in desperation, she left the broad street and the crowd again, and went, with panting breath and feeble, fleeing feet, through the narrower side streets, into a sordid ill-famed street, where few people passed, and sounds of singing or wild laughter broke now and again miserably upon the dingy stillness.

Then at last the woman stayed her flight; then at last, as she stood panting before a door and struggled to fit a key into the key-hole, she looked round to see if her pursuer were near.

Paul Garnet had turned the corner of the street; he came on with long, swift strides; he was beside her before she could turn the key.

'At last,' he said.

The woman, with her face towards the door, made an attempt to enter.

He put his hand upon her shoulder.

'Where you go, I follow.'

She stood passive, though all her body trembled.

'I must see your face,' he said.

She kept her face still turned away from him, and did not answer.

'We will go into the house,' he said, after a minute.

She answered in a gasping whisper.

'Oh no!'

'Then tell me who you are.'

Then she sank down upon the door-step, and drew her cloak across her face.

'I am a lost woman, who is trying to rise.'

Paul Garnet looked down at the shrinking figure before him; his face was trembling, but when he spoke his voice held no emotion.

'I am your husband,' he said, 'and I have come to take you home.'

CHAPTER XX.

For 'tis not in mere death that men die most.
E. B. BROWNING.

IT was a wild night. The wind whirled with a rushing moan through the trees about Fanelands Hall, flung itself in gusts against the lone walls of Heather Den, and swept in unchecked freedom across the heath.

At Fanelands there was an unwonted stir; now, after the many dark, quiet evenings of the past weeks, the hall and the white-walled sitting-room were lighted up again; fires burned in the lately unused grates; and dusting and sweeping had been going on all day. Paul Garnet and his wife were coming home again after their long holiday in London, and the half-inhabited house must be cleaned and warmed to receive them. About six o'clock everything was ready, and the old house-keeper was on the alert for sounds of her master and mistress's arrival ; before seven, Paul Garnet had written, they would be home.

At Heather Den old Wichelow sat in his usual corner with a little pile of silver in his hand ; there was nearly enough to be changed into a gold piece, and added to the hoard beneath the flooring. His interest in the money made him forget for a time the ex-pected return of his grand-daughter, although when he had first heard of her coming, a reality of emotion had stirred his deadened heart. He had missed her more than he owned even to himself; and the thought of seeing her again created in him a sensation of almost affectionate expectation, which was mingled with a malicious curiosity as to what Paul's attitude towards her and the outside world would be. But while he felt the money

in his hand, and looked at the faint shine of
the one candle on the dulled surface of the
shillings and half-crowns, there was no room
in his heart for thought of any human love or
suffering ; and he forgot that Rhoda would
pass through the battling wind outside, not
far from the walls that sheltered him.

Across the heath Rhoda and Paul Garnet
walked side by side.   The wind fled by them
in great flying sheets ; the heavy clouds made
a whirling darkness over the still, dark earth ;
the onward stretch of the moor was lost in
the blackness of the stormy night.   In the
tumult it would have been hard to make
speech audible ; but neither Paul nor Rhoda
made any attempt to speak ; side by side,
with faces set to the wind and resolute steps
that did not flag or pause, they moved on
steadily across the lonely, unsheltered space.
In the darkness, the bare ugliness of Heather
Den could not be seen ; though, as they passed
the nearest point to the house, Rhoda knew,

knowing the path so well, even when there was nothing more to guide her than the little ups and downs which her feet had trodden from her earliest days, that it lay a hundred yards away from her, and thought that within its gaunt strong walls her grandfather sat in his corner on the settle : but she did not turn her head and seek to pierce the darkness of the night ; the thought of the place that had once been her home was a thought instinct with bitterness.

The man and the woman, moving dumbly across the waste, were far from the woods that bordered the heath and broke the force of the wind, making a huge instrument that it touched with a sweeping rush and played on in divers tones ; as they went there was nothing but themselves to oppose its force ; and it uttered but one long whistling note as it struck them in its passage. They were a mile away from Heather Den now, far from the borders of the heath on every side, in the

very midst of the wind-possessed loneliness :
then Paul stopped and spoke.

'Wait here,' he said.

His voice sounded clear through the storm,
but his words were blurred by the rush of the
wind.   But Rhoda had paused involuntarily ;
feeling that he stopped, she stopped too,
yielding him intuitive obedience.   He came
and stood before her, almost touching her as
she waited ; she could not see his face, but
she felt that it was very near her own ; his
eyes seemed to pierce, not the outward darkness that hid her bodily form, but the veil
that divided her spirit from his, and to look
into her very soul.

'Can you hear me speak ?' he said.

His back was to the wind ; she could hear
him distinctly now ; and she answered :

'Yes.'

'What other sound do you hear ?'

'Only the wind.'

'It calls loudly.'

' Yes.'

' Does its strength lie in its voice ?'

She answered almost mechanically : ' I do not know.'

' Lie down,' he said, ' in the heather, that the wind may not strike you as it goes.'

She obeyed him ; he bent low beside her, and presently he spoke again.

' Can you hear the wind's voice now ?'

' No,' she whispered.

' The wind is silent,' Paul said. ' If there is nothing to bar its course it does not speak. It is only if it meets resistance that it cries aloud ; it is always noiseless when it is alone.'

Lying in the rough, bare heather, with a great darkness within and without her, and the mighty wind moving on voiceless above, with only a dim, far-away murmur where, in the distance, it met the woods, it seemed to Rhoda that death looked at her with the eyes of life, and that life held all the grim mystery of death.

Paul took her by the hand and lifted her up.

'You have seen,' he said, 'that the force of the wind is a silent force ; when its path is free it makes no sound. So shall it be with the punishment that you shall take and I will give. It will be unseen and silent ; yet it shall not fail to sweep on through all your life.'

He waited a minute, but she did not speak ; the feeling in her was too hopeless for fear ; the rush of the wind was like the wings of an irresistible fate that bore away her destiny in its flight.

Presently Paul's voice spoke again out of the moving darkness.

'I have kept the name of your honour pure,' he said. 'You have prostituted your body and your being, but your name is un-spotted as the day you left me.'

She clasped her hands ; she made a little inarticulate sound—of gratitude or wonder.

'I did it,' he went on, 'for my pride's

sake, and because of what you once had been to me. It is my necessity to hold you in contempt, knowing you for what you are; but no other man or woman in the world shall lightly use the name or scorn the presence of the woman who is my wife.'

' I am not your wife.'

The words broke from her in agony.

' No,' he answered, ' you are not my wife; but the world believes you to be my wife, and must go on believing it.'

' Why?' she whispered.

' Because I choose to have it so; because '—his voice grew harder in the effort to show no trace of the feeling in his heart— ' because I have loved you. No stone of slight or scorn shall be cast at you, if I have the power—and I have the power—to hold the hurling hands. I will neither abandon nor forgive you.'

It seemed to Rhoda that the wind shook her as it passed; she did not know that it was her own sick heart that caused her to sway and tremble.

'Why did you bring me back?' she said with a rush of despair.

'To punish and protect you.'

'Rather kill me.'

'I cannot kill you. The strange thing in you that binds your soul to mine will not let me take away your life; your adultery holds you back from mine. We must go on, side by side, together, yet for ever apart.'

She sank down in the heather, shuddering.

'Nay,' said Paul, 'there is no other way. And now you must begin to walk in it.'

Then she rose up again, and went in silence by his side through the black roar of the wind.

CHAPTER XXI.

Those that are betray'd
Do feel the treason sharply, yet the traitor
Stands in worse case of woe.

SHAKESPEARE.

IN the hall at Fanelands Mrs. Shand awaited her master and mistress's arrival. Everything was as it should be : the burning wood filled the wide space of the fireplace ; near by, a table stood ready for supper, the old silver goblets catching the life and sparkle of the flames ; in Rhoda's sitting-room the furniture had been uncovered and well polished, and fire and lamp light cast a warm glow upon the pure white walls.

The wind drowned all outward sounds, and it was no use to watch at the window

while the dark night blinded sight. Mrs.
Shand could only stand by the fire and wait.
At last came the signal of arrival, Paul
Garnet's peremptory knock on the big door.
The housekeeper hurried forward to open it,
a smile of welcome on her face, and stood
curtseying as the husband and wife entered.
The smile faded as she caught sight of Paul's
stern face ; and Rhoda looked strangely white
and weary.

'I hope I see you well, sir,' she began, in
a voice that grew timid at its own sound.

'Oh, quite well, very well indeed.' Paul
laughed harshly. 'We have enjoyed ourselves so much in London.'

'And the mistress ?' the woman said doubt-
fully.

'Your mistress is much the better of the
change,' said Paul. 'She wanted a change.'

'She doesn't look——' Mrs. Shand began.

'She is tired,' Paul said. His tone changed
suddenly. 'Bring supper,' he said sharply,

'as soon as it is ready.' Then he crossed the hall and mounted the twisting stairs.

'You are tired, ma'am,' Mrs. Shand said, turning to Rhoda, compassion in her failing eyes.

'Yes, very tired—and faint. I must wait a little before I can go up.'

'Can I get you anything?'

'I don't know—yes, a little water, if you will.'

'Come in here, ma'am,' said Mrs. Shand. 'The sofa's handy.'

She opened the sitting-room door and led Rhoda into the pleasant room. Entering, Rhoda's gaze met the pictured Leonardo face; the eyes seemed to look at her with a triumph of understanding. She drew back.

'No, not here,' she said.

'But you must lie down, ma'am.'

The woman spoke with kindly persistence; and Rhoda, too weak for combat, suffered herself to be guided to the sofa, and lay there while Mrs. Shand went for the

water.   Presently one of the girls who
helped the housekeeper in her task of ordering the house, came in with a tray and glass.

'Mrs. Shand hopes you'll excuse her,
ma'am; she's about the supper.'

'Very well.   Thank you.'

Rhoda took the glass of water and put it
on a little table beside her : presently, when
she was left alone again, she forgot all about
it.   The faintness had passed away, but the
stupor that is the antidote of excessive emotion, following close behind it and guarding
the reason and strength that would otherwise
be destroyed, had stolen over her ; and she
lay quite still, knowing that she suffered,
but feeling only the weight and not the
sharpness of pain.

But by-and-by, after only a few minutes
had passed, she was roused into acute consciousness again.   The wind moaned and
howled about the house, calling with a dreary
voice amidst the trees, and complaining at

the windows ; but through the cry of the wind
came a sound of tramping footsteps that
shuffled and scraped on the gravel-path outside the room where Rhoda lay. At first
she did not heed the sound, only half hearing
it amidst the tumult of the blast and through
the wall of her own suppressed consciousness ; but presently, with the footsteps, came
a murmur of voices ; and the voices caught
her ear and penetrated to her brain. She
sat up to listen ; as she raised herself the
voices ceased, and there was a pause in which
the wind spoke alone. Then a single voice
rose again ; Rhoda knew it ; it was Micah
Yates' voice, and it counted : One, two, three,
four ; one, two, three, four. She could almost
hear the words, and memory gave back to
her what the wind snatched from her ears.
Then, amidst the wild cry of the wind, a
chorus of voices arose, that quavered and
shook, and wandered the one from the other
for want of a firm leader ; and she knew the

wile the dark night blinded sight.
Sand could only stand by the fire and
Al last came the signal of arrival,
Grnet's peremptory knock on the big
The housekeeper hurried forward to o
a mile of welcome on her face, and
crtseying as the husband and wife e
The smile faded as she caught sight of
strn face ; and Rhoda looked strangel
ad weary.

'I hope I see you well, sir,' she be
a voice that grew timid at its own sou

Oh, quite well, very well indeed.
laghed harshly. 'We have enjoy
seves so much in London.'

'And the mistress ?' the woman sai
fly.

Your mistress is **the bette**
_ chnge,' said Paul. nted a
'She **doesn't** l Shan
She is tired tone
denly. ne said

'as soon ███████ ███████
the hall and ███████ the

'You are ████ █████.
turning to Rhoda, █████
eyes.

'Yes, very ████—and █
a little before I can go up █

'Can I get you ████████

'I don't know—yet, a █████

'Come in here, ████████.
'The sofa's handy.'

She opened the ████████
Rhoda into the ███████
Rhoda's gaze ███ the █

water. Presently one of the girls who helped the housekeeper in her task of ordering the house, came in with a tray and glass.

'Mrs. Shand hopes you'll excuse her, ma'am; she's about the supper.'

'Very well. Thank you.'

Rhoda took the glass of water and put it on a little table beside her : presently, when she was left alone again, she forgot all about it. The faintness had passed away, but the stupor that is the antidote of excessive emotion, following close behind it and guarding the reason and strength that would otherwise be destroyed, had stolen over her ; and she lay quite still, knowing that she suffered, but feeling only the weight and not the sharpness of pain.

But by-and-by, after only a few minutes had passed, she was roused into acute consciousness again. The wind moaned and howled about the house, calling with a dreary voice amidst the trees, and complaining at the windows; but through the cry of the wind came a sound of tramping footsteps that shuffled and scraped on the gravel-path outside the room where Rhoda lay. At first she did not heed the sound, only half hearing it amidst the tumult of the blast and through the wall of her own suppressed consciousness; but presently, with the footsteps, came a murmur of voices; and the voices caught her ear and penetrated to her brain. She sat up to listen; as she raised herself the voices ceased, and there was a pause in which the wind spoke alone. Then a single voice rose again; Rhoda knew it; it was Micah Yates' voice, and it counted: One, two, three, four; one, two, three, four. She could almost hear the words, and memory gave back to her what the wind snatched from her ears. Then, amidst the wild cry of the wind, a chorus of voices arose, that quavered and shook, and wandered the one from the other for want of a firm leader; and she knew the

voices and the faults and the weakness of
them; and she knew the sad air and the
words they sang :

> ' Sorrow and toil, and sin and passion rife,
>   Satan at hand to vex us in the strife ;
>   No hope of rest through all this struggling life ;
>   But oh ! for the rest beyond !'

The wind rushed between the verses, and
broke in upon the singing as it rose again,
muffling the sound ; but Rhoda heard with
her heart the sounds that did not reach her
ears, and the refrain swelled always full and
strong above the rushing of the storm. She
sat, still in the same strained attitude into
which she had first raised herself, her white
face drawn with pain, the last notes of the
last line lashing her suffering, when the door
opened and Paul entered.

' What is this ?' he said, standing just
within the room, his eyes cold upon his
wife.

She turned to him and moved her lips, but
she could not speak.

'Are you ill?' he asked.

She shook her head : then her voice came :

'It is the people—they are singing.'

'Your grandfather's people, do you mean?'

She bent her head.

Paul crossed the room to the window, and threw it open. At first he could distinguish nothing in the darkness; a confused murmur of whispering voices ceased suddenly as he appeared. Then the light, streaming out from the room behind, showed him a straggling group of dark figures, that bobbed up and down as he looked at them or raised stiff arms to their brows.

'What do you want?' Paul asked.

There was a pause, with some nudging and whispering amongst the dim group out-side : then Micah Yates stepped forward.

'Beg pardon, master,' he said; 'we'd heard as how she was to be home to-night, and so——'

Words came with difficulty to Micah : he

stopped now, unable to find enough to express what was in his mind. A woman's voice finished the sentence for him.

'So it come to us as we 'ld give her a welcome.'

'And the songs she'd taught us—what could be a better way?' Micah said, taking his position as spokesman again.

'What indeed?' Paul looked over his shoulder at his wife. 'They have come to welcome you home.' Then turning to the people again: 'Come in,' he said.

They hesitated, shrinking one behind the other; at last, Micah Yates was urged forward; and the rest followed him. They came in with shambling, awkward gait, blinking their eyes against the light, and pulling shamefacedly at the locks of hair on their foreheads, the women bobbing at almost every step. On all the faces there was a look of honest pleasure that battled with shyness; and the eyes held expectant welcome.

When all the people were in the room, Paul
shut the window, and the guttering candles
burned steadily again.

Rhoda had risen, and stood behind the
sofa ; she was perfectly pale.

'They have come to welcome you home,'
Paul said.

She bent her head with a stiff, abrupt
motion ; she spoke with a sort of jerk.

'Thank you.'

There was a minute's silence ; the men
shifted their weight from one foot to the
other ; the women cast swift, timid glances
about the room ; Micah Yates cleared his
throat again and again.

'We've missed you, ma'am,' he began,
'more 'n I can say. I speak for all,' he said,
looking round at his companions, who answered him by nods of the head and grunts
of assent, 'and it's a true saying and worthy,'
he added, with a sudden rush of words that
came he knew not whence to his grateful

utterance, 'and worthy of all acceptation. And the night you didn't come,' he proceeded more slowly, 'we was all—we was all—I can't put it into words ; but you'll be able to fancy the kind of way we felt bad.'

'Yes.'

Rhoda almost laughed in her misery ; the rising unshed tears made a pink flush about her eyes.

'We couldn't find heart to sing for many a day,' Micah went on ; 'and then we made a plan as how we 'ld practise up against your coming back.' He paused again, and looked round at his fellows for inspiration. 'If it's agreeable,' he said suddenly, 'we'll sing another hymn.'

'By all means.'

It was Paul who spoke ; without looking at his wife, who still stood gazing with shrinking, fascinated eyes at the well-known faces before her. There was a little more whispering and nudging ; but it was evident

that the 'practising up' had been limited ;
there was not a large number of songs to
choose from ; and after further clearings of
the throat Micah began to count once more :
'One, two, three, four ; one, two, three.'
And then the voices began, in a key that was
too high for them, the hymn that they had
sung that Sunday night when Anthony Dexter
had come to the wood, and had joined, at
Rhoda's command, in the singing.

'Oh come, sinner, come ! 'tis mercy's call ;
Here at Jesu's feet.
Oh come, and repenting, lay thy all
Down at Jesu's feet.'

Feeble and quavering, only a few voices
sustained that part of the air that Rhoda had
been used to sing alone. She listened now
with a catching at her heart, half thankful for
the faulty intonation and the drawling drag
of the voices that, jarring on the nerves of
her musical ear, thus broke into, and in so far
diminished, the stabbing pain that memory

forced upon her.   But when the chorus rose ;
when the many voices joined confidently in
the simple words and music that they all
knew :

> ' Oh lay it down, lay it down,
> Lay thy weary burden down ;
> Lay it down, lay it down,
> Lay it down at Jesu's feet !'

when, forgetting their shyness, the people let
their hearts flow out into their singing as they
had been used to do in the twilit woods : then
the familiar run of the tune, the simple in-
tention of the singers, the worn, dull, trusting
faces, touched something in Rhoda's bound,
stricken heart, that set the springs of suffering free, and loosed the torrent of her anguish
in a rush of uncontrollable emotion.   She
covered her face with her hands ; the tears
rained down ; sobs shook her as she stood.

The singing faltered, dwindled, stopped ;
the singers looked at one another in puzzled
dismay ; their welcome had produced an
entirely unexpected effect.   The men stood

with their mouths half open; the women shook their heads; old Micah Yates, with a slow glance at the group around him, said in a voice of awed disappointment:

'It's a'most too much for she!'

They waited a minute or two in awkward embarrassment; Paul Garnet, meanwhile, a little apart, stood without speaking and watched; then silently, with shuffling, creaking steps that sought to be noiseless, they moved towards the window. Very soon they were all outside in the eddying wind again; and the tramping steps went over the gravel and across the grass to the woods.

By-and-bye as they went, the men began to talk and wonder over what had happened: the women drew apart and whispered amongst themselves. It was bad luck they said, to cry hard when a child was on the way; it meant sorrow to the babe unborn.

CHAPTER XXII.

With travail of day after day, and with trouble of hour upon hour.— SWINBURNE.

THE months passed heavily. All the chill and darkness of the winter seemed to enter into and possess the life at Fanelands Hall. Paul Garnet, always stern in manner and sparing of speech, showed to outward, casual observation, but little change of habit or demeanour : he spent much time alone ; and the stormy nights drew him forth to match his restless spirit against their strength ; but it was only he himself who knew his own heart's bitterness, and the havoc that it wrought within him.

To Rhoda the punishment of these slow

months was almost greater than she could bear. The thought of the child that would be born to her by-and-by was a thought of anguish; sometimes it seemed that she must flee away and hide herself and her sin at any cost: but in all the world there was no hiding-place; Paul's sure determination would inevitably find her and bring her back to the silent hopeless endurance of the life he had willed her to lead. Yet, she told herself, she could still bear it, if she could be sure that her husband knew the fulness of her shame; but she could not be sure; and the doubt held the chief sting of her suffering. Day after day went by and week after week, and Paul said no word to her of scorn or of reproach; she seldom saw him except during the constrained, quickly finished meals; she was rarely alone in his presence; there came no self-given chance to say to him: 'Do you know?'

Each night when she lay prone before the God whom she dared not petition, she re-

solved that on the coming morning she
would seek her husband and tell him the full
measure of the dishonour she had brought
him ; and each morning her heart failed with
the failing opportunity ; and the gnawing
ignorance went on.　And then she began to
think he certainly could not know ; if he had
known, he would not have given her the outward position that covered the terrible hardness of his punishment ; he could not know.
The growing conviction became unbearable ;
goaded by it, she made an attempt to confess
the truth.

'Paul,' she said, one evening after supper,
when, as usual, he was about to leave her,
'Paul, I must speak to you.'

'He was half-way across the hall ; he turned
at once.

'I listen,' he said, and stood waiting.

She came a few trembling steps towards
him : he raised his hand, as though to bid
her pause.

'I can hear you quite well,' he said, 'from where you stand.'

'Oh, but I cannot——' She came forward quickly, quite close to him. 'I must tell you; you do not know. Do you know that——?'

She broke off; it was very hard to speak with those dark, cold eyes upon her.

'What?' he asked.

'The whole truth; how far my—your dishonour——'

He interrupted her; his voice had a sharp, hard ring in it.

'Did I ask you,' he said, 'what you had done those months that you were hidden from me? Did I ask you that night when I found you again?'

She shook her head.

'Or since?'

Again she signed to him without speaking.

'I know all I need to know,' he said. 'I have told you that I will shield your guilt with the name I gave you in your innocence.

That is enough.' A terrible cruelty flamed up in his eyes. 'You cannot be worse than I think you.'

He turned away abruptly, and left her to sink down upon the ground in the bitterness of her humiliation.

After that night, she passed through the dragging weeks with a dull endurance that refused to recognise the keenness of her suffering : she said to herself that it did not matter, and thought she believed what she said.

Spring had come, and the April air was sweet with blooming flowers when Rhoda's baby was born, a little puling, fretful child that came into a world that did not want it, two months before its time. There was a night on which it seemed that Rhoda must pay for the child's life with her own. She did not know her danger ; she did not know of anything that was going on around her ; in her half-conscious delirium, there was only one thought that rambled and twisted about her disordered brain. It was the same thought that had been locked there, clearly defined, for many months; and the burden of it found unceasing utterance in the words, muttered or shrieked all the night through: 'Does he know?' 'Oh, if he knew!'

She did not know that she said the words; she did not know that Paul heard them; she did not know that all night long he lay outside her door in an agony of dread.

But life came back to her, and she woke into consciousness again, with a passionate, yearning love stirring within her towards the tiny, delicate child that lay accusing and innocent by her side. The first day that she was able to be downstairs again, Paul came into her sitting-room as she sat near the window looking out at the fresh May beauty of the trees and grass. The child lay in her lap; instinctively she pulled forward the shawl she wore to hide him out of sight.

' Then the child will live ?' Paul said.

' They say so.'

' You are glad.'

His tone was half assertion, half inquiry. She hesitated, her mouth trembling.

' How can I but be glad ?' she said with sudden, desperate entreaty. ' It is all I have to live for.'

' Let me see him,' Paul said, coming close to her.

She drew the shawl aside slowly, as though she feared to expose the little sleeping face to the look in the dark eyes above it.

' You are glad,' Paul said. ' You should not be glad. The child that you hold so tenderly, will give you only enough joy to make you feel more keenly the pain that he will bring.'

Rhoda shrank back in her chair, pressing the child so closely to her that it waked out of its sleep and gave a little wailing cry. When it was hushed into peace, Paul spoke again.

'I pray God Almighty,' he said, 'to fulfil His promise that He will visit the sins of the fathers upon the children ; I pray that the music which was your ruin, may awake and strengthen in your son ; that as it ruined you, so it may ruin him ; that you may see the ruin ; and that I may be by to watch you feel such pain as you have given me.'

He spoke with a calm deliberateness that was far more terrible than any wildness of denunciation. Rhoda looked up at him with wide, horror-darkened eyes : she could not speak, but her bloodless face was a prayer.

He heard the speechless prayer, but would not answer it : he turned away and left her alone, and went out upon the moor to wrestle with the passion of a love that was too strong to cease and too little strong to forgive.

CHAPTER XXIII.

My freshness spent its wavering shower i' the dust ;
And now my heart is as a broken fount,
Wherein tear drippings stagnate, spilt down ever
    From the dank thoughts that shiver
Upon the sighful branches of my mind.
                   FRANCIS THOMPSON.

OLD Wichelow sat outside his door in the sun ; the air was still, and the warmth came down, unchecked by any clouds in the deep blue sky. Boniface had just come back from his morning walk round the farm, and he was tired ; he was glad to sit down and rest his stiff limbs ; and he was glad to let his mind relax from active vigilance to its normal state, a state of passive contemplation of his growing secret store of wealth.

The strong light dazzled his eyes; but the sunshine was as wine to his old, weak body; and he sat blinking and dreaming in a state of complete enjoyment. Sitting thus with the outward world blurred and dim, he did not see Paul Garnet and Rhoda come out of the woods and cross the road on to the heath: he did not notice them till they were close beside him. Then, at the sound of Paul's voice, he started and looked stupidly about him.

'There is nothing the matter,' said Paul. 'We have not come to rob you.'

'There's nothing to rob,' said old Wichelow, shooting out his under lip: 'I have neither money—nor wife.'

'Nor son's wife,' Paul said.

He went close to the old man and put his hand upon his shoulder, looking down into his face.

Old Wichelow's face changed.

'I meant no harm, Paul,' he said, 'I had no hidden meaning.'

'I had,' said Paul; 'how long it remains hidden, depends on you.'

He waited for half a minute, his eyes on the wrinkled face before them; then he turned on his heel.

'Rhoda!'

Rhoda had gone to sit down on the bench on the other side of the door; she was tired after her walk, and her face was pale and languid. She rose when Paul called her, and came towards him.

'We have not long to stay,' Paul said. 'You had better tell your grandfather what we have come for.'

'Yes.' She went to old Wichelow, still sitting blinking his eyes at the sunlight, and stood before him. 'Grandfather, I have come to ask you to be godfather to the child.'

'We have both come,' said Paul, 'to ask you to be godfather to the child.'

'To your son?' said old Wichelow.

'Yes,' Rhoda answered.

'And heir?'

'The property is not entailed,' said Paul.

Old Wichelow rubbed his hands.

'Well,' said Paul, 'your answer.'

'I—I don't know,' said the old man. He turned to his grand-daughter. 'I don't know, Rhody. Wouldn't it be better for some friend—not a relation—it's usual to——'

Paul interrupted him, speaking with slow sarcasm.

'In this case,' he said, 'we want no outsiders. We prefer to keep everything connected with the eldest son entirely in the family.' He paused. 'That is our wish, Rhoda?'

She bent her head; her pale cheeks flushed with sudden scarlet.

'I have no money, Rhody,' the old man said hesitatingly, 'no money I can lay my hands on just now for a present. I should like to give the child a present—but just now —in time for the christening, I'm afraid——'

' He wants no present,' Rhoda said.

' I am the other godfather,' said Paul ; ' I will give the presents. You need not be afraid that you will have to pay for the honour.'

' I shall be glad, very glad, Rhody,' said old Wichelow with sudden cordiality. He rose from his seat and kissed his grand-daughter. ' When is to be—the christening ?'

' The day after to-morrow—Thursday, at ten o'clock.'

' In the church ?'

' Yes, in the church.'

' I will be there, without fail—without fail, Rhody.'

On Thursday morning Rhoda followed Paul into the garden. He stopped in his walk when he heard her footsteps behind him, and waited till she came near.

' Yes ?' he said.

' Do you mind,' Rhoda said, with clasped

hands and downcast eyes, 'what I call the child?'

'Yes.'

She looked up at him quickly.

'Why? What can the name——'

'There can be no doubt about the name,' Paul said. 'An eldest son should not fail to bear his father's name.'

She gave a little cry.

'What is it?' said Paul. 'What other name can be so suitable?'

'Oh, if you knew!' she gasped.

He looked at her with a strange smile, and his look silenced her. She turned away without further words, and it seemed to her that she understood him at last.

Old Wichelow was early at the church. He had put on his best coat: it was thirty years old, and hung in creases upon his shrunken shoulders; but the cloth was still whole and good, and the old man, with his

well-cut face, had a certain air of breeding
and dignity.

Rhoda carried her child to the church herself; she stood with it during the service,
her eyes never moving from the little thin,
waxen face; it was with an effort that she
gave it out of her own keeping into the
parson's arms. He was a young man and
held it clumsily, but it did not wake as he
took it.

'Name this child,' he said.

He looked at Rhoda, but she did not
speak; she made an almost imperceptible
movement towards Paul. It was Paul who
answered. Old Wichelow started, but Rhoda
stood without flinching, when he said:

'Anthony.'

END OF VOL. II.

Lightning Source UK Ltd.
Milton Keynes UK
UKHW021305011218
333149UK00003B/200/P

CLEAN SLEEPING

HOW TO SLEEP BETTER NATURALLY

THIS IS A CARLTON BOOK

Published in 2019 by Carlton Books
An imprint of the Carlton Publishing Group
20 Mortimer Street
London W1T 3JW

10 9 8 7 6 5 4 3 2 1

Text and design © Carlton Books 2019

A CIP catalogue for this book is available from the British Library.

ISBN 978 1 78739 345 5

Printed in Dubai

Material in this book was previously published in *Sleep Better Naturally*.

CLEAN SLEEPING
HOW TO SLEEP BETTER NATURALLY

LISA HELMANIS

CARLTON BOOKS

CONTENTS

INTRODUCTION

Our lifestyles today are all about being stimulated, entertained and excited. We regard the 24/7 culture that we have created in the Western world as an essential part of living and getting the most out of life.

Yet, while most of us acknowledge the importance of good nutrition and regular exercise in enabling us to take advantage of these pleasures, many forget the other essential ingredient for maintaining a modern lifestyle – sleep. Sleep is central to our sense of wellbeing and general health, but today's culture is increasingly marginalizing its importance, and we are paying the price.

Despite the fact that we spend a third of our lives sleeping, research in this area is still relatively new. There is much debate on why we need it and the exact role it plays in our health, but all scientists agree that it is essential. Research at Columbia University in the USA has shown that little or poor-quality sleep can be linked to weight gain, with those who sleep only two to four hours a night being 73 per cent more likely to be obese than an average seven-hour sleeper. This is in addition to the more well-documented effects such as poor concentration, irritability, memory loss, a predisposition to diabetes and reduced immunity to illness. Add to this the immediate risk of accident and injury caused by fatigue (around 350 deaths occur annually on roads in the UK as a result of somebody falling asleep at the wheel, according to Awake, a body that advises the UK Department for Transport) as a result of somebody falling asleep at the wheel, and the scale of the problem becomes apparent.

Even if you have never experienced extreme symptoms of sleep deprivation, you have probably suffered the misery of insufficient sleep at some time in your life. It is that unpleasant sensation of crawling from your bed, fuzzy-headed and disorientated, feeling emotional and frustrated, and more likely than not taking your unpleasant mood out on your nearest and dearest through the sheer inability to cope. Compare this feeling with the bright, positive glow you get from a well-rested comfortable night and it is clear why a good night's sleep is so important for tackling, and enjoying, the day's challenges.

Sleep is also important for learning. Tests by Robert Stickgold, a cognitive neuroscientist at Harvard Medical School, have shown that subjects who were allowed to sleep after learning new information or skills recalled them better when asked to repeat them. Those who had performed the same task later in the day with no sleep in between had poorer results. A lack of sleep quickly affects our ability to perform even simple tasks, articulate ourselves or control our emotions. It is also important in your body's fight against disease. When your body is fighting a viral infection, it will break up the virus's wall – the fragments of which are sleep inducing. These go into your system and make you lethargic and sleepy, thus giving your body a chance to concentrate on fighting the infection.

Whether you believe sleep is a golden elixir or a nuisance that just makes the day shorter, its benefits can't be denied. It is important for your emotional life – depression, relationship breakdowns and inefficiency at work are all results of, or exacerbated by, lack of sleep. It is also vital for good health, helping to prevent obesity, the onset of diabetes and the damaging effects of stress. Even your looks will benefit from a good night's sleep. Good sleep, in both quality and quantity, can dramatically improve your everyday lives and future happiness.

SLEEP PATTERNS
and THE NEED FOR SLEEP

SO HOW DO YOU KNOW IF YOU ARE GETTING ENOUGH SLEEP? RESEARCH FROM BRITAIN AND THE USA HAS FOUND THAT MORE THAN ONE IN FOUR ADULTS FEEL THEY SUFFER THREE BAD NIGHTS OF SLEEP EACH WEEK.

On a very simple level, it does depend on how you feel – poor sleep will leave you feeling tired and sluggish the following day – though there are other tests you can do to see if you have a more serious sleep problem. First, let's look at a 'normal' day.

Our lives are governed by a biological 'clock' deep inside the brain. It sets out the rhythm of peaks and troughs we experience during the day. This clock, consisting of roughly 100,000 nerve cells, is formally called the suprachiasmatic nucleus, and the patterns it produces are called the 'circadian rhythm'. It governs everything from hormone production to when we feel like going to bed. We are all at our most sleepy in the early hours of the morning and again in the early afternoon, which might be why work can seem like a chore just after lunch. The circadian rhythm doesn't work alone, however; there are other nerve cells that collectively are called the 'sleep homeostat', and they measure how long we have been awake. The longer we are awake, the greater the pressure for sleep. The biological clock counteracts this pressure during the day but in the evening, shortly before bedtime, it winds down and, all being well, sleep begins. Light has a big effect on the clock. There are even specialized nerve cells that lead from the eye to the clock. Light can actually reset our clock – for example, when we travel through time zones.

The clock controls the release of the hormone melatonin. Light blocks the release, but as it gets dark melatonin levels increase, telling our body, a few hours before we go to bed, that sleep is approaching. By influencing the release of the stress hormone cortisol into our bloodstream, our internal clock also prepares us for the new day a few hours before the alarm sounds. For our body clock to get the release of hormones correct, light is essential. This is why the glare from a streetlight, or even a night light, invading your bedroom can make it hard to sleep – you might know it's night-time, but your body can't tell the difference between electricity and the sun.

So, if you feel perky in the morning, a little sluggish after lunch and then more alert in the evening, you are probably getting your sleep balance right. However, if you dread the sound of the alarm and spend the morning in a daze, tetchy and distressed, and you find yourself suffering from frequent colds and viruses, you are probably sleep-deprived. There can be a large number of reasons for this, such as:

- Birth of a new baby
- Ageing
- Menopause
- Bereavement
- Illness
- Shift work
- Overuse of stimulants such as coffee, alcohol and nicotine
- Penchant for late-night parties
- Pressure at work
- Overactive thyroid gland
- Anxiety
- Depression
- Post-traumatic Stress Disorder
- ME, or Chronic Fatigue Syndrome
- Snoring partner
- Sleep apnoea (a breathing difficulty)
- Jet lag
- Biological clock disorders like Delayed Sleep Phase Disorder (DSPD), making it impossible to fall asleep until early morning.

It may even be the short-term, regular effects of another cycle; premenstrual syndrome (also known as premenstrual tension) is known to cause sleeplessness. Although chronic sleep deprivation (which means you are literally falling asleep during the day, and which can even be caused by missing a single night of sleep) can be rectified over a couple of nights, a slow buildup of sleep loss, by an hour or so a night, can affect your long-term health and make you susceptible to illness, weight gain and even premature death.

HOW SLEEP WORKS

While we are still unclear about the exact role of sleep, scientific research has revealed more about the form it takes. Sleep has two main states – REM (Rapid Eye Movement) and non-REM.

Within the non-REM stage there are four distinct stages. The first stage is short, not lasting many minutes, and is really an in-between state of sleep and wakefulness. The muscles start to relax and the brainwave patterns begin to slow down. During this stage you are very easy to wake, and as it begins, you may have that sensation of 'nodding off', with little rouses into consciousness.

To an observer, Stage Two looks very much like Stage One, but an EEG (a graph called an electroencephalogram which depicts the pattern of brain waves produced by the brain) shows that there is a change in the type of brain waves being produced. A single wave, called a K complex, is followed by a sleep spindle (named after the spindle shape it makes on the EEG screen). There may be a train of these, or it may be intermittent, but it would take a louder noise or firmer prod to rouse you from this stage, though you are still considered to be in the 'entering' stage of sleep. As more and more of these appear, you start going into deeper sleep.

About 10–30 minutes after the onset of Stage Two, you enter deep sleep. The brain waves are now slow and make rolling shapes on the EEG screen, indicating a very deep sleep. Your heart rate and

blood pressure fall, your breathing is slow and regular, and you will need a ringing phone, shouting or shaking to bring you back to the waking world, which would find you groggy and disorientated and probably not very happy (which is also how you would feel if woken during Stage Four). This stage gets deeper and deeper. Your muscles are now totally relaxed and you are very difficult to wake up – an onlooker might be tempted to use the phrase 'dead to the world'. It is during these deep stages that our body carries out its repair work, fights any illness or damage and, in men, releases the growth hormone. This sleep is essential to refresh us.

These non-REM stages described above take you approximately one hour into your first sleep cycle. You will then re-emerge towards consciousness and experience a brief awakening that you won't remember; this is often when you turn over or grab back some of the sheets. (Dr Paul Caldwell in his book *Sleep Really Well* suggests that this may be due to an evolutionary need to check our environment for danger, as in deep sleep we are very vulnerable.) After this you start REM sleep, where high-frequency waves begin to appear on the EEG screen. Your brain has now started to create some alpha and beta waves, which are similar to the ones produced when you are awake. You are probably dreaming and your eyeballs are moving under their lids, which is what gives REM sleep its name (you can also dream in non-REM sleep, but these dreams tend to be simple and dull). Although dreams seem very real and physically active, a healthy person's body won't act out your dreams because your muscles are paralyzed in this stage and you remain motionless (some scientists believe that this is the body's way of preventing you from harming yourself). Sleepwalking is likely to happen in the deep, non-REM part of your sleep, which isn't accompanied by paralysis.

A full cycle of non-REM and REM sleep takes about 90 minutes: about 60 minutes in the various forms of non-REM sleep, and between 10 minutes and up to 30 minutes of REM, with the REM sleep periods lengthening and deep sleep decreasing gradually throughout the night. In total, 20 per cent of an average night will be spent dreaming. (Age also affects the proportion of sleep types you have, with less deep sleep as you get older.) Once you have completed a full cycle, you return to the first, non-REM, stage and the cycle repeats itself. The number of cycles you perform depends on how long you sleep, but most people wake up in REM sleep, which is why we often remember our dreams. As you are naturally closer to the waking state at this time, you will feel more refreshed emerging from this sleep stage.

Various sleep monitors have been developed, which mainly monitor your body movements and look for these 'almost awake' moments, triggering your morning alarm clock and ensuring you wake during these parts of your cycle. Of course, getting the right amount of sleep would make this a natural occurrence, but for those who need to be up at certain times, setting a window of about 20 minutes for the watch to seek out the optimum, least distressing time to sound the alarm can make the interruption less painful.

There can be a few unexpected additions to this sleep pattern. For instance, despite a conviction that we may have slept soundly throughout the whole night, we usually wake up from the shallower phases of sleep several times – we just don't remember doing it. Some research has shown that muscles in the body do not need sleep, just periods of rest. All research does agree that sleep is essential for the brain. Electroencephalogram (EEG) results show that the parts of the brain which deal with emotional issues, for example, are very active. This has fostered the new belief that we need sleep to process our daily feelings and consolidate our memories. Some scientists say we only dream the memories and situations that are meaningful to us, while others consider dreaming to be a way of shedding information that is surplus to requirements or trivial. Either way, it seems to be an essential part of our mental wellbeing.

NATURAL EFFECTS ON YOUR SLEEP PATTERNS

There are two other factors that need to be considered when understanding your sleep patterns. Both are entirely natural and exert a profound influence on the way that we sleep.

Ageing
As well as the circadian rhythm (see page 7) and our lark or owl status (see below), we are ruled by the basic cycle of life. Ageing

greatly influences our sleep patterns; six-month-old babies sleep for up to sixteen hours a day, teenagers need about nine, adults need about eight, and from middle age the length and quality of sleep often gradually decreases. Older people report more instances of night-time awakenings, insomnia and unwanted early waking. They can often find sleep affected by illness or other problems, such as a snoring partner, but, due to more frequent night-time awakenings, may remember more dreams.

Larks and Owls

Many of us are 'larks' (or 'early birds'), which means we prefer to rise early and go to bed early, or 'owls', which makes us prone to late nights and later rising times. This can change during our lifetime – most of us will remember being owls when we were teenagers! Your lifestyle pattern, such as taking children to school or shift work, may force you into a set regime, but your natural inclination will decide whether or not you will be at your best when you wake up. Larks are often breezy and perky in the mornings, but fade fast in the evenings. Owls, on the other hand, will loathe an early-morning start but find that they are full of energy at night. In an ideal world, we would start work at the time best suited to our disposition, but try telling that to your employers!

SLEEP AND YOUR IMMUNE SYSTEM

In our hectic everyday lives, it is easy to sacrifice sleep in order to meet the many demands of chaotic schedules. We need to realize, however, that in doing this we are depleting our natural resources that fight infection and help us to cope with daily demands. The immune system is our defence against illness and it filters out the

HOW LIKELY ARE YOU TO DOZE OFF IN THE FOLLOWING SITUATIONS?

Never – 0 | Occasionally – 1 | Often – 2
Most of the time – 3

- Sitting and reading
- Watching television
- Sitting in a public place, such as a theatre or at a meeting
- As a passenger in a car for an hour without a break
- Lying down in the afternoon
- Sitting talking to someone
- Sitting quietly after an alcohol-free lunch
- In a car, stopped for a few minutes in a traffic jam

If you score 10 or more, you are probably not getting enough sleep or getting poor-quality sleep.

damaged and defective body cells. A well-operating system can seek out a virus and minimize it to a snuffle, rather than a sledgehammer that wipes us out for weeks. The lymph nodes produce the cells that attack invaders. They are located in your neck, armpits and groin, which is why they feel swollen when you are ill – it means they are doing their job properly. A healthy immune system needs vitamins and nutrients to maintain it, and most importantly it needs sleep. A lack of sleep suppresses your immune system and prevents it from being able to fight infection effectively.

Recently it has been discovered that the brain is also connected to the lymphatic system. Apart from its nerve cells (neurones), the brain also consists of glia, or supporting cells. These are supportive and also provide nutrients and a waste disposal system for the neurones. The lymphatic system in the brain is connected to the glia and so has been called the glymphatic (gl[ia] [l]ymphatic) system. This system is most active when you are asleep, particularly deep sleep when the metabolism of the brain is the slowest. It has been found that the beta-amyloid protein, which is associated with Alzheimer's, accumulates during the day and is cleared out during sleep by the glymphatic system.

HOW MUCH SLEEP IS ENOUGH?

The standard figure that has been recommended by most healthcare professionals over the years is eight hours per night, although older people sleep less and children need a lot more, as they are growing. Everyone's needs vary, but research carried out at Stanford University, California, under the eye of William Dement, one of the founders of the field of sleep research, showed that most people had a sleep deficit of around 25–30 hours. Once people had recovered from their sleep deficit, they generally settled into a natural pattern of around eight hours a night, with women sleeping twenty minutes more a night than men.

When you consider the fact that scientist Paul Martin (in his book *Counting Sheep*) estimated that most adults average 6.7 hours before a working day and 7.1 hours before a day off, you can see how easy it is to create a sleep deficit that leaves you yawning.

So how do you work out your needs? The time that it takes us to fall asleep from lying down to attempting sleep is called the Sleep Latency Period, and this can be used to measure how tired you are.

You lie in a darkened room in the middle of the day, ready to take a nap. Everything is normal except that you have your arm hanging off the edge of the bed and with it you hold a spoon, over a metal tray, or something else that will make a clattering noise when the spoon is dropped. You write down the time you lay down and the time you are awoken by the clatter when the spoon slips out of your hand and onto the tray. If it takes you between 15 and 20 minutes, you are probably okay; around 10 minutes and you may have accumulated a sleep deficit; less than 5 minutes and you are suffering from a problematic lack of sleep.

If this method seems unscientific, try the Epworth Scale, developed by Murray Johns at the Sleep Disorders Unit, Epworth Hospital, Australia, and first published in 1991. Answer the questions in the box opposite using the points system.

THE ROLE OF EXERCISE IN GOOD SLEEP

While most people would agree with the idea that physical exhaustion promotes sleep, the issue isn't quite as simple as it would first seem. Exercise too close to bedtime can be stressful and disrupt sleep. Studies have shown that muscles can remain healthy if given periods of rest, but that does not have to be sleep. The growth hormone repairs and maintains the body, and in men (not women) is made mainly during sleep. After exercise, the amount of slow wave sleep when this hormone is released is shown to increase – although some scientists argue that the change and the effects are modest.

So why do people feel that exercise so greatly improves their sleep if it is not wholly reflected in research? Well, exercise is wonderful for the body and our state of mind. Many conditions, from depression to premenstrual tension, are improved by taking exercise. As well as weight loss (which can help eliminate snoring), it can also reduce tension in our muscles, which can contribute to RLS (Restless Legs Syndrome, see page 21), and boost the brain chemical serotonin, which is associated with making us feel good and pacifies all those little anxieties that can keep us awake. Doing some physical exercise three times a week, even only 20 minutes at a time, will help your frame of mind and your physical frame.

NAPPING – A QUICK RESTORATIVE

There was a time when only cats and grandparents could get away with napping, but as the restorative power of sleep becomes better understood, health professionals have now begun to advocate its advantages. Far from being the habit of a sloth, a well-timed nap

can improve your state of mind and your energy levels. In many cultures, napping is an accepted and promoted way of living, the Spanish siesta being a prime example.

The optimum length for napping is still open to debate, but if you find that groggy feeling after a nap disruptive or unpleasant, limit your nap to between 10 and 20 minutes. For a proper break, nap for between 60 and 90 minutes. Everyone has slightly different needs, so experiment, but also make sure you don't overdo it. If you nap too much during the day, you won't sleep well at night, so you shouldn't be using napping in order to catch up on the sleep you missed by being awake the night before.

GETTING BACK ON TRACK

Whatever the reason for losing your natural balance, there are many ways in which you can regain control. Losing sleep can often result in a nasty feeling of being overtired, and unable to sleep, no matter how desperate you are. This situation can bring on insomnia (see page 18), a condition all the more frustrating in that worrying about it seems only to exacerbate it. Feeling tired magnifies the helpless feeling that accompanies insomnia – spotting a pattern yet?

The great news is that, far from being helpless, there are many ways in which you can improve the quality of your slumber. In the following chapters we will look at some of these ways, such as techniques to combat negative stress and lifestyle pressures, how to eliminate aggravating dietary factors and integrate sleep-friendly foods, and how to create a sleep-inducing haven, including pleasurable pre-sleep rituals. In addition, all-natural alternative and holistic therapies and retraining techniques can replace or supplement orthodox medicine.

ASSESSING
your SLEEP
PROBLEMS

WE ALL KNOW HOW IT FEELS TO BE SLEEPY, AND HOW COPING WITH THE FOLLOWING DAY'S STRESSES AND STRAINS CAN FEEL LIKE YOU ARE WADING THROUGH MOLASSES, BUT MOST OF US UNDERESTIMATE THE FAR-REACHING EFFECTS OF SLEEP DEPRIVATION.

From waking, you may find the transition into daytime mode more difficult to make. You feel sluggish and disorientated, and simple tasks, such as making breakfast, may take longer to perform.

You may find yourself much more irritable and snappy with anyone who has the misfortune to cross your path. Added to this, you may also feel a sensation of light-headedness and your coordination may be impaired — this is when you stub your toe or spill your coffee!

Other changes in mood, such as sadness and lack of emotional resilience, become apparent. You may become emotionally detached and, slowly, all your communication, social and memory skills start to deteriorate. Overtired people lose their ability to make clear decisions and, as a result, often exhibit poor judgement by making snap decisions. The biological clock and lack of sleep are thought to have contributed to some of the biggest manmade disasters of the last century — the 1986 Chernobyl nuclear reactor accident; the capsizing of the passenger car ferry *Herald of Free Enterprise* in the Belgian port of Zeebrugge; and the 1997 Korean Air flight 801, which crashed killing 228 people. Paranoia, aggression and apathy may also make an appearance, which can obviously have serious effects on personal relationships.

Excessive sleep deprivation has quite radical effects on the body. Experiments have shown that animals will eventually die if they are kept constantly awake, so it can be assumed that it would have a similar effect on humans. Don't panic too much, though, it would take months of total sleep deprivation to have this effect. From sleep deprivation experiments conducted on human beings, we know that the body will begin to exhibit the following range of symptoms, to some degree, after only a few days without sleep:

- Dry, itchy eyes
- Bad skin
- Chapped lips
- Drop in body temperature
- Increased appetite
- Impaired vision
- Increased pain sensitivity

You can liken the effects of being tired to being drunk. Going without sleep for only 21 hours is the equivalent to having 0.8 per cent alcohol in your system, which is over the legal limit to drive in many countries. As well as the physical similarities to being drunk, such as swaying and bumping into things, when you are tired you may also lose your social inhibitions, act overconfident or behave badly without any embarrassment, and be unable to communicate properly, including losing interest in sentences halfway through. Strangely, you may also experience an increase in libido, although no one knows quite why.

Our lifestyle often has a major effect on how much sleep we get and therefore how sleep-deprived we are. Unfortunately — say because of shift work, long commutes, babies, caring, etc — it's not always possible to control this. The best one can do is to optimize, and a lot of this book describes how.

Sometimes lifestyle or illness can lead to a full-blown (intrinsic) sleep disorder. Sleep disorders are roughly divided up into insomnias (not being able to sleep when appropriate or desirable), hypersomnias (not being able to stay awake when appropriate), parasomnias (undesirable behaviours or experiences while going into, emerging from or in sleep), and disorders associated with poor breathing.

TYPES AND CAUSES
OF INSOMNIA

Although most people associate the term insomnia with endless nights lying awake staring into the gloom and waiting to drop off, it is actually a catch-all term used to describe a wide variety of symptoms with varying degrees of severity and covering problems such as staying asleep or waking up too early in the morning.

The definition of insomnia and how to treat it has been changing over the recent decades as we understand more about sleep. It used to be regarded as primary and secondary. The latter was sleeplessness caused by some condition, either environmental (e.g. noise, heat, babies, etc) or internal (e.g. depression). The former, primary insomnia, was sleeplessness without an apparent cause, and there were different types. These have been dropped recently, as they turned out not to be useful for treatment, but it is worth describing some to give an idea of the different 'flavours' of insomnia.

One primary type is called psychophysiological insomnia, which describes 'learnt' insomnia. A period of sleeplessness may have been triggered by grief or stress, and can persist long after the negative event. Or, the sleeper can have become anxious about sleeping well, making it a source of stress and stimulus in itself. Idiopathic insomnia describes a life-long sleeplessness that is usually attributed to an abnormality in the neurological or neurochemical control of the sleep-wake cycle, and usually makes itself known from childhood. There is also sleep state misperception, where a patient imagines they have slept much less than they actually have, but this can still leave them feeling dreadful and distressed.

Insomnias were also categorized as early-, mid- and late-sleep wakefulness. This was useful for pharmaceutical products but otherwise unhelpful. Simply classifying insomnia as acute, transient and chronic did not help. The primary and secondary distinction endured longer but has also now been dropped in favour of considering insomnia as a 'co-morbid' condition. Many disorders can cause insomnia, and that insomnia may develop a life of its own; it begins to co-exist with the other disorder. Therefore, the best plan is to try to deal with the insomnia directly rather than waiting to see whether it disappears.

Nowadays, the recommended treatment for insomnia is cognitive-behavioural therapy for insomnia (CBT-I). As the name implies, there is a cognitive part and a behavioural part. For cognitive there is an analysis of whether there are any pernicious anxieties surrounding sleeplessness which feed into maintaining wakefulness during the night. These anxieties are challenged and dispelled. The behavioural part usually consists of 'stimulus control', basically being in bed only when sleeping, and going to bed only for the period that you are likely to sleep (though usually not less than five hours).

A good way to work out the cause of your poor sleep is to keep a sleep diary, to help pinpoint any recurring themes. If you can track a pattern, such as deadlines and late dinners directly affecting your ability to drop off, you can start by eliminating them, or managing them differently; in some cases, simply moving the TV out of the bedroom can have startlingly effective results (see Chapter 4).

Even if you need to approach a healthcare practitioner to address the problem, the diary will be invaluable in finding a treatment to fulfil your specific needs. It will also help ease the feelings of helplessness and frustration that so often accompany insomnia.

WHEN THE BODY WORKS AGAINST US

In this section we will look at the most common complaints, from body clock problems and snoring to more serious conditions.

Clocked Off

When our body clock works well, we feel sleepy when it is dark and ready to take on the day when there is daylight. However, this isn't always the case, and there are certain types of insomnia that are related directly to our circadian rhythm.

Those who find themselves fighting to keep their eyes awake as soon as dinner is over may be suffering from Advanced Sleep Phase Disorder (ASPD). This is not merely a 'larks' tendency to go to bed early so they can enjoy their preferred 6 a.m. start; it often has sufferers fighting a ridiculously early bedtime, as they know that they will find themselves wide awake, having had their full quota of eight hours, at 2 a.m. Their sleep is often refreshing, but simply out of step with the rest of their lives (and those around them). Resetting the circadian rhythm might be possible using light therapy and 'chronotherapy', which moves the bedtime back gradually until they return to their normal pattern. This can also be helpful when tackling jet lag (by gradually adapting your bedtime to the new destination before you begin your journey).

The opposite syndrome is Delayed Sleep Phase Syndrome (DSPS). This is defined as the inability to fall asleep within two hours of the socially desirable sleep time. It can often be exacerbated by the anxiety caused by knowing that one has to rise early for work. Both can be accompanied by depression as a result of the frustration and isolation they can cause. Light therapy, chronotherapy and melatonin are used to try to reset the body clock (see page 45 for melatonin details).

Snoring

Anyone who lives with a snorer can tell you how draining and frustrating snoring can be. Some people seem to snore so loudly that they wake themselves up, though in reality they could be suffering from the more serious form of sleep apnoea. Snoring affects around 3.5 million people in Britain, according to the British Snoring and Sleep Apnoea Association, and it is mostly men who snore, later joined by post-menopausal women. Men have thinner air pipes than women, but both lose muscle tone as they age, which makes us all more susceptible to snoring as we get older.

Snoring occurs when the soft palate tissue at the back of the throat relaxes too much and obstructs the entrance to the throat. As air tries to pass through, the soft palate vibrates and produces the snoring sound. Alcohol can aggravate the symptoms because it is a muscle relaxant (sleeping pills can have the same effect). Another factor that can make snoring worse is excess body weight. People with a collar size of more than 42 cm (16½ inches) are more likely to snore because of the extra weight on their throat muscles. Snoring can also be caused by nasal congestion; avoiding dehydrating drinks like coffee, tea and alcohol, using a humidifier or putting eucalyptus oil on your pillow can help clear the passageways.

For most snorers, sleeping on the back exacerbates the problem, as the tongue falls backwards into the throat, which can narrow the airway and partly block airflow. Try sleeping on your side. If this doesn't work, pillows designed to help prevent snoring, losing weight to reduce pressure on airways, and even a mandibular device (which you wear like a mouth guard at night to bring the lower jaw forward and open up the airway at the back) can all help.

Sleep Apnoea

Sleep apnoea is caused by the same muscles that cause snoring, but it is more dangerous because it alters normal breathing patterns. With breathing during sleep there is a continuum: normal, snoring, hypopnoeas and apnoeas. 'Apnoea' means completely stopping breathing, while 'hypopnoea' means shallow breathing. While asleep, apnoea sufferers may stop breathing for between 10 and 25 seconds at a time. This depletes the bloodstream of oxygen and deprives the brain of vital supplies, which then sends out an emergency signal, telling the person to wake up and take in a big gulp of air. In a single night, sufferers may experience up to 350 apnoeic events and usually find themselves waking up sweaty, with a dry mouth and a headache. Sleep apnoea can be a potentially life-threatening condition, associated with strokes, heart attacks and high blood pressure, and therefore requires medical attention. It is also strongly associated with road traffic collisions.

A sleep test is usually carried out to diagnose sleep apnoea and its severity. This test is often very simple and sleep centres will loan the equipment to take home. The measurement may just involve a finger transducer to measure blood oxygen levels, a chest band to measure breathing and a nasal transducer to measure airflow. Mild cases can be effectively treated through lifestyle changes – losing weight, cutting down on alcohol or sleeping on your side, for example. A lot of cases will be prescribed a Continuous Positive Airway Pressure (CPAP) device, which supports your breathing during the night. More severe cases, which have been cited in some heart and respiratory failure fatalities, demand medical intervention, such as observation in a sleep clinic.

Restless Legs Syndrome (RLS)

This condition is mainly associated with old age but it can strike at any time, and may be caused by low levels of iron in the brain. RLS is a tingling, itching or burning sensation and unexplained aches and pains in the limbs, mainly the legs. The problem ranges from being simply uncomfortable to painful. Sleep is disturbed because people often have a strong urge to move the legs to relieve the discomfort by stretching, rubbing the legs or getting up and pacing around. It may be inherited, but pregnancy may also bring on the condition. Caffeine and alcohol aggravate the sensations, so should be avoided. Massaging the legs, using a hot or cold pack, leg stretches, magnesium and iron supplements, and a warm bath can all help ease the symptoms. It is worth getting your general practitioner to measure your ferritin levels. Ferritin carries iron into the brain, and even low levels are associated with symptoms.

Periodic Limb Movements of Sleep (PLMS), a similar disorder that impairs sleep and causes daytime sleepiness, is characterized by involuntary leg twitching or jerking movements during sleep which typically occur every 10 to 60 seconds, sometimes throughout the night.

Narcolepsy

This is a condition that makes sufferers uncontrollably fall asleep at apparently random intervals. It is often associated with cataplectic attacks, where people have physical symptoms of sudden sleep, such as collapsing, but are actually wide awake. An attack is often brought on by intense emotions, such as anger or sexual arousal. One person in a thousand suffers from narcolepsy and there are various causes – it can be a result of a virus triggering an autoimmune disease, or head injury. The symptoms arise because the wakefulness-promoting parts of the brain are damaged. "Sleep pressure" builds up and there is nothing to counteract it. Many of the symptoms are associated with REM intruding into wakefulness; hence the REM paralysis becomes cataplexy.

Narcolepsy can also be accompanied by headaches, lethargy and poor concentration and, although hard to diagnose, it requires medical attention and treatment to find techniques that will help the sufferer and their loved ones to cope better.

A lesser, but still debilitating, condition is hypersomnia, which is long-term excessive daytime sleepiness with no clear cause. Sufferers go into long phases of deep sleep, which can last up to two hours at a time. Occasional patches of hypersomnia can happen several times a day with problem-free periods in between. Excessive tiredness can also happen after periods of intense stress on the body or emotions; this is known as post-traumatic tiredness.

Seasonal Affective Disorder (SAD)

As the winter nights begin to draw in, many people find themselves sleeping longer, eating more and generally feeling low and lacking in motivation. Many of us may recognize these symptoms, as it is a common complaint, although the extent of the problem can vary between every sufferer. Treatment is usually in the form of light therapy, exposing the patient to a light source of about 2,500 lux; lux is the measurement of light – average room lighting is about 250–500 lux. The light mimics the effect of the sun, which is thought to control the production of melatonin – one theory is that darkness means more production of melatonin, which makes us more lethargic. The best way to control this ourselves is to make the most of any available light by taking a daily walk outside. Also make sure that your curtains and blinds are wide open when the sun is out. Use brighter,

THE HAMILTON ANXIETY SCALE

If you have anxiety disorder, your doctor may use a special list of questions or statements to measure your symptoms. A popular one is the Hamilton Anxiety Scale. This scale lists 14 types of symptoms. You and your doctor rate each symptom on a scale from 0 (meaning you don't have that symptom) to 4 (meaning you have it very badly). The total score can range from 0 to 56. A total score of 18 or more means you should seek treatment for an anxiety disorder.

1. Anxiety, including worry, insecurity, irritability, fear, dread and panic.
2. Tension, including nervousness, muscle tension and trembling.
3. Fears, such as fear of enclosed spaces or fear of open spaces, and avoidance of these situations.
4. Lack of sleep or poor sleep.
5. Poor concentration or difficulty making decisions.
6. Depression, including sadness, gloom and hopelessness.
7. Muscle pain or weakness.
8. Trouble hearing, poor vision or unusual sensations on your skin (such as prickling).
9. Symptoms affecting your heart, such as palpitations (you feel your heart beating faster than normal) or feeling faint.
10. Trouble breathing.
11. Constipation, diarrhoea, nausea or other problems with your digestive system.
12. Needing to urinate too often; abnormal periods.
13. Nervous symptoms, such as sweating, dizziness or a dry mouth.
14. Feeling anxious, nervous or agitated while talking to your doctor.

As with depression, which is closely related and often accompanies anxiety, talking to a counsellor, practitioner or even a friend will help relieve the symptoms and speed the recovery process.

daylight bulbs in your home to kickstart your daily cycle and get a 'sunlight' alarm clock to help your body prepare for the day. Also consider changing your annual holiday; two weeks in the sun in winter could perk you up dramatically.

Anxiety

Ranging from a nervous feeling when awaiting news to a full-blown, physical panic attack, anxiety can be terribly debilitating. It may have a reasonable cause, such as financial or personal uncertainties, but the symptoms may persist long after the initial trigger has been resolved – and this is known as 'free-floating anxiety'. It may even be that an unpleasant sleep association has developed, making the process of trying to get some much-needed – and healing – sleep traumatic, and resulting in sleepless nights, which makes things seem even more unbearable and the chances of recovering without help less likely.

Depression

Sleep disorders and depression are frequent bedfellows. Symptoms may include a sense of hopelessness, weight loss, withdrawal from social interaction, fatigue, feelings of guilt, low libido, negative thought patterns, indecision and lack of focus; some sufferers also have suicidal thoughts. Depression can vary in its intensity and duration and affects twice as many men as women, but it is treatable. A problem with depression is persuading sufferers that their feelings of shame regarding their situation are actually part of the condition and that, with treatment, they can begin to live again. It is not clear why sleep disorders and depression are linked. Disrupted sleep leads to lowered pain sensitivity and perhaps it also leads to lower emotional resilience; whatever the theory, both are worth treating.

A LIFESTYLE OVERHAUL

Sleeplessness, or what was once called extrinsic insomnia, is likely to affect us all at some point. According to research by the Better Sleep Council, 65 per cent of American adults claim they are losing sleep through stress. Stress itself can take many forms, but it mostly results in some form of constant, low-grade sleep deprivation. Some life events cause a 'natural' insomnia, such as a new baby, menopause, the death of a loved one or illness. That is not to say that it is any easier to cope with, but it is an expected part of these life-changing events and should rebalance in time, although you can help the situation along. Other forms of insomnia, or the creation of a sleep deficit from sleeping for too short a time, need treating at the root of the problem. Life in the fast lane and pressure at work demand a re-evaluation of your way of living.

The way we sleep changes constantly, with the amount we need gradually decreasing throughout our lives. For women, sleep patterns change throughout the month; the best sleep occurring immediately after menstruating and the worst in the run up to it. Pregnant women also experience a change in sleep patterns. They have more REM sleep and may find it hard to get comfortable or need to urinate in the night. Even women taking the oral contraceptive pill will have more shallow sleep than a woman using another form of contraceptive.

Work-Life Balance

In the current work culture, where we are expected to show our commitment through long hours and demanding schedules, it is easy to feel that we have no choice but to fall into line at the expense of our personal lives. But next time you decide to work into the small hours, consider the fact that you are less able to think laterally and creatively when you are tired. So those extra hours trying to come up with an idea, when your body is sagging and your mind wandering, would really be better spent sleeping. Some scientists even believe that sleeping helps to filter out all the useless information of the day and helps us to process the more important stuff; a theory that might be supported by anyone waking up with the solution to a nagging problem they couldn't resolve the day before. The lack of interest and motivation that results from sleep deprivation has led to some US companies encouraging executives to take naps during the day to refresh themselves, and make them more focused, as a nap can instantly sharpen your powers of concentration.

Shift Work

Working shift hours is the result of our demand for a 24-hour society. Those caring for an elderly or sick friend or relative may experience similar sleep patterns to those doing shift work. The very existence of the 'darkness' hormone melatonin, which is produced at night to tell us to go to bed, is a clear sign that we are not nocturnal creatures. People who work shifts for a number of years are more likely to suffer from depression, heart disease and certain cancers, such as breast cancer in women. According to family physician and author Dr Paul Caldwell, switching from one shift to another is the most disruptive form of shift work; sticking to the same shift makes it much easier for the body to cope. The usual problems that flow from sleep deprivation, such as impaired personal relationships, becoming increasingly accident-prone and suffering from a suppressed immune system, all apply here; even though you are virtuously working away, the body makes no distinction. There are, however, some ways to make shift work more bearable.

TIPS FOR SURVIVING SHIFT WORK

- When you are working, make sure the light is bright, and when you are meant to be sleeping, make sure the room is dark.
- Don't wait until the night you start your shift to change your sleeping patterns. Try to go to bed a little later each night in order to anticipate the change it will make to your wake-sleep patterns.
- Try to get 'power naps', especially if your job involves making important decisions. Even a 15-minute nap can sharpen your decision-making process.
- Make nutrition central to your wellbeing. Shift workers often resort to convenience food and alcohol to help them to wind down. Your body will cope better if you have nourishing meals.
- Make sure your partner or friends understand the toll on your system and emotions. It will help keep your relationships on track.

Stress

Everyone has some stress in their life. At best, it can motivate us to achieve our goals and respond to constantly changing demands; in its worst form it can give us horrible symptoms such as anxiety, depression, guilt, isolation, back pain, insomnia and headaches. Learning to manage our reaction to stress is essential to achieving a good night's sleep. In terms of feeling good, American women identify getting a good night's sleep as their top priority for personal wellness. The US Better Sleep Council discovered that 27 per cent believe that sleep is more important to wellness than eating a balanced diet (24 per cent) and exercising for 30 minutes a day (19 per cent). However, while 45 per cent of women say they feel most energized after a good night's sleep, only 16 per cent say that they are likely to sleep more to improve their overall wellness. Most people still leave sleep at the bottom of their priority list.

The main problem with stress is that it demands quick solutions. We tend to use quick fixes, such as caffeine, chocolate and processed snacks and meals, to make us feel instantly better so that we can get on top of the demands made of us. Finding time to buy nourishing fresh food or to do calming exercises can often seem totally implausible, but finding time to do them is vital if we are to arrive at a place where we can enjoy challenges and adapt to them, rather than feel desperate.

The Day-to-Day Effects of Stress The effects of poorly managed stress on the mind and body are wide-ranging. The general, most noticeable symptoms are listed below.

THE SYMPTOMS OF STRESS

- Muscular tension, especially in the jaw, neck and shoulders
- Insomnia
- Poor concentration
- Infections, such as colds
- Lack of appetite
- Loss of sex drive
- Panic attacks
- Depression
- Low self-confidence
- Inability to make decisions
- Mood swings
- Hyperventilation
- Inability to change thought patterns
- Digestion problems, such as constipation, diarrhoea
- Anxiety
- Headaches, dizziness or light headedness
- Palpitations
- Heartburn
- Tingling sensations on the skin
- Exacerbation of skin complaints, such as psoriasis, eczema and acne

The Adrenaline Rush

Every time we find ourselves faced with a new challenge, our body activates the 'fight or flight response'. The intensity of this reaction can depend on the type of situation we are in. The part of the autonomic nervous system that kicks into action is called the 'sympathetic' branch. It increases our rate of breathing, heartbeat, perspiration and production of the stress hormones cortisol and adrenaline and sends blood to muscles while shutting down our digestive system. We find ourselves with a sharpened mental awareness and a surge of physical energy and tension – this is what helps us to act quickly or meet that deadline. Once things have calmed down again, the 'parasympathetic' branch comes into play. This slows down all the mechanisms that speeded up and gets our digestion running again. Unfortunately, some people can start to rely on this 'rush' in order to get things done. This can have disastrous effects on long-term health and cause fatigue and exhaustion. Balancing the two systems is thus essential to our emotional and physical wellbeing. Repeatedly pushing ourselves past our limits will lead to burnout, a condition that will take far more than a few nights of extra rest to sort out.

Acknowledging our dependence upon these highs and the importance of taking control of our own state of mind is the first step to restoring a balance. Next, we need to make time to wind down through relaxation, visualization, meditation and breathing techniques, all of which can help us to drift off into a more refreshing sleep. We often assume that all our worries are valid rather than acknowledging that sometimes we may simply fall into negative patterns of thinking. Relaxing effectively is a learned pattern of behaviour, in just the same way as negative thinking is, so why not choose the more pleasurable option?

Mastering relaxation techniques can have powerful physical and emotional impacts. If you find your concentration wandering to your 'to do' lists, start your recovery programme with an aromatherapy massage and let someone else take over the technical side. Soon you will see the relaxing effects that such a practice can exert.

Jet Lag

Whether it's for pleasure or business, air travel is now common for many of us. While it may be a quick and convenient mode of travel, it also has its drawbacks. Jet lag, the awful 'travel hangover' that comes from skipping time zones, can wreak havoc with our body clocks and sleep patterns. Our bodies are designed to adjust to seasonal time changes, but not at the speed required when we travel across the world by aeroplane. The feelings of disorientation, nausea, headaches and insomnia are all a result of the disparity between the external indicators in our new destination conflicting with our body's expectation of where we are in our circadian rhythm cycle.

The biological clock for most people tends to run slowly. Left to its own devices, and synchronized by light and activity, our sleep would start later and later and we'd be waking up later and later. Normally

TIPS FOR ENJOYING A RESTFUL FLIGHT

What with jet lag, the noise, sleeping in the company of sometimes hundreds of strangers, children crying, cramped conditions, poor air quality, reheated food and the general chaos and stress of the airport, there is very little to make you have a restful and refreshing journey. Try some of the techniques listed below for making your recovery time shorter.

- As soon as you get on the flight, make sure you change your watch to the new time and act accordingly — if it's 3 a.m. at your destination, try to sleep.
- Don't wake up for the airline meals. Take your own snacks to eat at the right time, rather than just eating at a time that is convenient for the airline — more often than not, you won't be missing much!
- Eat well the day before the flight. Eat lots of fresh fruit, vegetables and lean protein so that your body is running at an optimum level to handle the stress.
- If you are travelling a long way, make changes in the week before you fly. Get up an hour later/earlier to adjust to the new time.
- Keep drinking water to help your body deal with the changes.

Needless to say, dehydrating substances such as tea, coffee and alcohol won't help.
- Get out and about in daylight when you arrive. Lurking in the hotel room will only prolong the jet lag.
- Earplugs, eye masks and the reading light can help you make your own sun and moon. Use them to control your sense of the time of day.
- Do exercises, such as flexing and pointing your toes, stretching your arms above your head and walking around the plane, to help relieve muscle cramp and avoid Deep Vein Thrombosis (DVT).
- Natural sleep preparations can help if you need to sleep on the plane but also use carbohydrates to help you reach a soporific state.
- Vitamin B complex can help your body to cope with the strain of flying. Take it when you don't want to sleep, as it can be stimulating to the brain.
- When you arrive, use a power nap (no more than 90 minutes) to refresh your brain, and then get on with the day, no matter how much your body pleads for bed.

dawn light resets the clock to the new day. When we travel west, it is like artificially lengthening our day and so we cope better than on an eastbound flight where we're artificially trying to speed the clock up. When we travel east our day shortens and we lose time, making our sleep time less. Your body will still want to rest and you end up struggling not to sleep in the afternoon, when you should be at a meeting or, more importantly, out in the sun enjoying yourself. It has been estimated that the body adapts one hour a day when flying eastward, and one and a half on westward journeys. So if you travel four hours east, it will take six days for you to feel fully recovered; travel six hours west and it only will take four.

New Kid on the Block

A baby in the house is a joyous thing, but it can also have a profound impact on the sleep quality of everyone else. Understanding the sleep process and patterns of your growing child can help in this situation, but ultimately the best thing to remember is that each phase is just that, a phase. As difficult as it is to do – and sometimes it will not be practical or possible – try to sleep when your baby sleeps in the first few months. This will help refresh you and prevent exhaustion.

1–2 months Newborns can sleep between 10$\frac{1}{2}$ and 18 hours a day and, as any new parent will tell you, at irregular hours. Exposing them to light and noise during the day can encourage them to sleep more at night. The National Sleep Foundation of America suggests putting the baby in the cot (crib) when he/she is drowsy, not asleep, with their face and head clear of blankets and other soft items.

3–11 months When infants are put to bed drowsy but not completely asleep, they are more likely to become 'self-soothers', which enables them to fall asleep independently at bedtime and send themselves back to sleep if they wake during the night. After 6 months, infants may experience separation anxiety, but by this time, if you're a lucky parent, many will sleep through the night, for about 9–12 hours with naps during the day.

1–3 years The standard sleep time at this age is 12–14 hours, with one long nap during the day of between 1 and 3 hours. Nightmares, the ability to get out of bed and separation anxiety can all make sleep difficult. A security blanket or stuffed toy should help, as will firm enforcement of the sleep ritual.

3–5 years Children will sleep between 11 and 13 hours a night by this age, although falling asleep and waking is common. Sleepwalking and sleep terrors may start around this time. Maintaining a sleep schedule that ends in a cool, dark room should help.

5–12 years Daytime naps should end about this time. Children aged 5 to 12 need 10–11 hours of sleep, but there are now increasing demands on their waking time from school and social schedules. Watching TV close to bedtime has been associated with bedtime resistance, difficulty falling asleep and sleeping fewer hours. Make sure they don't have a TV in their bedroom, so that you can monitor how much they watch.

TO SLEEP, PERCHANCE TO DREAM

In our time-pressured culture, sleep is often seen as a nuisance that gets in the way of more enjoyable or essential pastimes. This may be work, but it is also often drinking, dancing and generally having fun. A good, rewarding sleep, however, can bring a great deal of pleasure in its own right.

Sleep can impact positively on your personal relationships, making you relaxed and happy and helping you deal with stress by making you more emotionally prepared to cope with the strains of everyday living. This will help you to enjoy more of the life around you by keeping you sharp, alert and engaged. Your levels of creativity and mental agility are also fine-tuned by sleep, as is your immune system, which is boosted by sleep, keeps infection at bay and improves your resistance to disease. Don't forget that lovely warm feeling you get from waking from a restful night's slumber to a bright summer's morning, full of energy and ready to make the most of what the day has to offer.

FOOD, DRINK *and* SLEEP

FOOD AND DRINK, LIKE SLEEP, ARE AN
ESSENTIAL PART OF LIVING A HEALTHY AND
FULFILLING LIFE, BUT WE OFTEN FORGET
THAT OUR BODY WORKS AS A WHOLE.

Most of us, for example, fail to acknowledge the effect that alcohol, caffeine and rich food might have on our patterns of sleep, and feel frustrated when we sleep the requisite amount of time yet don't feel refreshed.

In reality, most people are unwilling to live an entirely abstemious life. Try wrestling a cup of cappuccino from the hands of a caffeine addict just before they leave for work, and you will begin to appreciate how many of us rely on such props to help us make it through the day. With that in mind, it's worth admitting your weaknesses and planning out your daily diet sensibly to avoid the food and drinks that keep you awake, and to begin to appreciate more soporific foods later in the day.

SLEEP AND WEIGHT

For those trying to lose weight, good sleep could be essential. A study by Columbia University in New York indicates that there is a link between sleep and the US's obesity epidemic. The research suggests that the more you sleep, the less likely you are to become obese. People who get less than the recommended amount of sleep each night are up to 73 per cent more likely to be obese although, obviously, obesity is also usually the result of several other lifestyle factors. It has also been shown that there is a connection between middle-aged spread in men and the quality of sleep they have. Vicious circles abound... Lifestyle reduces the amount of time to sleep, but increases the amount of time to eat. Weight goes on, which disrupts sleep. Disrupted sleep affects appetite and more food goes in. The weight leads to sleep apnoea (poor breathing), which disturbs sleep and so on. Women join in after menopause when the neck musculature relaxes (along with other parts).

THE BAD STUFF

Caffeine, in beverages such as tea, coffee and fizzy drinks, will keep some people awake well into the night. If you're one of them, you need to enjoy your last cup at least five hours before bedtime. The same goes for heavy, rich foods. Although scientists say that there are no direct chemical reasons why such foods should keep you

33

awake, your digestive system still needs to break down the food. As this is one of the functions that the body winds down during sleep, it can keep you up, or affect your sleep quality, until it has finished its work. So a rich meal with alcohol at 10 p.m. is not the best idea; neither are stimulating meals that contain spicy foods, onions or peppers, which can give you indigestion and delay the onset of sleep.

As a general rule, you should try to avoid the following foods late at night:

- **Fatty foods can cause heartburn, which leads to difficulty in falling asleep and discomfort throughout the night.**
- **Foods containing tyramine (bacon, cheese, ham, aubergines [eggplant], pepperoni, raspberries, avocado, soy sauce, red wine) might keep you awake at night.**

Caffeine

This is the most widely used drug in the world, and probably the most socially acceptable, but its effect should not be underestimated. Reactions to caffeine differ depending on a person's sensitivity. About 99 per cent of the caffeine contained in a drink will enter your bloodstream. On the positive side, it can generate sensations of increased alertness and enhance performance in mental and physical tasks. On the negative side, it can create or exacerbate anxiety, depression, restlessness, headaches, flushes, tremors and heartburn, as well as aggravate high blood pressure. It also has a profound effect on our ability to sleep, which is often the reason it is so popular in the first place.

Caffeine enters the blood stream quickly (in about 5 minutes) and its effects are felt for between 15 and 45 minutes. It then takes between five to six hours for half of it to be filtered out of your blood stream. The remaining half takes another five to six hours again, which is why addicts are often reaching for the coffee filters before they have even changed out of their pyjamas.

As well as your waking time, caffeine also affects your sleeping time. It suppresses feelings of sleepiness and pushes back the time you hit the pillow, in which case that last coffee or tea of your working day keeps you perky for much longer than you would expect. Remember that, as well as coffee and tea, caffeine is also found in cola drinks, chocolate, cocoa, energy drinks, cold remedies and painkillers. Make sure, if you do want to give up, that you don't just end up reaching for it in other forms.

Life After Caffeine If you believe that some of the symptoms caused by caffeine are affecting your quality of life, the good news is that caffeine leaves your system quickly. Detoxing from it might give you withdrawal symptoms of a nasty headache, for a few days, with some irritability and nausea, but you should be able to cope. Increase your daily intake of water and fresh juices to help flush caffeine out, and deal with the temptation by making herbal tea instead; this means you won't have to miss out on the sensation of a comforting warm drink as you work or relax. If you would like to keep coffee as part of your daily life, give yourself a cut-off time of around noon to allow the caffeine adequate time to leave your system, or drink de-caffeinated.

Nicotine

This is the largest preventable cause of death in our society, yet it still plays a huge part in many people's lives. It is a major cause of cancer in the lungs and heart, heart disease and high blood pressure – the risks are manifold. Smokers might cite suppressed appetite (they tend to be an average of 2.2–4.5 kg [5–10 lb] lighter than nonsmokers) and increased memory ability as bonuses, but the undisputed deterioration of their overall health is a high price to pay. Smokers might also note that the good sleep quality they lack thanks to the nicotine in their body could help them to maintain a good weight and memory recall without the health hazard. Unfortunately, the highly addictive nature of nicotine stops many people from acknowledging the risks. Like most drugs, the pleasant, calming sensation created after the initial intake can turn into a jittery, angst-ridden feeling if you don't keep the levels in your body up.

Smoking also affects blood sugar levels, which makes you irritable and prone to sugar cravings. As a stimulant, nicotine acts on the central nervous system and delays sleep as well as increasing the frequency of night-time wakings, which results in a light and less refreshing sleep. Anyone who lives with a heavy smoker and suffers from poor sleep may also be experiencing the effects of passive smoking on their systems.

Life After Nicotine Giving up is hard, but the health benefits will more than outweigh the effort you put in. When inhaled, nicotine quickly stimulates the heart, brain, gastrointestinal tract and adrenal glands, giving the buzz or peak in alertness that comes with a drag on a cigarette. As it is a brain stimulant, it can stop the onset of sleep, but also increase the number of night-time wakings and shorten the duration of sleep; and remember, if it is affecting your sleep, it will affect that of your partner and children, too, as they passively inhale your smoke. Initially, those giving up smoking will experience disturbed sleep from the nicotine withdrawal, but patches and supplements can help ease this transition. Once you are past this point, you will be rewarded with a much deeper and nourishing sleep, as will anyone else in your home.

SMOKERS ARE STATISTICALLY MORE LIKELY TO DRINK MORE CAFFEINE, WHICH ONLY COMPOUNDS THE SIDE EFFECT OF DESTROYING SLEEP QUALITY.

Alcohol

A great deal of self-deception is at work when people use the term 'nightcap' to describe alcohol. Although, as a sedative, it helps you to fall to sleep by making you feel drowsy, it then proceeds to ruin the rest of your night.

Drinking is a hugely popular aid to relaxation, especially for those working long and strenuous hours. Those who drink on an empty stomach will feel the sensation quicker, as drinking with or after food can delay its effects for up to an hour and a half. How tired you are when you start drinking is also important. After five nights of partial sleep deprivation, three drinks will have the same effect on your brain as six would have on a regular night.

If you find the sedative effect more pronounced when drinking in the afternoon, this is because it exaggerates the natural ebb and flow of your circadian rhythm. The energy lull you feel in the afternoon becomes more pronounced, whereas you are naturally more alert in the evening a few hours before bedtime, so its drowsy effects are less dramatic. We all know the general results of drinking, but its impact on sleep is often ignored. Even a small amount of alcohol can change the type of sleep quality we have. REM sleep and the length of sleep we have are reduced, with more wakings and shallow sleep, which results in an unrefreshing sleep. It also has a detrimental effect on sleep conditions, such as apnoea and snoring, making both more pronounced. Alcohol is also a diuretic, which means it encourages you to urinate, which is never welcome when you are trying to sleep.

Life After Alcohol The benefits of regularly drinking a small amount of alcohol, such as a glass of red wine with a meal, are well recognized – the wine contains antioxidant properties and plays a role in helping to reduce the risk of heart disease. If drinking plays a larger part in your life, however, you must allow your liver at least two to three days off a week in order for it to recover. Nights off will also allow you to attain deeper, and more refreshing sleep, giving you the chance to clear the sleep deficit it inflicts. You should also see the benefit to your skin as eye-bags and skin problems caused by drinking will clear. And don't forget the essential glass of water between drinks; avoiding dehydration will stop you waking at 4 a.m., desperate for a glass of water, then finding yourself unable to get back to sleep.

Sugar

In all its forms, sugar can play havoc with our sleep patterns. This is mainly because our blood sugar levels can 'crash' after a big dose of the stuff, leaving us even more tired, and hunting around for another snack to give us a quick energy fix, often washed down with our old friend caffeine. This cycle can leave us too fatigued to make a substantial dinner for ourselves, even if we feel ravenously hungry, and this is where convenience food comes in – offering even more hidden sugars and chemical sweeteners. And so the cycle continues.

Life After Sugar Cutting down on sugar means committing to eating foods in their natural state. This means avoiding processed foods and weaning our sweet tooth on to more natural sugars, such as honey (in moderation). Balancing out the peaks and troughs of blood sugar can aid in weight loss, as we are not overeating and always hurtling from one unhealthy food fix to another, and balance our energy and concentration levels. This will mean you arrive at bedtime ready for a good night's sleep. The key to healthy snacking is to be prepared; a bag of roasted pumpkin seeds in your bag, a fruit bowl on your desk, will make them an easier option than finding a vending machine full of energy-sapping sugary and salty snacks. Aim to graze through the day rather than find yourself suddenly starving and willing to eat whatever you can find (it's always easier to find junk food). Little and often is best, and will stop you suddenly obsessing about what to have mid-morning.

ENERGY-STABILIZING FOODS

The effect on mood and concentration from jolts in blood sugar can make coping with everyday problems more difficult. When the blood sugar level is raised, the pancreas produces insulin to bring it down again (and if this happens too often diabetes can develop). The short-term effect on our energy is to make us feel exhausted, irritable and stressed. We should choose foods that keep our energy levels at a fairly constant level, which helps us to concentrate and frees us from the urge to keep refuelling. It also improves our general mood, making us calmer and more balanced, so we are less likely to lie awake at night fretting over details or wound up from the theobromine in the emergency chocolate bar that we consumed before going to bed (theobromine is similar to caffeine).

When looking for ingredients to create meals, keep in mind the following:

- Water aids digestion, so try to drink at least 2 litres (3$^1/_2$ pints) a day.
- Fresh fruit is the best slow-release energy source.
- Eating protein-rich foods for lunch, such as lean meats, cheese, eggs, natural yogurt and fish, will keep your levels balanced as you enter the natural dip in your circadian rhythm. Eating refined carbohydrates, like white bread, will cause your sugar level to soar, then crash, and only exaggerate this natural dip.

- Pulses, beans, lentils, nuts and seeds are all great for slow-release energy – try them with wholegrain bread.
- Chromium-rich foods, such as shellfish, cheese, baked beans and wholegrain bread, help your body overcome extreme low blood sugar.
- A ravenous hunger the morning after a night of drinking is because the alcohol affects your blood sugar levels, making you reach for quick fixes the next day. Drinking on an empty stomach makes it worse.

The Glycaemic Index

The body needs glucose for energy. It is obtained from starches and sugars in the food we eat and either used or stored as fat. Everything we eat is processed this way, but it is the speed at which this happens that makes the difference to our weight and general health – this is what gives food its GI rating. The faster that food is broken down, the higher its index rating (a high rating is about 70 or above). Low-GI foods keep us fuller for longer, have more fibre, and are usually full of minerals and vitamins.

The lower the glycaemic index (GI) rating of food, the better it is for maintaining a balanced sugar level. Eating foods with a low GI rating, such as pulses, lentils and beans, is a great help when you are giving up stimulants such as caffeine and nicotine because they help prevent the swings in mood and hunger. The more processed the food is, like white bread, white sugar and junk food, the higher it tends to be on the Index.

Choosing energy-balancing foods and drinks during the day can help you feel healthily tired and unwound by bedtime. A large breakfast of complex carbohydrates, such as porridge, fruit, nuts, seeds and lean protein, will keep you balanced.

Tryptophan, the Insomniac's Friend

The good news is that for all the foods and drinks which overstimulate us and keep us awake at night, nature has provided sleep-inducing alternatives. Some calm us down while others actively deliver sedative effects. This is mainly down to a chemical called tryptophan.

Tryptophan is an amino acid and an essential chemical for life, as it helps us to build protein. We consume about one to three grams of tryptophan a day, but we can boost our intake by seeking out foods that have a higher concentration. It's reputed to speed up the onset of sleep, decrease the number of spontaneous wakings during the night and increase the overall length of sleep during the night. Elderly people, who suffer from increased sensitivity to noise, may find it especially helpful.

Eating a main meal around four hours before bedtime with a low to medium GI rating, including complex carbohydrates or some of the vegetables listed below will help start the relaxing process.

If needed, a tryptophan-rich snack before bedtime, such as the snacks listed below, should greatly improve your chances of getting a good night's rest. Remember, however, that the same rules apply as before; make sure you give any snacks enough time to digest (an hour or so) before you go to bed.

FOODS RICH IN TRYPTOPHAN

- Bananas
- Turkey
- Poultry
- Eggs
- Milk and other dairy products
- Almonds
- Cabbage
- Kidney or lima beans
- Oats
- Poppy seed
- Pumpkin seed
- Spinach
- Wheat
- Evening primrose seed (has the most tryptophan of any food source)
- Red meats
- Soybean
- Tofu
- Basil
- Dill

Sedative Snacks That Aid Relaxation

Combine 'sleepy food' with other foods that contain bromine, such as avocados, mandarins and lettuce, to help ease that short-fused feeling, for a light, easy-to-make and easy-to-digest snack.

Lettuce has a longstanding reputation for promoting healthy sleep. This may be due to low concentrations of an opium-related substance, combined with traces of the anticramping agent hyoscyarnin, that are both present. Lettuce should be an integral part of your evening diet if you are suffering from sleep disorders. Juiced, and mixed with a little lemon juice for flavour, it makes an effective sleep-inducing drink and is highly preferable to the synthetic chemical agents in sleeping pills. You can also try carbohydrates, including pasta, brown rice and oatmeal.

Try one of these delicious snacks an hour before bedtime to help you to relax and unwind:

- **Wholegrain toast with a little almond butter**
- **A small portion of a healthy, fat-containing food, such as olive oil on your salad or an avocado**
- **A small pot of natural yogurt with a little honey**
- **Fresh, dried or cooked fruit for dessert**
- **A small cup of warm milk, with nutmeg for flavour and digestion**
- **A small banana**
- **A handful of unsalted nuts or seeds.**

Soothing Drinks

The traditional drink of a glass of warm milk before bedtime does indeed consist of calming properties – the tryptophan, calcium and magnesium presumably all help the mind and body to relax. Try adding a sprinkling of cinnamon, which is excellent for digestion and can ease a sore throat or night-time cough.

Difficulties in breathing can sometimes be aggravated by dairy products, so consider other relaxing drink options. Herbal tea blends can be wonderful at sending you off to sleep; experiment with different blends to find your favourite.

Passionflower The passionflower vine is a sedative and digestive aid. The herb is considered to be a mildly effective treatment for anxiety and insomnia, and is often combined with other herbal preparations, such as valerian and hops. It isn't as potent as some of the other natural sedatives, but it is ideal for those who also get a nervous stomach, especially in the tea form, taken three times daily.

Camomile The familiar camomilla plant is used in varying degrees to help calm and relax. As well as being drunk, it can also be used to create a soothing, sleep-inducing bath before bedtime: simply put a teabag or two into the bath, or float some of the dried flowerheads in the water. Camomile is quite easy to grow if you fancy a constant supply – just dry it out and use. Add a little honey if you need a sweet kick, but not too much!

Lemon Balm Also known as *Melissa officinalis*, this strong lemon-smelling member of the mint family can be made into tea. Also try using it to season soups and salads, or as a cooling iced tea on hot, restless summer nights.

Verbena Also known as lemon verbena, this is similar in flavour to lemon balm, but with a stronger taste, and has similar effects.

Lime Flower Also known as linden, lime flower has soporific effects. Infuse a handful of dried flowers in 1 litre ($2^3/_4$ pints) of boiling water, and drink two large cups before going to bed.

Mandarin Juice A great alternative to tea in the hot summer months is the natural sedative mandarin, which is packed full of calming bromine.

ESSENTIAL VITAMINS & MINERALS

With our hectic daily schedules it is not always possible to eat as well as we would like to, which can leave our systems depleted of much-needed vitamins and minerals. There are ways of combating these lapses, but the most important thing to consider when buying a supplement is that each brand has a different concentration level; often buying a cheap version with too low a level will have little impact. Some also need to be taken together in order to promote absorption, and some should not be taken with food for the same reason.

Some vitamin and mineral supplements should not be taken at night because they can stimulate brain activity, especially if they contain vitamin B complex, which will erode your good night's sleep. When choosing a supplement, don't just assume that the more you take, the better you will feel. Some products can be harmful when consumed in high amounts or in combination with certain other substances. If in doubt, check with your healthcare provider before taking a supplement, especially when combining them with or substituting them for other foods or medicine or if you are pregnant.

As you will see below, you can maximize your intake of several vitamins and minerals by simply increasing your intake of certain foods.

Vitamin B Complex This helps the body to cope in times of stress; helps prevent depression and aids women who suffer from premenstrual syndrome, B6 specifically. It is especially effective if taken at times of extreme pressure, helping to banish feelings of helplessness and the often resulting insomnia. To be most effective, a vitamin B complex must contain thiamine, riboflavin, niacin, folate and B12.

Naturally occurring: You can boost your intake by eating poultry, green leafy vegetables, fish, nuts, seeds, wholegrain products, red meat, soya, potatoes and yeast.

CALCIUM PROMOTES A GOOD NIGHT'S SLEEP, SO IT NEEDS TO BE REPLACED, ESPECIALLY BY WOMEN, WHO OFTEN SUFFER FROM OSTEOPOROSIS AFTER MENOPAUSE.

Calcium Our stressful lives often trigger the 'fight or flight' mechanism that switches on the stress hormone noradrenalin, which causes the body to excrete calcium from the bones. Take calcium with magnesium and vitamin D to aid absorption.

Naturally occurring: You will find calcium in dairy products, such as milk and cheese, pulses, canned fish with bones, green leafy vegetables, soya, sesame seeds and tofu.

Magnesium Magnesium is the fourth most abundant mineral in the body and is essential to good health. It is needed for more than 300 biochemical reactions and helps to maintain normal muscle and nerve function, keeps the heart rhythm steady, supports a healthy immune system and keeps bones strong. Magnesium also helps regulate blood sugar levels, promotes normal blood pressure and is known to be involved in energy metabolism.

Naturally occurring: Magnesium is found in apples, nuts, sesame seeds, figs, dried apricots, lemons and green vegetables.

Vitamin C Like vitamin B, vitamin C is needed to turn glucose into energy. Smoking depletes it, as does alcohol, which also depletes vitamin B – this is one of the reasons you feel so awful after a night indulging in such activities. Vitamin C is an essential antioxidant that repairs the damage caused by free radicals (harmful molecules in our body) and maintains healthy skin and the operation of many of our main organs. Try not to cut vegetables and fruit into small pieces before eating them because vitamin C is oxidized by air. It is also soluble in water.

Naturally occurring: It is found in oranges and other citrus fruit, berries, strawberries, broccoli, cauliflower, raw peppers and kiwi fruit – in fact, all fresh fruit and vegetables contain vitamin C.

Chromium An essential mineral that helps stabilize appetite and prevents cravings, as well as maintaining a healthy heart. A lack of chromium can mean daytime drowsiness, cold hands, excessive thirst and an addiction to sweet foods.

Naturally occurring: It is found in wholegrain bread, brewer's yeast, oysters, potatoes, chicken, green peppers and wheatgerm.

Evening Primrose Oil As well as its high levels of tryptophan and gamma-linolenic acid (GLA), which helps balance hormone production, this is a great aid to women suffering from sleep problems connected with premenstrual syndrome/tension (PMS/PMT) or menopause.

Kava Kava Native to the South Pacific, the root of the kava (*Piper methysticum*) is renowned for its successful use in the overall treatment of anxiety, depression, restlessness and insomnia. Kavalactones appear to act primarily on the limbic system, the primitive part of the brain that affects all other brain activities and which is the principal seat of the emotions and instinct. It is thought that kava may produce its anxiety-relieving and mood-elevating effects by altering the way in which the limbic system influences emotional processes. Unlike many preparations, it does not lead to an increased tolerance, so kava won't lose effectiveness over time. It is useful for anxiety and insomnia resulting from the menopause. For sedative effects, it should be taken one hour before you want to go to bed. Kava is restricted in many countries, and although not available in unlicensed form in the UK or Canada, it is legal in the USA and Australia.

Melatonin This hormone is created by a group of nerves in the brain, found just behind the eyes, called the pineal gland. Its name comes from the Greek word *melas*, meaning dark or black. Melatonin is released by the pineal gland as the sun sets and makes you feel sleepy and ready for bed. It is how the body knows that it is night-time, and even what season it is. Melatonin also lowers the body temperature, which is needed to slow down the heart rate and allow the body to enter sleep mode. Sleeping in an utterly dark room increases the production of melatonin.

Clever as it is, your body cannot tell the difference between electric light and sunlight – this is one reason why we get less sleep than our ancestors. In days gone by, candles were expensive, so people would spend more time in bed sleeping and in a waking state of rest. With the invention of the electric light, the hours in which we can and are expected to work and play have been extended.

Melatonin is a hormone and as such is not available for purchase in some countries, although it is available in the USA. Taking melatonin as a supplement facilitates sleep when the natural cycle is disturbed, and is particularly effective for coping with jet lag (see also page 28).

Ginseng If your insomnia is stress-related, ginseng could help you to control the attendant anxiety and protect you from stress 'burnout'. It stops you from producing excess cortisol, the stress hormone that can tip from good to bad when too much is produced and it starts to impair concentration. Ginseng keeps up the production of serotonin and norepinephrine, which guard against depression. The dip in our immune system brought on by a lack of sleep can also be corrected by ginseng, when taken in small amounts.

CREATING
a SLEEP
HAVEN

THE IDEA OF GOING TO BED HAS ALWAYS BEEN SYNONYMOUS WITH COMFORT, PEACE AND RELIEF. SADLY, THE REALITY IS OFTEN A PALE IMITATION OF THE FANTASY.

Many people's bedrooms are a muddle of furniture, entertainment systems, clothes and office or exercise equipment. Despite the crisis of space many of us suffer from, to ensure the best night's sleep the bedroom needs to be a retreat from all the stimulants that keep you hooked into your daytime concerns.

First, try this quick quiz to determine whether your bedroom is a sanctuary or a cell. For each yes answer score one point, for each no, zero.

- **Do you take longer than 20 minutes to fall asleep?**
- **Do you have one light source in the bedroom?**
- **Do you have a TV in your bedroom?**

- **Is your bedroom dual-purpose (e.g., an office)?**
- **Do you lack adequate storage in your bedroom?**
- **Do you sleep near a busy road or experience other forms of noise pollution?**
- **Do you wake feeling groggy?**
- **Do you ever wake up repeatedly in the night?**
- **Do you share a bed regularly with someone else?**
- **Are you reliant on tea or coffee to start the day?**

Answering yes to three or more means you need to re-evaluate your sleep space. The following section will give you ideas for improvements.

THE RIGHT EQUIPMENT

Sound a bit scientific? The reality is that you need the right conditions to get a restful night. Just a small investment can help you to reap the rewards with a more refreshing night's rest.

The Bed

The first step when carrying out a review of your sleep is to take a look at your mattress. If you are having painful or disrupted sleep, it should be your first port of call, as it could be your body's way of simply saying that you need a new bed. We move around in our sleep up to 60 times in the night, so your bed needs to give enough room to manoeuvre. If you share your bed, you need to buy the largest you can; bear in mind that a standard double gives both partners less space than a single bed for each would.

A good mattress will last you 10 years at best. After 10 years, a bed that is used regularly will have deteriorated by as much as 75 per cent from its new condition. Considerable back pain or restlessness can be put down to your deteriorating level of support. Mattresses come with various types of internal spring unit (open coil, pocket sprung or continuous springing), ordinary foam, visco-elastic or latex foam (which mould to the body) or can be filled with cotton or other fibres, or be designed to relieve particular orthopaedic difficulties. In general, the higher the spring count in a mattress, the better the support. As a guide, the higher the spring count, the more you will pay.

A divan bed has springs in the base as well as the mattress, which are designed to work together. If you have a more basic bed frame, without springs, make sure you buy a good mattress to compensate for the lack of support in the base. A myth that persists is that the firmer the mattress, the better it is for your back. The level of firmness should actually relate to your body weight − the heavier you are, the firmer your bed needs to be. The mattress should allow your 'sticking-out bits' − your hips and shoulders − to press into the mattress so that your 'sticking-in bits' − your waist or the small of your back − is supported. If you have a specific joint or back problem, take advice from an osteopath or healthcare professional who will be able to advise you.

Make sure you test lots of mattresses because they vary massively from one manufacturer to another. If you share your bed with someone, make sure they try it too, in order to ensure you both have enough room and don't roll together. If you can't compromise, then look at zip and link beds, which join two single beds together. These have welcome advantages for those who have widely differing comfort and support requirements.

When buying your bed there is still one last element to consider − to store or not to store. A lack of storage in the bedroom can be simply solved by purchasing a bed base with drawers underneath, but bear in mind that these are not as good for your back as a sprung base. In some cases, however, losing a degree of comfort more than makes up for getting rid of the piles of boxes or clothes that distract you from rest.

Pillows

Good-quality pillows are vital in the fight against neck and back pain. Choose a mix of duck down for comfort and feathers for support. If

you suffer from a feather allergy, there are good synthetic versions, although they won't last as long, so be aware that they will need replacing sooner. As with duvets, pillows should be cleaned regularly every four to six months. Feather pillows can be dry cleaned, hand washed or machine washed. Make sure there are no holes in the casing, then wash on a cool wash with a mild detergent. Afterwards, dry on a hot setting in your tumble dryer or hang out in the sun; whichever method you choose, make sure the pillows are thoroughly dry. Placed in a pillowcase, a damp pillow will get mildew and be ruined. For those with dust allergies, pillows that can be regularly laundered in the washing machine are ideal.

If you tend to wake up with a sore neck, this could be down to the positioning of your pillows. As you enter REM sleep, your muscles are relaxed and only the ligaments are holding your head in place. Your head, therefore, needs to be held in a straight line with your body; not bent towards the bed or towards your chest when you are flat on your back. Experiment with one or two pillows to see what works best for you.

Duvets

The common choice for bedding these days is a duvet or comforter, so when selecting one you need to understand the 'tog' rating that is usually applied to them. Tog is a measurement of warmth: the higher the tog, the warmer the duvet. A child should be fine with a 4.5 tog duvet all year round in mild climates, but in winter an adult may need a duvet with a rating of between 12 and 13.5. A good way to match the rating with the season is to buy a low-tog spring duvet, about 4 togs, and a heavier one, about 9 togs, and combine them in the winter. Men and women control their body temperatures differently. I won't dictate who's right in an argument over bedroom and bed temperature... Everyone's different! There are now duvets with a separate tog rating on each side to allow for couples with different preferences.

Sheets

Choice of sheets is a case of personal preference, but linen is kindest on the skin because it is natural and pH neutral. It can absorb up to 20 per cent of its own weight in moisture, thus absorbing some of the 280 ml ($1/2$ pint) of water we lose every night in perspiration. The higher the thread count, the finer the weave and the softer it will feel on the skin. Although linen is more expensive than cotton, it will last for many years, so it will be a good investment. If cotton is your preference, apply the same thread count rule as per linen for softness; anything with fewer than 180 will feel rough on the skin.

Nightwear

Unless you like to sleep as nature intended, wear nightwear that is made of natural fibres to help the skin to breathe and cope with fluctuating body and external temperatures. The clothing should be soft, warm and comfortable. Ensure you don't choose items that are too tight or likely to get caught up in the bedding.

Bed socks work for those who suffer from chilly extremities, and can even comfort and aid restless sleepers with no temperature problems. By keeping the extremities warm and thus making you more comfortable, bed socks allow the core body temperature to drop further, which promotes deeper relaxation – intense relaxation through meditation has also been shown to lower the body temperature.

ALLERGIES

Some allergy sufferers can find that bedtime exacerbates their symptoms, causing them to lie awake trying to catch their breath and sneezing. To help keep dust and dust mites to a minimum, vacuum and launder bedding frequently, use hypoallergenic pillows and bedding and keep pets out of the bedroom. As well as the bed, take a good look around your room for possible triggers – padded bed heads, carpets and cushions can all harbour dust and mites. One very common misconception is that feathers should be avoided, as people often think that feathers irritate all allergies – in fact, they only affect those with a feather allergy! Natural bedding is often a good option for allergy sufferers because it is usually enclosed in a tighter woven casing, so is pretty dust-mite-proof. If you are unsure about the cause of your problems, ask your doctor about being tested.

AMBIENCE

Now that you have all the equipment in place, it is time to consider the ambience of your sleep space. We are especially sensitive to our environment when entering the first stage of sleep, as we can be easily disturbed (see page 8), and it is essential that we feel relaxed, comfortable and safe in order to go to sleep. Here are some ways you can improve the environment where you sleep.

Lighting

Most importantly, you need to get the room lighting correct. For the brain to activate the 'it's sleep time' hormone melatonin, it needs darkness. Gentle, low-level lighting in the bedroom, therefore, allows the body to prepare for sleep. With this in mind, choose low-level lamps that give off a diffused light; this also has the advantage of creating a relaxing, intimate mood.

Architects and designers call this kind of gentle lighting 'mood lighting', but because in winter months you also need your bedroom lighting to be bright enough to allow you to dress and prepare for the day, you will need brighter 'task lighting' – your lighting plan should allow for both. Fitting a dimmer switch to the overhead light will give you the most range. If you share a bedroom, bedside lamps are invaluable for allowing one person to read and the other to snooze. The ultimate luxury used to be a switch by both the bed and the door, or even voice-activated ones, so that you don't even have to get out of bed to turn off the lights. Nowadays, there are various app-controlled lights too. When tackling children's rooms, low-level lighting, such as a night light, means you can leave it switched on without disturbing the child's sleep, though darkness is the ideal. Dimmer switches can also be used to help your child recognize that bedtime is approaching.

The light as you wake is just as important as the light when you are trying to sleep. While it is necessary to keep strong light, such as irritating street lights, out of the room to allow you to nod off, you also need to make sure there is enough light coming in to let the body know when to start rousing you from your slumber. A window treatment that shuts out the emerging dawn will encourage the production of extra melatonin, which will lead to a drugged and disorientated sensation upon waking up. Thick, heavy curtains will keep you warmer in winter, but will also produce this effect. If you have no other choice but to opt for total blackout, buy a light-activated alarm clock that imitates the onset of dawn and helps the body prepare for waking up by releasing the 'wake up' hormone cortisol. To allow natural light to wake you, try diffusing it with voile or muslin curtains.

A good tip is to treat yourself to a visit to a sumptuous hotel to see how the experts create appealing sleep spaces. Perhaps steal a few ideas, such as bedside lamps mounted on the wall or downlighters – you can always justify it as research!

Temperature and Humidity

Key to a really good night's sleep is the correct temperature. The body needs to cool down to allow the core temperature of the internal organs, like the heart and lungs, to slow their rate. This is why hot summer nights can make it so difficult to sleep. Cool – not cold – conditions are the best for good sleep and the ideal temperature should be between 16–18°C (60–65°F). Even on chilly winter nights, when it might be tempting to turn up the heating, you should try to maintain this level. If you are cold, don't just throw a heavy blanket over the bed to keep you warm, as this can affect the efficiency of the duvet. Instead, replace your duvet or team it with another one for a heavier tog value. Alternatively, put the blanket under the duvet or buy a thin electric blanket.

Humidity is also an essential element for good sleep. Central heating can dry the air in living spaces and make breathing become difficult or uncomfortable. If you wake up with a sore throat or dryness in your nose, the room probably has too little humidity. You may be unable to sleep with the window open, because of pollution or noise, but humidifiers, which release moisture into the air, can prevent the room from seeming dry and stuffy. You can achieve a similar effect by placing a bowl of water near the radiator or heater in your room.

Blocking Out Noise

Noise is not always such a bad thing. Although it would be wonderful to sleep in total silence, sharing a planet with lots of other people means this is frequently unachievable. People often wake up, roused by noise, as they enter the lighter part of their sleep cycle – this is often more a problem for older people who spend less time in deep sleep and more in the kind that is easily disturbed by noise. You can, of course, use sound insulation if you live on a busy road, such as double glazing, insulation between floors and walls, or choose a room in the quietest spot of the house away from main roads, or use good old-fashioned ear plugs. However, an effective trick can be to add some noise of your own. The low-level whir of a fan can often block out distracting noises, and once you have become used to the sound, you may find that it no longer disturbs you at all. If you have ever fallen asleep in front of a flickering TV, the effect of a comforting low-level background noise will be familiar.

COLOUR YOURSELF SLEEPY

Colour has an incredibly far-reaching effect on our emotions; for example, orange is known to stimulate mental activity and red represents power, drive, action and passion. When choosing a colour for your bedroom, therefore, it is not always wise to go with your favourite colour. If you have a colour that you really want to use, like purple, try a paler version of it such as lilac; it will be much more restful. You can then use it in its bolder form as accents such as cushions or throws.

The most reflective colours are associated with calm in nature: dusky pinks of late summer skies, soft greens of pastures, pale blues of wildflowers. Other colours can be used in more intense shades and still feel restful, such as turquoise and pink.

In conjunction with the Colour and Imaging Institute at the University of Derby in the UK, Angela Wright created a software system that analyzes the most appropriate use of colour based on emotional and psychological principles. In their pure form, the following colours are most suitable for a bedroom environment. The key to choosing a colour that creates calm rather than coldness, for example, is selecting the right shade; look at several samples and choose the one that draws you to it when you think of a calming, rather than cold space. A 'warm' shade (such as a white with a yellow undertone rather than a blue undertone) will always seem friendlier (and less like an old-fashioned hospital ward).

Blue: Essentially soothing, blue affects us mentally, calming the mind and aiding concentration. A strong blue will stimulate clear

COLOUR YOURSELF SLEEPY CONT.

thought. Too much, or the wrong shade, can be cold.

Violet/Purple: This colour has the shortest wavelength, making it nearest to ultraviolet, and lending it mystical qualities. It encourages spiritual contemplation, and has associations with luxury, truth and awareness. Too much can cause introversion and a sense of suppression.

Pink: A physically nurturing colour, pink evokes feelings of tranquillity, warmth and love, and is also the colour of femininity. It is physically soothing, but can be draining if used to excess.

Green: This colour is at the very centre of the colour spectrum, and therefore represents balance. It suggests harmony, refreshment, peace and rest. Too much can indicate stagnation or boredom.

White: White creates a heightened perception of space, and represents purity, clarity, sophistication and simplicity. However, when used with warm colours it can make them seem garish, so accessorize carefully. White used in the wrong shade (there are many 'whites') can seem cold and unfriendly, so choose a yellow-based shade. The colour works well with texture to soften its hard implications.

Brown: Warm and soft but serious, brown communicates earth and nature. A useful neutral, it is quietly supportive in interior design. Too much can look heavy, so is best used as an accent, such as a dark wooden floor in a white room, which will help achieve softness.

SENSORY STIMULATION

Keeping outside influences, and reminders of the active daytime world, from creeping into your sleeping environment will go far to aid rest and relaxation. There are also ways you can create sense experiences that induce sleep, from introducing comfortable fabrics to using relaxing aromas to scent the bedding and air – which can form a welcome contrast to the rest of your home and help coax the body into a state of deep relaxation.

Electronic Equipment

Two-thirds of British children have a computer, games machine or TV in their bedroom, which could mean they are losing sleep as a result. The adult population is no better. To avoid the temptation to stay up past your bedtime and send just one last email, or watch one last episode of that TV show, electronic equipment needs to be moved from your sleeping space if you are to get a good night's sleep. If space is at a premium, however, and you have to work from your bedroom, use a storage system that you can fold away or, at the very least, use black tape to cover the red stand-by indicators.

THE
RED 'STAND-BY'
LIGHTS CAN IMPAIR
YOUR SLEEP QUALITY BY
AFFECTING THE BRAIN'S
ABILITY TO SWITCH OFF.

Clear Up the Clutter

There are other distractions that should also have a veil drawn discreetly over them. Open storage might seem like an efficient way to grab a cardigan before work, but being able to see a mess out of the corner of your eye is enough to keep you wide awake just thinking about clearing it up. A clear demarcation of space is needed. Doors, or even muslin drapes, can help you to shut out mess and muddle and to switch off. Think of clutter as intellectual noise. If you leave things heaped about the room, you are doing the equivalent to your brain of inviting a brass band to play while you try to sleep. Even if you are too tired to tidy that night, throw everything into a basket and put it outside the bedroom door. You can deal with it tomorrow when you are more refreshed.

Introduce Texture

Texture is essential for bringing interest and comfort to a bedroom. A neutral relaxing colour scheme, such as a mixture of off-whites and camel colours, can be given extra depth and interest by throwing a woven blanket over the foot of the bed, or hanging some heavy, chunky cord curtains. Don't just opt for one type of texture. If you would like some personal mementos to keep the theme fun and sleep-inspiring, a collection of black-and-white photographs of loved ones is stylish without making you forget why you are there.

You can also use texture to try something new. If you are getting over a sleep problem, or just want to shake off old associations, try a gauzy canopy over the bed, a string of tiny lights around the bedhead instead of a reading lamp, or a dramatic window treatment; choose a focal point and make the most of it.

Pep Up the Passion

Use music and scent to quickly change the energy in your bedroom after a long, demanding day. Choose something sultry, rather than distracting, for background noise (yes to easy jazz, no to heavy rock, unless you want your partner to break off to do a guitar solo halfway through). Scent acts very quickly to alter an atmosphere: try ylang ylang in an oil burner, as the flickering light will also enhance the mood. A row of candles standing on a long mirror will also add a sense of occasion. If your partner still can't shake off the stress of the day, get them to try this simple 'state breaker', which will instantly encourage them to release themselves from their mood. Sit straight with your eyes closed, then breathe in deeply through the nose and out slowly through the mouth; repeat three times to attain a more relaxed state.

SLEEP RITUALS

Bedtime rituals are known to help children to prepare for a good night's sleep. The repetition of the same routine gradually unwinds the mind and body and indicates to them that nearing bedtime can be wonderfully soothing and achieve effective results. It's obvious, but easy to forget, that creating a slightly more sophisticated version can have the same success for adults.

A Bathroom Retreat

One of the most effective routines is to have a nightly bath. The calming properties of water have clear effects on our senses and can be used to refresh and revive, or improve, our mood and calm us. Creating different atmospheres in your bathroom will help achieve both ends, and using different fragrances will enhance the effect.

A warm, but not too hot, bath works by increasing the body temperature, which then begins to drop, mimicking the body's reaction to the onset of sleep. For many of us who share a home, have a chaotic work schedule or even work from home, it is a great way to change the pace of your day by signifying some time specifically for yourself and your relaxation needs. Even preparing your bathroom for your soak can be restful. Research has shown that low-level tasks, such as cleaning or organizing, can help balance the mind and relieve stress. If you repeat the same process nightly, you will start to relax as soon as you hang your towel on the radiator.

First, you need to eliminate all the unnecessary clutter in your bathroom. This may seem difficult because many bathrooms tend to be small, but there is room for improvement in most situations, so invest in some stacking boxes that won't take up much floor space, and pack away children's toys or the products you don't use every day but would like to keep. Before you simply put things away, though, ask yourself when was the last time you used them – a lot of perfumed products go 'off', so as a rule if you haven't used something in two months you should use it up quickly or throw it away. Replace open shelves, if you aren't disciplined enough to keep them tidy, with slim cupboards with doors. If you don't want to get shampoo or conditioner from the cupboard every day, swap half-empty, sticky bottles for more aesthetically pleasing pump-dispenser containers that go with your colour scheme. Getting rid of a multicoloured chaos of plastic junk will immediately make a space more calming. Don't forget to look up – a shelf above a door utilizes often 'dead' space and can be used to house clutter-containing baskets or rolled up towels; you could even put your homemade relaxation kit up there, out of the way of small prying hands.

Once decluttered, you should put together a kit designed especially for you. A sumptuous bath sheet to wrap yourself in when you emerge is essential, but try not to use fabric softener on your towels because it coats the fibres with a substance that tends to stiffen them.

Candles that contain aromatherapy oils, or oils in an oil burner, will provide a soothing, flickering, melatonin-triggering low light and a calming fragrance. Finally, include something scented in your bath to promote rest. As you become accustomed to your ritual, the evocative nature of scent, which is known to generate memory recall, will make you associate this daily routine with calm and peace. Try one of these relaxing, stress-balancing recipes:

- **The colour and pretty daisylike shape of camomile flowers are lovely to look at; sprinkle the heads into the bath and sip a cup of camomile tea while soaking.**
- **A combination of Dead Sea salts with a few drops of sandalwood and lavender essential oils will rest both aching muscles and a tired mind. For a choice of other calming scents and their properties, see pages 70–72 on aromatherapy.**

Before you go into the bathroom, deal with annoying stresses so that you don't lie there fretting. Put the washing machine on, have any chats about the day's demands with those who need filling in, then make it clear that you are not available for the next 30 minutes. You may even want to hang a 'Do Not Disturb' sign on the door; someone knocking to ask if you've paid the phone bill can be very disruptive.

Bathtime might be the time to get out your notepad. Write down any of the stresses that have happened during the day, errands you feel you need to deal with, or things that worry you. Writing them down will help you put them aside while you sleep, and sleeping well will allow you to cope with them much better the following day. You will often find that half of the things you are worrying about don't actually need any attention; they are just the product of an overwrought mind. If you don't want to write them down in the bath, keeping a notepad by the bed is also a good way of 'doing' something about worries that may cause insomnia. You also need to grant yourself 'permission' to go to bed, and not feel that you are shirking responsibilities.

Self Massage

While you are warm, clean and peaceful, it is a great time to perform some self-massage techniques. You can make your own massage oil, but be careful to avoid using stimulating blends by mistake or just because they are the only ones you have to hand. Try this aromatherapy blend to encourage the onset of slumber:

4 drops of lavender
3 drops of camomile
3 drops of clary sage

Carrier oil such as olive, sunflower or almond oil (25 ml/1 fl oz of carrier oil should have only 12–15 drops of essential oil added).

Shoulders

Our shoulders are often the area that holds the most stress and tension, especially if we spend the day hunched over a desk. You may want to sit in a comfy chair or on the floor for the following two massages. For the first massage, use the first two fingers of each hand.

1   Begin by placing them in the hollow just inside your collarbone, at the base of your neck – you will know when you have hit the right spot, and you will feel the tension. Press gently once, and release.
2   Repeat the pressing action along the shoulders, outwards and towards the shoulder joint.
3   Repeat the whole process five times, then change hands and work on the other shoulder.

For the next shoulder massage, you will start by using the middle three fingers of your right hand to work on the left shoulder, and then switch sides.

1   Use a firm pressure here, not enough to feel painful, but enough to release the build-up of tension.
2   Find the large triangular-shaped muscle where a lot of tension is stored, just below the shoulder.
3   Starting from the outer edge of the shoulder and working towards the spine, use your fingers to massage in a circular motion.
4   Repeat for as long as you need to, before using the same technique, with the left hand, on the other side.

Hands

A great deal of stress and tension can be held in the hands. This technique is especially beneficial if you use a computer as part of your everyday routine. Your thumb and index finger will do the work here. Start with your right hand working on the left, and then switch over.

1   Make a gentle pinching movement along each finger in turn, starting at the base and moving along towards the fingertip.
2   Repeat three times on each hand, before returning to the left palm.

3   Loosen the palm with your right thumb, working in a circular motion. Repeat with your other hand.
4   Return again to your left hand, loosening the back with your three middle right-hand fingers and working from the base of the fingers to the wrist. Repeat on the other hand.

Feet

They carry us around all day, but feet are often neglected. A simple foot massage can relieve tension and ease aches. A foot massage benefits the whole body, stimulating the many thousands of nerve endings there.

1   Use a little foot cream or olive oil to nourish the foot as you work.
2   Hold your feet with your thumbs facing inwards towards the sole, and gradually work around it, kneading firmly but gently.
3   Rub in small circular motions on the sole, then work on the upper part of the foot. For a great boost to circulation, carry on working up the calf, towards the heart, in gentle pressing motions.
4   Press the inside back of the ankle (the slight hollow) with the thumb to promote circulation further.

RELAXATION METHODS

Learning to relax effectively, and when you want to, should have a dramatic effect on your ability to go to sleep, stay asleep and generally get more from your waking hours. After activating our stress responses, we need effective ways to rebalance; this is where relaxation exercises like meditation, muscle relaxation and yoga can help. Here are some very immediate ideas that you can try when you are lying in your bed. First, prepare your environment to ensure it is conducive to relaxation. The checklist below may be helpful when setting the scene.

• When you are relaxed your body temperature drops, so make sure the room is warm enough to accommodate this change, but not too stuffy.
• Dress in your sleepwear, and then you won't have to disrupt your mood by changing before bed.
• Use a 'Do Not Disturb' sign to ensure peace and quiet; you may also want to put on low music to drown out background noise.

Meditation

As well as unwinding tight muscles, which can mean an uncomfortable and unrefreshing rest, meditation can calm an anxious mind and keep us from lying awake until the small hours, fretting needlessly over small worries.

The classic image is of someone sitting cross-legged with their eyes closed, quietly chanting. This, of course, is just one way of approaching meditation. If you are pressured for time and feel pulled in several directions, the mere thought of meditation may seem impossible, so give yourself permission to take time out from your stressful environment. Sit in a quiet space, on a straightback chair (the support will help open up the lungs), and place a hand on your stomach. Consciously try to fill your lungs with slow, long breaths, in through your nose and out through your mouth. It may take a little practice, but you will know it is working if you feel your stomach rise and fall under your hand. Repeat this until you feel calm again. Once you have mastered the practice, you can use it anywhere – in your own living room or even in the office.

Those who find it hard to attain the requisite discipline for meditation could benefit from focusing on an object, such as a candle or flower. An initial worry when people begin meditating for the first time is the way that many thoughts start crowding into your mind, just as you are trying to escape from them. This is a natural process, and with time and practice you will find it much easier to leave those thoughts to one side. To block these thoughts out, try to concentrate instead on your object or your breathing.

Breathing

Sometimes, no matter how much you need it, sleep just won't seem to come. Learning simple breathing exercises can help. In yoga this is called diaphragmatic breathing, and is profoundly relaxing. Using your abdomen, not your chest, breathe through your nose for three seconds, then breathe out through your mouth for three seconds. Pause for three seconds before repeating. Practise for 10 minutes each night, and you may find that you don't remember doing the last few exercises! Research has shown that imagining a place of calm, like a favourite holiday destination, can also help speed the onset of sleep – it has even been shown to be more effective than counting sheep. This method, called creative visualization, is a very simple process to learn. Lie in your bed (try the 'Corpse' yoga position on page 63) and visualize a serene place. Imagine all the sensations that come with this place – the warmth of the sun on your skin, the babbling sound of a mountain stream and even the sweet scent of the grass. This process can be used in conjunction with progressive muscular relaxation (see overleaf).

Once relaxed, you can start focusing on your breathing, and imagining the stresses and tensions of your muscles, as a colour or sensation, leaving your body as you breathe out.

Progressive Muscular Relaxation

This systematic relaxation of the muscle groups is a useful technique for anyone who finds themselves tense and agitated at the end of the day. It is a widely acknowledged fact that anxiety, stress, depression and emotional distress can all cause muscle fatigue and tightness. Working on these muscle groups and releasing contractions can therefore help ease the problems that put the tension there in the first place. A physiologist called Dr Jacobson devised PMR to achieve this state of relaxation.

Concentrate on tightening a specific group of muscles, hold the contraction and then slowly release the tension, breathing out, with a sigh through the mouth as the tension ebbs away. Visualizing this outward flow of stressful energy will enhance the effect. Repeat on various other muscle groups. As with any form of relaxation, the effectiveness of the technique and your sensitivity to it will improve with practice and you will soon be able to relax at will.

Yoga

Designed to unify the body and mind, yoga promotes strength, good health and inner peace. It has many separate disciplines and can be invaluable in combating insomnia – even a beginner can reap the benefits. Central to effective yoga practice is learning to understand and gain control of your breathing. This can be of great help, even when we don't combine it with the specific poses. Breathing helps us to calm anxieties and clear our mind when we find ourselves under pressure.

Although there are many yoga books and videos available, it is useful to attend a class while you are getting to grips with the basics. Once these basics are mastered, you can then do them pretty much wherever you like. If practised regularly, stamina, flexibility, muscle tone, strength and energy levels will all improve. The ability to calm the mind, enter a relaxed state and improve your mood and sense of wellbeing will also be in your grasp.

Choosing the right class and exploring new forms are vital for anyone hoping to get the most from yoga. The main types are explained below.

• **Hatha yoga is the most accessible type for a beginner to take up and** you will find that many classes practise this form. 'Ha', meaning sun, and 'tha', meaning moon, join to mean 'union', and the practice is designed to unite physical and spiritual harmony, and promote good physical health.

- Iyengar yoga is very precise, with 12 tightly controlled postures. It can appear slow and seemingly straightforward to the untrained eye, but it takes time to master and to find the correct balance. It is excellent for muscle tone, posture and peace of mind.
- Kundalini yoga includes chanting and breath work as well as postures. It is said to be the best form for those looking for a spiritual element. It is also good for prenatal women and those after a youthful appearance.
- Sivananda and Jivamukti yoga are more meditative forms, and include an incense-scented ritual. Clearing the mind of stress is integral to these forms of yoga, so it is good for those hoping to alleviate worries and negative thought cycles.
- The most athletic form of yoga is Astanga yoga, which offers a cardiovascular workout. It has fat-burning and toning results, but is very demanding and not always ideal for a beginner. It is, however, excellent for those with experience and who are looking for a bigger challenge.
- Bikram yoga uses the principle that heat will help aid movement and flexibility. The room is heated to around 38°C (100°F), and you sweat out all your toxins while getting your body into some amazing positions.

Unwinding the body is essential if you want to get a good night's sleep, so the following basic yoga posture for relaxation should help free up your mind and body.

The Corpse
In yoga this pose is often practised between especially difficult poses and used to take the muscles and mind into a place of deep relaxation.

Lie on the floor with your legs slightly apart and your arms slightly outstretched. You should feel utterly natural, as if you have just flopped down on the grass in the sunshine. Avoid pointing your toes or clenching your fists. The back of your hands should be touching the floor and your palms should point skyward. You may find that your muscles twitch or you want to stretch out your limbs, and this is the tension in your muscles making itself known. To combat this, try to imagine that you are extremely heavy and that the floor is supporting you. You can lie for as long as you like, but stay for at least five minutes. This is also a useful pose for meditation (see page 61).

INVITING PARTNERS
TO THE SANCTUARY:
ADVICE FOR LOVERS

Around two-thirds of us do not regularly sleep alone. Sometimes, however, our sleep problems mean we don't sleep together at all – in all senses of the word. Sleep problems are infectious; lying next to someone with sleep difficulties can mean that we soon end up sleepless, too.

One of the first areas to suffer when we are overtired is our sex life. Physical exhaustion and emotional hurt from unpleasant exchanges as a result of short fuses may leave us defensive and shaken. These upsets are just some of the reasons intimacy is neglected. The benefits of physical intimacy and an active sex life are well documented. Sex relieves stress and boosts our immune systems. By making it a rewarding part of our lives again, we can experience a renewal in our physical energy and our relationships.

Making Time
We are often so busy trying to make the most of our free time, because of demanding schedules, that time alone together becomes low on our list of priorities. Refusing a dinner invitation to stay in together alone, not always eating in front of the TV in a distracted daze after a long day, and asking the simple question, 'How was your day?', are all ways of getting your relationship back on track. Take advantage of our 24-hour society and get your groceries delivered so that you can spend Saturday morning in bed, instead of trailing round the supermarket. You have to put time and talking back at the top of your list in order to rediscover the desired level of intimacy.

Deploy the Aphrodisiacs
Assuming you have followed the earlier advice on making your bedroom a serene and sensuous space, you are now ready to use the rest of the tactics in the lover's campaign.

Before They Get Home
Take a relaxing bath with 3–5 drops of oils of lavender or mandarin oil in it before your partner gets home. Then put on an outfit you know they like and that you feel confident wearing. Essential rose mixed as body

oil is said to heal matters of the heart and release anger at the self and others, including the feeling of betrayal or resentment. It replaces any negative feelings with ones of love and affection – great if you have been arguing.

On the Table

A dinner away from the clamour of a restaurant is a clear sign that you have something special in mind, and anticipation is wonderfully arousing. Try serving aphrodisiac foods, such as asparagus, oysters, celery or parsnips, ginger or cinnamon. Even if your loved one isn't sensitive to them, the message you send by serving them can be an aphrodisiac in itself.

Seductive Scents

As smell is the most evocative of all the senses, aromatic oils, candles and incense can be very effective in initiating a mood for romance and intimacy. Jasmine, rose, patchouli, orange, sandalwood, rosewood and ylang ylang are an ideal accompaniment to seduction. Use oils in a burner or to make up a massage blend. Massage is a great way to make each other feel valued and central to each other's world and can be an effective prelude to lovemaking; the self-massage instructions on pages 59–60 can be adjusted to include you both. The more you use it, the more your mind will associate it with romance. Try this blend of essential oils to promote tenderness and connection:

    2 drops of geranium
    2 drops of cedarwood
    3 drops of ylang ylang
    3 drops of lavender
    10 drops of a carrier oil of your choice, such as olive,
        sunflower or almond oil.

HOLISTIC THERAPIES

FOR MANY PEOPLE, ALTERNATIVES TO TRADITIONAL WESTERN MEDICAL PRACTICE ARE BECOMING INCREASINGLY POPULAR. ONE OF THE POSITIVE ASPECTS OF USING HOLISTIC THERAPIES IS THAT THEY ARE ALL NATURAL AND OFFER TREATMENT WITHOUT SIDE EFFECTS OR DRUG DEPENDENCY.

Among the many alternative therapies you may find suitable in the fight against insomnia and other sleep disorders are aromatherapy, homeopathy, acupressure, acupuncture and Western medical herbalism.

When choosing any form of treatment, however, you must always make sure your practitioner is aware of any health issues, such as kidney or liver disease, pregnancy, Alzheimer's disease, or other medication you may be using to help with your condition, such as antidepressants. Natural, alternative treatments are not entirely innocuous and could affect, or be detrimentally affected by, any of these factors. Make sure you find a registered professional who practises these treatments; details are listed on pages 123–125. And do be cautious of the many remedies on the market advertised as natural – always buy from a well-respected source and follow the manufacturer's advice fully.

SIMPLE ADVICE TO HELP YOU SLEEP

Before moving on to look at the various treatments that professionals can offer, here are a few simple, no-expense ways you can try to improve your sleep yourself.

- Make sure you go to bed and wake up at the same time every day. This helps programme the body and lets it prepare for the hour when you will want to retire.
- Don't answer your telephones at least 45 minutes before you go to bed. This will make sure you don't end up caught in a lengthy chat. If you do use your mobile phone, make sure it is in night mode (blue light surpressed).
- Have a milky drink, herbal tea or sleepy snack before you go to bed, and practise other pre-sleep rituals (see page 56).
- Don't toss and turn if you cannot sleep, as this can have a stimulating effect on the body and mind, working you up into even more of an agitated state. Try lying on your back and – working upwards from your feet – tense and release every muscle in your body while breathing deeply. Repeat this for as long as necessary.
- Zone your time and manage it. If you haven't finished a chore, set it aside and learn to move on to the next thing. Stress management is essential for good rest.
- Rather than lying there and getting frustrated if you can't sleep, get up.

SIMPLE ADVICE TO HELP YOU SLEEP CONT.

Catch up with the ironing, do the washing up, anything as long as it's boring – avoid re-stimulating your brain, however, by reading or watching TV.

• If random noises are disturbing you, put on a radio on low level to make soft monotonous noise that drowns the other noises out.

• Exercise is great for promoting sleep, but don't do it too close to bedtime because it will increase your metabolism and over-stimulate your brain.

• If you still haven't slept well, resist the urge to sleep in longer than normal. Getting up on schedule keeps your body in its normal wake-up routine.

• Keep a sleep diary. This will help you to spot whether there are any patterns. For example, do you find yourself unable to sleep the night before important meetings or after working very late? Sleep diaries often show that it is rarely true that their author has been awake all night, despite what they believe. The journal will likely help give you a more hopeful perspective.

• If you still have trouble falling asleep night after night, or constantly suffer from daytime tiredness, you might have a serious sleep disorder. At this point it is advisable to seek more advice from your doctor.

CONVENTIONAL CURES

For sleep problems, your GP may have offered a prescription sleeping drug. Most of the drugs will belong to a group known as benzodiazepines, which came into use in the 1960s and include the now-famous Valium. They can lower anxiety levels, a major cause of sleeplessness, by inhibiting the chemical action of the neuro-transmitters. This slows the flow of information from one cell in the brain to another and quells the anxiety that speeds up this process. These drugs come in short-, medium- and long-acting forms and can have an effect from a few hours to a few days. All of them reduce the amount of time it takes to fall asleep and can reduce the number of night-time wakings. Unfortunately, they lose their potency with continued use, which means that doses must be increased, and so they are highly addictive. Side effects can include dependency (with withdrawal symptoms), impaired reactions and nightmares.

There is a new generation of drugs that were introduced in the 1990s, the most common of which are zopiclone and zolpidem. These speed the onset of sleep, but have a shorter life of up to four to five hours. Headaches and drowsiness can still occur as side effects and it is also possible to become addicted.

ACUPUNCTURE AND ACUPRESSURE

Acupuncture has evolved over thousands of years. Like all forms of Chinese healing traditions, it is based on the concept of maintaining balance and harmony within the body. As with most non-conventional therapies, it is difficult to run scientific studies. Nonetheless, some have reported that it is helpful for insomnia, showing that those who have received it fall asleep faster and sleep more soundly. It can also relieve insomnia by addressing other issues, such as illness or anxiety that can disturb sleep patterns.

Ancient sources suggest acupuncture works on the principle that illness and disease are a result of the disruption, or blockage of the flow of chi or qi (life energy). Qi consists of equal and opposite qualities – yin and yang – and when these become unbalanced illness may result. By inserting fine needles into the channels of energy, an acupuncturist is said to stimulate the body's own healing response. The flow of qi can be disturbed by a number of factors. These include emotional states such as anxiety, stress, anger, fear or grief, poor nutrition, weather conditions, poisons, infections, hereditary factors and trauma. To release the flow, needles are inserted into points along the meridians (energetic pathways) of the body. There are more than 350 points on the meridians of the body, so the acupuncturist will determine which to use by questioning and examining the patient. This method ensures that the cause of the sleeplessness, and not just the effect, is treated.

Acupressure works on similar principles, but is non-invasive. It works to relieve, calm and enliven the body and mind, and its most frequently found form is shiatsu massage. Zero-balancing is a newer addition to the acupressure arts, but this also encourages harmony within the body. Reflexology works on a similar principle and dates back to ancient Egypt, India and China. It concentrates on massaging specific points of the feet, which correspond to organs and systems in the body, thus encouraging the body to rebalance – it can be particularly soothing for those with sleep difficulties. Each session tends to last about an hour, and you should talk through the resulting sensations; for example, some patients may feel weepy, tired or faintly nauseous after reflexology or energy work, but this a perfectly natural indicator that the treatment is working and changes are occurring.

AROMATHERAPY

We all use aromatherapy, in its most basic form, every day. The smell of baking bread, a rosewater perfume or an aversion to bad smells are all powerful stimulators of memory and sense. In its technical application, it is an effective and soothing way to balance moods and manage energy and it is an effective way to relieve sleeplessness. The oils provoke a variety of different responses by stimulating the olfactory organs, which are linked to the areas of the brain that control emotions, causing a series of reactions effecting a physical or emotional change in the body. If you don't appreciate a particular scent, it won't relax you and you should try something else. Oils can be used by adding them to a bath, burning them in a diffuser or using them in a compress. For sleep problems, they can be particularly effective in the form of massage, especially if your poor sleep is due to muscle tension.

Always buy pure oils, rather than synthetic oils. Most essential oils require a 'carrier' oil, such as olive, sunflower or almond oil, and should be mixed before use in massage because they are highly concentrated and can cause skin irritation. Their potency means you need only a very small amount. For massage on adults, 28 ml (1 fl oz) of carrier oil should have only 12–15 drops of essential oil added. When using it in the bath, 10–12 drops of essential oil should be used. The water temperature should be sufficiently hot to ensure that the oil mixes fully with the water. This has the dual effect of helping the oil to soak into the skin and producing an oil-enhanced steam that is breathed in – make sure the doors and windows are closed to encourage maximum inhalation. When properly stored in a cool, dark place, essential oils can last for years. Once they are combined with a carrier oil, however, they will turn rancid within three months, so use them up.

The following essential oils are recommended for aiding a good night's rest (there is little scientific backing, but many people believe in the effects). In their dried form, some can also be used to stuff 'sleep pillows'. Herbs such as basil and marjoram can be ingested in food dishes or made into teas.

Basil This herb can promote calm and rest for those suffering from nervous insomnia or fatigue. It is also regarded as an aphrodisiac, which is ideal if you are feeling too tired to even contemplate sex. The flower heads and leaves can be used in cooking, so ingest their benefits with a refreshing mozzarella, tomato and basil salad.

Clary Sage This is regarded as an all-round panacea, and supports the central nervous system in many of its duties. From fatigue, depression and headaches, it can relieve many of the problems associated with poor sleep. Its benefits can be gained from eating it fresh, as well as in an essential oil form. Add it to salads, or stuff chicken breast with it.

Frankincense This is an ancient and widely used gum resin from Africa and the Middle East, which can aid meditation. Place a few drops on a piece of cotton wool or in a small dish of water near a warm radiator before you start to meditate. Inhale the fragrance deeply throughout your session.

Geranium Use geranium essential oil for renewing and reviving a tired mind. It is also a great antiseptic and insect repellent and one of the most useful and important aromatherapy oils. Use it in self-massage to fight the fatigue caused by poor sleep or stressful demands.

Lavender A classic recommendation, thought to encourage sleep and relaxation. It can be effective as sleeping pills for the elderly. A great way to promote rest is to add a few drops to your linen spray when you are ironing your sheets. This way you can subtly infuse your whole sleep space with the scent. You can always freshen up the scent by spraying directly onto your pillow. Alternatively, put a few sprigs in the linen cupboard. Lavender has traditionally been used to provide relaxation and drowsiness, but be careful: using more than 1–2 drops can have the opposite effect.

Melissa or Lemon Balm This has a sedative effect when the fragrance is inhaled. Originally from Southern Europe, it was spread by the Romans and it is ideal for insomnia, and sleep enemies such as depression, migraines and PMS. It is also very effective as a tea or in foods – the lemony flavour is great for soups and desserts.

Mandarin A member of the orange family, the oil comes from the skin of the fruit rather than the flowers. The bromine content, which calms the nervous system, is very high, so following dinner with a couple of these for dessert will have a sedative effect on anxious people. It can also be used in the bath.

Marjoram This has a powerful sedative effect and is great if you are sleeping badly owing to nervous tension or are just generally tired. It can be used in a massage oil or oil burner, mixed with a drop of orange oil on a tissue by the bed or as a soothing drink in its dried form – a pinch of marjoram and one of dried lime flowers in hot water, half an hour before going to bed, will encourage sleep.

Neroli Originating from the flower of the orange tree, neroli oil can be used to treat depression, anxiety and insomnia, either in a relaxing bath, as a drink or just in its fruit form. Using it in hot water and steaming the skin can treat acne and poor skin conditions, which may often be exacerbated by poor sleep.

Petitgrain Another product from the orange tree, this is derived from the leaves, twigs and unripe fruit. It is a very effective relaxant and has similar effects to neroli. It is especially good if you are coming off tranquillizers, which may have been prescribed to treat insomnia symptoms. Like neroli, its benefits can also be gleaned from placing an orange plant in your room.

Rose This is particularly helpful for treating women who are suffering from insomnia due to anxiety or a nervous disposition. Whether massaging rose oil into the solar plexus, drinking a rose infusion tea or putting it in the bath, it is an easy oil to work into your routine because it has such a pretty scent. It can be used to fragrance desserts or as a salad dressing when mixed with white wine vinegar.

Sandalwood This has been used in Ayurvedic, Asian and Arab forms of treatment for centuries, and is very calming. Keeping sheets in a sandalwood chest can have a very relaxing effect when you put them on the bed. It is also a good aid for meditation.

Tangerine The fruity, sweet scent is calming and ideal for treating not only anxiety and insomnia but also muscle pain and ageing skin.

Insomnia Blend
Blend these oils for a truly restful sleep:

    10 drops of roman camomile
    5 drops of clary sage
    5 drops of bergamot.

Mix the oils well in a clean, dark-coloured glass bottle. Add one to two drops to a tissue and place inside your pillow to aid you in falling asleep. If you prefer to make a diffuser blend to enjoy during the hour before bedtime, make a blend with a ratio of two drops of Roman camomile to one drop of clary sage to one drop of bergamot and add to your diffuser.

HOMEOPATHY

Used by an estimated 30 million people in Europe, homeopathy is designed to work with your body through a holistic system of healing, which works on physical and emotional symptoms. There is no scientific backing, and little in the way of proof of the basic principles, but a homeopath will ask you about your lifestyle, worries and hopes as well as your physical worries, and attempt to work on those too.

To stimulate your body's own healing process, a remedy that is tailored especially for you is prescribed. The healing begins from within your body, strengthening your health and immune system without the danger of damaging side effects. No synthetic products are used, but you should avoid eating, drinking, smoking or using toothpaste for 20 minutes after taking a homeopathic medicine.

Conventional and homeopathic medicine can be taken at the same time, but if you are unsure always consult your healthcare provider. The following treatments are most useful for sleep-related problems.

Cocculus Ideal for insomnia following a tiring long journey or being in a hectic, smoky atmosphere. It is also recommended for anxiety and sleep that is disturbed by nightmares.

Acid phosphorus Helps to overcome mental and physical debility caused by a prolonged bout of grief, whatever the cause.

Ignatia This can help those who have received shocking news that consequently leads to disturbed sleep. Rapid mood swings, weepiness or tiredness can also be alleviated.

Camomilla Useful for sleeplessness in crying, angry and restless children, especially when they are teething or suffering from colic. Sometimes the child may demand things, then refuse them, and is hot, thirsty or irritable.

Arnica Can aid the exhaustion that follows extended physical and mental effort, and can also help with jet lag if taken before the journey.

Kali Phos. Can be used to treat weakness and tiredness, especially after worry, excitement or overwork.

Nux Vomica When the mind is overstimulated or strained, this can help calm your thoughts – anger at being unable to sleep is often one of the symptoms. It can aid in regularizing sleep and it also helps sleep patterns that are disturbed by too many stimulants, such as alcohol, coffee and stress.

Coffea For physical restlessness and insomnia when the mind is churning up difficult thoughts and worries from the day. The alertness of the mind can result in light and interrupted unrefreshing sleep; coffea will slow down a racing mind.

Lachesis Repetitive insomnia can result in a fear of going to bed, which this treatment can ease. If you suffer from menstruation-related insomnia or jolting limbs when trying to fall asleep, this remedy helps both complaints.

Arsenicum Album Use this to tackle the unpleasant experience of waking in the middle of the night fretting over problems. This sign of anxiety responds well to this treatment.

WESTERN HERBAL MEDICINE

Herbalism has its roots in the indigenous practices of the British Isles, Europe and North America. A significant proportion of orthodox Western medicines were originally derived from herbal medicines, but Western herbal medicine also has a holistic attitude to health. The patient, rather than the disease or condition, is the focus here. The background to the patient's condition is assessed through family and health history and lifestyle, and therapy is directed at the causes, not just the presenting symptoms. The practitioner then uses this information to assess the vitality and constitution of the patient, using this for the choice of herbs in the prescription. Prescriptions may vary substantially between individual patients with apparently similar conditions, and the herbal treatment is used as part of a bigger approach to understanding effects such as lifestyle and nutrition. Scientific backing is limited.

There are a huge number of conventional, over-the-counter sleep medications. These have their side effects and price to pay, not least of which is dependency. One of the key advantages of herbal medicines is that they are not believed to interfere with the sleep stages, something that can occur with conventional, chemical ones. Various plants are said to have sedative effects, such as hops, skullcap and black cohosh, and the effectiveness of these plants is very much down to the individual – a degree of experimentation can bring about the right blend for you, but most herbal supplements carry a mix of them, usually in conjunction with the most effective, which is valerian. A well-known hypnotic and sedative, it comes from the root of the heliotrope (*Valerian officinalis*) plant. It appears to improve sleep gradually, although it is also effective when taken for occasional insomnia. It is one of the most potent natural treatments available and can be taken alone, although many over-the-counter preparations mix it with a combination of other sedatives such as hops, passionflower and lemon balm. A good example of this is Avena Sativa Compound, an effective sleep medicine comprising a number of the herbs, including passionflower, valerian and hops. It should be taken in water just before going to bed.

BACH FLOWER ESSENCES

Flower remedies were originally the brainchild of Dr Edward Bach, who studied medicine at the University College Hospital, London. In the 1930s, after developing an interest in alternative health, he gave up his lucrative Harley Street practice and left London, deciding to devote the rest of his life to a new system of medicine that he believed could be sourced from nature.

Bach found that when he treated the feelings and personalities of his patients, their unhappiness and physical distress was alleviated. This 'unlocked' the natural healing potential already in their bodies, allowing them to recover. His system is composed of 38 tinctures. Each is aimed at a particular mental state or emotion and all have a specific 'vibration', which can be used alone or together to treat different states of mind from panic to forgetfulness.

The emotions described are often quite specific; listed below are three recommendations for dealing with insomnia.

White Chestnut When your mind is so cluttered with thoughts that you are unable to fall asleep.

Impatiens When you get irritated and impatient with yourself as you start counting the hours until the alarm clock goes off.

Vervain When your mind is too wound up with plans and excitement to sleep.

If you are unsure which remedies are best for you, an alternative health practitioner can help you decide. You can combine them in a single bottle, or use them individually as you need. Each bottle has a pipette (dropper) to administer them exactly. They can also be added to a bath – you need to soak for 30 minutes if this is your preferred method.

FAST-TRACK STRATEGIES

SLEEP CAN BE WONDERFULLY RESTORATIVE AND RENEWING. A LACK OF IT, HOWEVER, CAN CONSUME LIFE WITH A RANGE OF DEPRIVATION SYMPTOMS.

This section is designed to give you a practical helping hand for dealing with some of the most distressing and common complaints associated with poor sleep.

If you are on medication or feel unsure about the suitability of a particular remedy, talk to your doctor, pharmacist or local alternative health practitioner about finding a combination that works. And keep experimenting; we're all different and have changing needs, so we can always benefit from trying out new remedies.

ANXIETY

At one end of the scale, anxiety can feel mildly troubling and slightly disconcerting; at the other end it can be totally incapacitating and isolating. Anxiety can become an ever-present problem; you feel unable to handle the feelings of panic and unease, which often seem to have no rational trigger. It can be the result of one singularly traumatic event, such as the death of a relative, redundancy or the end of a relationship, or it can be a more gradual process, such as a continually stressful work environment. Free-floating anxiety is a continual undercurrent that is not attributable to any specific situation or reasonable danger, and can be associated with panic and panic attacks.

Ideally, the most effective approach to the management of anxiety would be the removal of the source of stress, a rebalancing therapy and support from a good diet and a willing ear. In reality, this isn't always possible, but the following methods of treatment can offer relief. If you are concerned at any time, do approach a heath practitioner to ensure you find the best solution. The conventional medical approach might offer some form of tranquillizer to break the cycle, but the problem with this can be a dependency. There are also many alternative treatments to consider.

Common Symptoms
- **Palpitations**
- **Nausea**
- **Perspiration**
- **Digestive problems (diarrhoea or constipation)**
- **Light-headedness**
- **Tingling in the hands and arms**
- **Rapid shallow breathing**
- **Muscle discomfort**

DIAPHRAGMATIC
BREATHING, USED
IN YOGA, LETS US PULL AIR
DEEP INTO OUR LOWER
LUNGS TO ADDRESS THE
IMBALANCE OF OXYGEN AND
CARBON DIOXIDE IN OUR
BODIES AND CALM
US DOWN

Breathing

Learning to master your breathing can be a great way to control feelings of anxiety and distress. When we feel panicked, we often take shallow, quick breaths. This leads to an imbalance between the carbon dioxide and oxygen in the bloodstream and makes the anxiety much worse. See page 61 for how to master the diaphragmatic technique.

Reset Your Mind

'Reframing', taking the same set of facts and applying a different meaning to them, is a technique often employed by psychotherapists to help clients get a more positive perspective. For example, if you have an argument with a friend, rather than blame yourself for it, try to see it as a chance to change the dynamics of how you relate to each other. In its most basic form, it is about looking for the positive in everything. Most people can improve their perspectives by reprogramming their minds to think of themselves as fortunate. Start by resisting the temptation to relive your past failures and worries. It can dampen your spirit and encourage you to stress over difficulties during your day. Get things in perspective, look for opportunities in disaster and see taking chances as a natural part of the process of fulfilling your dreams – this will help you to persist in the face of failure. The more often you do it, the quicker it becomes your default mechanism.

Aromatherapy

It's important, when you are suffering from anxiety or stress, to make sure you have a safe space in which you can unwind. Make time every night to have a soothing bath, at least an hour before you go to bed because this will help you sleep. Add a few drops of essential camomile, melissa or jasmine oil to the water to treat the lack of confidence that can result from anxiety.

Diet

Stimulants, such as tea, coffee and sugar-laden products, may seem comforting but they will only exaggerate your feelings of angst. Tryptophan is ideal in this situation, so look for genuine comfort foods that contain it (see pages 39–40). Bananas are a great snack, as is a turkey and lettuce sandwich or a handful of almonds. Replace regular tea with caffeine-free roibosh or soothing camomile. And don't leave long gaps between meals; you may feel too anxious to eat but you will only make your symptoms worse by making your sugar levels unstable. If camomile tea isn't for you, try an alternative such as lime flower (also known as linden), passionflower or valerian. A little honey can be a nice addition, but not too much because it is a sugar and should be used in moderation to keep your blood sugar levels stable.

Essential Supplements

Vitamin B complex is good for overall health and helps the body cope with the stress you may be under.

Homeopathy

Acid Phosphorus Free-floating anxiety can be debilitating, and this treatment can help very sensitive people who need a lot of reassurance.

Gelsemium Anxiety that has developed gradually over time should be treated with this remedy. People who suffer from long-term anxiety may become withdrawn and irritable and suffer headaches as side effects – gelsemium should address all these needs. It can only be sold by registered pharmacies, and it's advised that it be used under the supervision of a pharmacist.

Arsenicum Album A worried or tense expression often signifies the need for this remedy, which treats patients who are pressurizing themselves over achieving goals and perfectionism. Sleeplessness, irritability, restlessness and sensitivity to the cold can also accompany this obsessive anxiety.

Calc Carb SP This helps those who are mentally, physically and emotionally exhausted from overwork and stress, who can become anxious, apprehensive and occasionally confused, all factors that lead to disturbed sleep and being run down.

Flower Remedies
Keep a bottle of Bach Rescue Remedy with you at all times to cope with the symptoms of anxiety. As soon as you begin to feel unsettled or experience the signs of panic and fear, take a few drops in a glass of water or straight under your tongue. Other remedies that might help are white chestnut, for calm and clarity of mind, and rock rose, which helps to allay feelings of fear.

LACK OF CONCENTRATION, FOCUS AND MOTIVATION

An inability to concentrate or focus and a general lack of interest are common in those suffering from poor sleep. These symptoms are often compounded by the sufferer's lack of concern about the outcome of their poor performance, as they are simply too tired to care. This can cause serious problems in situations where close attention is demanded, such as driving or health and safety issues in the workplace.

The most effective way to improve this situation is to take a nap. Even 20 minutes is shown to improve concentration and make you more alert and capable of performing the tasks in hand.

Common Symptoms
- **Dulled mental skills**
- **Forgetfulness**
- **Repetition of ineffective approaches**
- **Inflexibility**
- **Bad decision-making**
- **Impetuous decisions**

Diet
Avoid self-medicating with too much caffeine and sugar, which just gives you quick highs of energy followed by troughs of exhaustion.

A little dose of caffeine can focus your mind and give you a boost, but limit yourself to no more than three cups of tea a day, two of coffee. (Even though tea contains as much caffeine, it tends not to be served in such concentrated measures). Do not drink them after 5 p.m., or they will affect your ability to fall asleep and exacerbate the problem. Dehydration is a classic cause of bad concentration, so make sure you are getting enough water. Increase your intake to at least 2.5 litres (4¼ pints) a day. Start the day with porridge, a slow-release energy source that will help you focus. Eat lean meat and vegetables that are low in carbohydrates, such as green leafy vegetables, for lunch. This will help you through the afternoon dip in energy caused by the natural cycle of your circadian rhythm.

Aromatherapy
If you have a project you simply must finish or an important deadline, diffusing geranium oil in the room when you have to keep working late should help renew and refocus you.

Flower Remedies
Try the Bach Flower remedy white chestnut to regain clarity of mind and bring you back to the matters in hand.

Meditation
Simple exercises can focus your mind and clear distracted thoughts. See pages 60–62 for how to master these useful breathing and meditation techniques.

Homeopathy
Arnica is helpful if taken before a long, tiring journey. It helps counter fatigue when you need to concentrate.

MOOD SWINGS

Anyone who has lived with a sleep-deprived person can attest to the presence of mood swings. As well as the physical feeling of being overtired, hormonal imbalances, which are exacerbated by lack of sleep, can also cause mood swings. This is often an integral part of other conditions, such as menopause and premenstrual syndrome/tension (PMS/PMT) in women. Hormone replacement therapy is usually offered for menopause, and taking the contraceptive pill is sometimes recommended by doctors in order to regulate and alleviate symptoms of PMS.

Very tired people are also often found hanging around the coffee maker at the office, offering to buy snacks or looking exhausted just after lunch. This is because tiredness can induce cravings for a sugar hit, and one stimulant often quickly needs to be followed by another.

Common Symptoms
- Irritability
- Aggression
- Anger
- Sadness
- Exhaustion
- Feeling weepy and unable to cope
- Hot flushes
- Aches and pains
- Cravings
- Tendency to eat sweet, processed or snack foods; reliance on stimulants
- Energy slumps during the day

Aromatherapy
A feeling of being unappreciated can often come with mood swings, so making time for yourself is essential. Taking a hot bath with an aromatherapy candle is wonderfully indulgent. Also try adding a few drops of essential oil to the warm water to complement the candle, such as lavender, camomile, marjoram and/or frankincense.

Diet
High-fibre foods can help lessen mood swings caused by hormonal imbalance. Increase your water intake to 2.5 litres (4¼ pints) a day to help the fibre perform its duties properly. Eat chromium-rich foods, such as cheese, shellfish, baked beans and wholemeal bread, to help overcome the symptoms of hypoglycaemia (low blood sugar). Fresh fruit is a slow-releasing food that will stop you reaching for sugar-rich snacks.

Flower Remedies
The Bach Flower remedy white chestnut will help soothe and restore your clarity of mind when you are feeling unbalanced.

Supplement
Phytonutrient herbs, such as liquorice, that boost levels of oestrogen, and ginseng that helps balance the body's adrenal hormones (related to stress) can be used to balance hormone levels. Women who eat phytoestrogens, such as wheat, green and yellow vegetables, citrus fruits, oats and rhubarb, have fewer problems at menopause.

DAYTIME SLEEPINESS

Most people experience this to some degree, as our natural circadian rhythm has a dip early afternoon. Everyone will have their own particular 'low' point, but for many it passes by about 5 p.m. and is followed by a more energetic period in the evening. If you find yourself fighting sleep at your desk or nodding off in the supermarket, this is usually a sign that you are sleep-deprived. More serious sleep problems, like sleep apnoea which is common (see page 21), or narcolepsy which is rare (see page 22), may be possible reasons, so if you are seriously concerned and altering your sleep routine and the number of hours you sleep is not resulting in an improvement, see your doctor. To check if your daytime sleepiness is a result of being sleep-deprived, check your Sleep Latency Period (see page 13).

In the battle against sleepiness, falling asleep could help. If you can barely keep your eyes open during the day, set aside a little time for a rejuvenating power nap. Even 20 minutes can help improve your performance and mood. Make sure it is no more than 20 minutes, though, or it will affect your night-time sleep. Even losing an hour a night over several nights will leave you with a sleep deficit that can result in daytime sleepiness, so prioritize your sleep until you have caught up.

Common Symptoms
- An overwhelming desire to sleep
- Falling asleep less than 10 minutes after going to bed in the day
- Lack of concentration
- Irritability

Diet
Avoid refined carbohydrates, such as white bread, for lunch which will emphasize the natural lull in your circadian rhythm. Opt for slow-releasing energy foods, such as porridge, for breakfast. Caffeine can give a boost, but avoid it after 5 p.m., or it will keep the cycle going.

DEPRESSION

Emotional resilience can be seriously impaired by lack of sleep, making you susceptible to depression. Whether the depression has been triggered by sleeplessness or the insomnia is a symptom of depression, the depression will be unlikely to lift without some intervention. If you are prescribed anti-depressants (usually an SSRI or serotonin reuptake inhibitor, the most famous being Prozac) you must ensure that any other treatments can be used safely with them, as they are not always compatible. An essential part of emerging from depression is talking. No matter whether or not you feel you want to discuss the origin of your depression, it can help to talk about the feeling of being depressed in itself. Talking can also alleviate symptoms of isolation, speed recovery and help resolve the issues that may have caused the depression in the first place.

Common Symptoms
- Disturbed sleep (such as insomnia or oversleeping)
- Anxiety
- Loss of appetite
- Poor concentration
- Loss of motivation
- Mood swings
- Lowered libido
- Negative thought cycles
- Hyperventilation

Aromatherapy

Essential oils, such as basil, marjoram, lemon balm, neroli, thyme and verbena are all known for their ability to help treat the symptoms of depression. Dilute two or three drops of them in five drops of grapeseed oil and rub it into the back of your hand, stomach or solar plexus; alternatively, drop it into a soothing bath. This may also be a good time to visit an aromatherapy practitioner, as the feelings of isolation that come from depression are often soothed by contact with others and a nurturing treatment such as an aromatherapy massage.

Diet

A disturbed sugar balance can also exacerbate depression, so make sure you eat a balanced diet and avoid stimulants that can give you mood and energy spikes. It may be tempting to reach for the chocolate, cigarettes or wine for comfort, but they will only add to the problem. Season food with marjoram and thyme for their antidepressant effects. Switch to teas such as mint, verbena and thyme to give you a lift and stop you from turning to stimulants such as tea and coffee. Wheatgerm is a great energizer, so sprinkle it over your salads or cereals, and eat bromine-packed pears and apples for their soothing effect on the nervous system. In general, add more tryptophan-rich foods to your diet for their soothing properties (see page 39–40).

Supplements

5-HTP, a precursor to tryptophan that helps the body to produce serotonin, is a useful supplement. Boosting your intake of omega 3 oils, B complex, vitamin C, vitamin E and ginseng will also improve your ability to cope with the stress of depression. If your diet is suffering from a loss of appetite or an inability or lack of interest in cooking, make sure you take a good all-round multivitamin.

Exercise

Make sure you get outside and walk every day, even if it's only for 20 minutes. Being in the daylight can also help with depression induced by seasonal affective disorder (SAD).

Herbal Help

St John's wort is a popular herbal alternative to prescribed antidepressants, but it can affect other conventional medicines used to treat illnesses such as asthma, heart problems and HIV. Anyone currently on medication must speak to his or her doctor about the suitability of taking this herb. Assuming all is well, St John's wort can be incredibly effective.

Homeopathy

Depending on the cause of your depression, or just your resulting feelings, you may find it helpful to try one of these remedies. Each works on a slightly different manifestation of the condition.

Pulsatilla Good for those who are excessively weepy and tend to cry easily, but feel better after a cry.

Natrum Mur Good for those who cannot accept sympathy and tend to become introverted, shunning other people's company. They may find it hard to talk about their feelings or ask for help, and become irritable.

Sepia Can help those whose depression stems from a physical or mental exhaustion and who display feelings of apathy or indifference. They may feel weary and are easily offended. It is especially beneficial for men.

Arsenicum Album Useful for helping those who wake in the night worrying about things and who berate themselves for their failure to meet their own exceptionally high standards.

Lycopodium This remedy is useful when there has been a loss of confidence, such as when a person's ability to cope with a job has been affected, making them forgetful and sensitive to criticism or contradiction. They may feel needy and dislike being on their own.

Flower Remedies

Bach Flower remedies can help rebalance some of the negative feelings associated with depression. Try using holly for alleviating anger, willow for bitterness and pine for guilt.

PERSISTENT FATIGUE

There are several reasons for the occurrence of persistent and chronic fatigue. As well as poor sleep, a diet lacking in nutrients can often be to blame. The two usually go hand in hand as we grab food on the go, especially sugar- and stimulant-crammed food to keep us going. The result of this kind of lifestyle is a body that is overloaded with toxins and that is hard to detoxify.

Common Symptoms
- **Feeling weary**
- **Weepiness**
- **Feeling tired upon waking**
- **Falling asleep early**

Aromatherapy
When you really need a perk, but can't take a break, geranium essential oil is a great pick-me-up. Mix 10 ml (2 tsp) of soya oil and five drops of geranium oil together, and massage it into the back of your neck, sinus area, back of the hands, temples and clockwise into the solar plexus, then lie flat, resting for five minutes.

Body Brushing
Dry body brushing your skin is a very hands-on way of getting your lymphatic fluid, which carries toxins out of the body and takes much-needed nutrients to the tissues, working at its best. As well as shaking off fatigue, it has the added bonus of helping prevent premature ageing. Using a firm, natural bristle brush (but not so firm that it scratches) work in large upward movements from the feet, up the front and backs of legs and including your buttocks. For the upper body, the action should be in circular motions towards the heart, in an up or down direction (be careful over any damaged or sensitive skin). Body brushing also improves your skin's tone and texture, getting rid of dead skin cells, and leaving the skin smoother and fresher looking.

Homeopathy
Kali Phos. can be used to treat weakness and tiredness, especially if it has been caused by worry, excitement or overwork.

Exercise
Gentle exercise will get the lymph drainage system, and everything else, moving. No matter how reluctant you feel about attempting it, even getting off the bus a stop earlier or walking rather than driving will give you a boost.

Diet
Eat little and often (but don't overdo it!). Choose slow-release carbohydrates, such as porridge, and fresh fruit. Avoid all stimulants, such as tea, coffee, sugar, cigarettes, chocolate, cola drinks and alcohol.

Supplements
Vitamin C (1,000 mg) and an antioxidant complex will help your body detoxify. An antioxidant complex will help mop up the damaging toxins.

VANISHED LIBIDO

Exhausted new parents may have 'making more babies' low on their list of priorities, but for many of us a missing sex drive can be a saddening and frustrating experience. A low libido can be due to hormone imbalance, depression or simply fatigue.

Common Symptoms
- **A lack of interest in sex**
- **Avoiding physical intimacy with your partner**

Your Environment
Make sure your bedroom is more 'boudoir' than dumping ground. It's hard to relax and feel sexy if you can't switch off from the pressures of the day because you can see them out of the corner of your eye. Take a look at pages 64–65 for some good ideas for getting back in the mood.

Diet
Increase your intake of seafood, wholegrain bread, green leafy vegetables, crumbly cheeses and lean meat. These all contain zinc, a lack of which can result in a low libido. Don't rely on alcohol to get you in the mood; it can cause impotence in men and make it difficult for many women to achieve orgasm.

Aromatherapy expert Daniele Ryman, in her book *Aromatherapy Bible*, recommends a glass of this basil aphrodisiac drink before meals to encourage your sex drive:

1 litre (1³⁄4 pints) of red wine from Cahors
50 g (2 oz) of fresh basil leaves

Uncork the bottle of wine, pour a little out to make room for the basil leaves, push the leaves into the bottle and replace the cork. Leave for two days to mature in the dark, shaking from time to time.

Supplements
A zinc supplement can help if your diet is lacking.

FEELING 'HUNGOVER' WHEN YOU WAKE UP

Even if you have been working on improving your sleeping patterns, you can occasionally wake with a muggy-headed sensation. This can be a result of the body still trying to work off a sleep deficit, over-sleeping or poor-quality sleep. It may also be that you are grinding your teeth, producing pressure in your jaw. Your dentist should be able to tell if this is happening and may be able to give you a mouthguard to help counteract it.

Common Symptoms
- **Reluctance to get out of bed**
- **Feeling of not being sufficiently rested**
- **Irritability**
- **Lack of coordination**
- **Craving for stimulants, such as tea or coffee**

Your Environment
Making sure your room is not too dark or too light is vital. Too much light in the room will suppress melatonin secretion, which means you will have a lighter, more broken sleep. Too much darkness, on the other hand, means an overproduction of melatonin which will leave you feeling as if you are being woken up in the middle of the night. Curtains that darken the room sufficiently to allow sleep, yet let the dawn's emergence become visible, are essential. If you cannot achieve both, try heavy curtains and a sunlight alarm clock that impersonates the dawn and lets the body start its natural production of cortisol to prepare it for the day ahead. Making sure you get up at the same time every day also helps the body to prepare for daytime demands.

Acupressure
This ancient system can pep you up in minutes. For quick relief, squeeze your ears quite firmly between your thumb and forefinger, starting with the lobes and going around the edge, holding each pinch a few seconds at a time. Alternatively, seek treatment with a practitioner.

Aromatherapy
Lemon oil will give you more energy, and an aromatherapy soap, such as grapefruit, will wake you up. If your poor sleep has been caused by catarrh or congestion, try inhaling essential oils before you go to bed to clear your sinuses. Cajuput, tea tree or geranium essential oils dropped into hot water to make vapours are all great for clearing the sinuses. The next morning, a bath with pepper or juniper oil will liven you up.

Diet
Cutting out dairy products can help stop the build-up of mucus caused by illness or poor congestion.

BAD BREATH

Occasional bad breath upon waking can have several causes. Breathing through the mouth, perhaps due to a cold or congestion, can be a cause, or it may be an oral health issue, such as tooth decay, saliva and mouth bacteria or gum infections. Bad breath can also be an indicator of other health problems, such as poor food digestion or lung and respiratory problems. Try over-the-counter mouthwashes and a visit to your dental hygienist. If these fail, consult a doctor.

Common Symptoms
- **Pungent odour**
- **Unpleasant fuzziness in the mouth**
- **Discoloured tongue**

Herbal Help
Make your own mouthwash from one drop of myrrh essential oil in a cup of cooled, boiled water. If you find the taste unpalatable, camomile, fennel, mint or thyme can be used instead.

Diet
Chewing parsley, thyme, tarragon, anise seeds or a cinnamon stick can all help. Take a note of your diet and see if there are any foods that cause you particular problems; spicy foods and garlic are often problematic.

Homeopathy
Kali Phos. Should be used if the mouth is dry and the tongue is coated yellow/brown.

Mercurius Solubilis Should be used if you suffer from bad breath and a sore tongue, especially noticeable while chewing, accompanied by excessive thirst.

RECURRENT COLDS AND INFECTIONS

Lack of sleep is often accompanied by a general run-down sensation, making you feel even less resilient and in control. This is partly due to a depressed immune system, which struggles to fight off the infections that attack us every day. Regardless of external pressures, you really must try to prioritize sleep at this point. When your body shuts down non-essential functions, it concentrates on repair and maintenance.

Common Symptoms
- **Increased frequency of coughs and colds**
- **Propensity to catch any bugs that seem to be circulating**

Herbal Help
Replace your regular brew with cat's-claw tea with ginger, four times daily. Drinking an infusion of rose petals, or gargling with them, will help settle a cough that may be keeping you awake. Echinacea reputedly shortens the length of a cold and helps protect against the onset of new ones.

Diet
A good balanced diet should maintain your system, but too much protein can suppress vitamin B6, which is essential for recovery. Avoid saturated fat, as it can affect immunity, whereas essential fats, those present in cold-pressed seed oil such as pumpkin or flax, can boost it. Watermelon juice, carrot soup and a snack of berries can all boost your immune system, too.

Supplements
For the immune system to function properly it needs vitamins A, B1, B2, B6, B12, folic acid, C and E, and the minerals iron, zinc, magnesium and selenium. A good-quality multivitamin should ensure you get all of these. If you still feel exhausted, take grapefruit seed and elderberry extract.

POOR SKIN

When lacking good-quality sleep, your skin can quickly indicate the stresses, and this is often exacerbated by a poor diet. A lack of sleep reduces your immunity, making you more prone to infections, including skin infections. The skin gains access to nutrients during the night and repairs any existing damage then, so poor sleep will disrupt this process. Your doctor may suggest topical steroid treatment creams for application directly to the problem skin areas.

Cold sores are caused by a herpes virus. If you notice the tingling sensation as it develops, then retrovir (anti-viral) can halt development. If you don't stop it, it'll disappear over the course of 10 days. The pharmacist can help with pain-reducing creams.

Common Symptoms
- **Spots, pimples and cold sores**
- **Sallow and dull appearance**
- **Flare-ups of conditions like psoriasis or acne**

Skincare Routine
Make sure you cleanse, tone and moisturize your skin each morning and night to reduce the chance of any flare-ups. A good-quality night cream, loaded with antioxidants and vitamins, will help the skin in its repair work. Smokers should look for oxygen creams to help counteract the damage caused by smoking. For a quick boost, a gentle exfoliator will slough off dead skin and bring back a fresh glow.

To get the blood circulating, try this quick exercise. Stand with your legs about half a metre (2–3 feet) apart. Place your hands on your hips, bend from the waist out and down towards the floor, keeping your legs straight. Now place your palms on the floor and keep stretching gently downwards. Slowly creep your hands forwards for a bigger stretch and then breathe deeply for 10–15 breaths. Reverse your moves, bringing your hands back to your feet, then up to your hips. Make sure you do all of this slowly so that you don't feel dizzy.

Diet
Strawberries, blueberries and raspberries are all very rich in vitamin C, which helps strengthen the collagen in the skin. They also have a high concentration of anti-ageing antioxidants. Try blending these ingredients in a smoothie:

100 g (3¹/2 oz) mixed berries
1 small banana
1 small pot of plain yogurt
150 ml (¹/4 pint) skimmed or soya milk.

RECURRENT HEADACHES

Headaches or migraines can come in many different forms, as anyone who frequently suffers from them can tell you. Try and write down the symptoms and times to see if there is a pattern. You may find that you have a headache after staring at your computer screen or when your blood sugar drops after a lunch on the go.

See your GP if they keep coming back and painkillers don't help. If it is severe and your jaw hurts when eating, you've got blurred vision and/or your scalp feels sore, get medical help quickly.

Common Symptoms
- Dull, throbbing pain around the head, neck, and temples and/or behind the eyes
- Feeling like a tight band is fixed around the head
- Sensitivity to light or noise

Aromatherapy
Effective in relieving headaches, aromatherapy is also a soothing treatment that can help with anxiety and tension that may be related to the headaches. Try blending the following:

2 drops of essential peppermint oil
3 drops of essential lavender oil
5 drops of eucalyptus oil.

Add to a cream or gel base and apply to the temples and the base of the neck. If these scents do not appeal, then try a single drop of basil, camomile, juniper (this also gives off a small amount of heat so is great for muscle tension in the neck), rosemary or clary sage in 5 ml (1 tsp) of grapeseed oil. This will bring relief when massaged onto the neck, temples or around the eyes (always be careful when putting any oils near your eyes).

Acupressure
Try this simple acupressure treatment on yourself, wherever you are. Press a finger into your eye sockets near the nose for a few seconds, several times. Alternatively, press the web of skin between your thumb and forefinger for two or three minutes (using the thumb and forefinger of your other hand). Swap hands and repeat.

Homeopathy
A good homeopathic remedy is gelsemium, especially for help with 'tight band' headaches. Acid phosphorus can help with headaches brought on by eye strain or tiredness.

Herbal Help
Lime flower, valerian or verbena will all help tension headaches.

Diet
Headaches are often due to low-level dehydration, so increasing your water intake should help – 2.5 litres (4¹/4 pints) is the recommended amount. Eat often and in

small amounts so you avoid blood sugar crashes, making sure you choose something with a low glycaemic index (see page 39).

High-fibre foods can help cushion the mood swings that bring on headaches. Avoid acidic fruits, such as citrus fruits, as they can aggravate headaches and migraines; opt for pears instead.

DARK CIRCLES AROUND THE EYES AND PUFFY EYELIDS

Often seen as a sign of a late night, dark circles around your eyes are, according to Chinese medicine, a sign of the body's inability to drain impurities. The purplish colour, along with puffiness, is the result of poor circulation in tiny blood vessels. The skin under the eyes is so thin that if the blood vessels are swollen, they show up very clearly and are a definite sign that you are not getting enough sleep. They can also simply be hereditary. A doctor may prescribe a vitamin A-derivative cream or refer you to a dermatologist for a prescription bleach cream. If you are going to indulge, set aside a few nights for the body to recover; it will make the areas around your eyes look much clearer.

Common Symptoms
- **Dark patches under the eyes**
- **Dull texture to the skin**
- **Swollen lids**

Skincare Routine
Dark circles under the eyes can be hidden, to some extent, with cosmetics. Select a concealer that is one shade lighter than your foundation. One with a pale yellow undertone will help hide blue- or grey-toned circles. A blue or mauve underbase masks brown-toned under-the-eye bags. Dab concealer under your eyes gently.

Eating well is good for general eye health and can help reduce the effects of poor sleep, such as dark circles and red eye. Vitamin A improves night vision and is found in dark green, leafy vegetables, carrots, spinach, broccoli, eggs, cheese and butter. Carotene allows the formation of visual purple in the eyes, which helps improve weak eyes. Good sources of carotene are carrots, broccoli, cabbage and peas. Vitamin B complex is excellent for reducing redness in eyes and it can also help eyes that are sensitive to light. Good food sources for vitamins B1, B2, B3, B6 and B12 are pasta, bread, milk, dark green vegetables, tuna, nuts, mushrooms, avocados, bananas and liver.

Don't just eat the food, though. Take slices of cucumber straight from the refrigerator, for its cooling and soothing effect, or use one small slice of potato. Put a slice under each eye and leave them for 20 minutes. This will firm the skin and constrict the blood vessels. Alcohol, smoking and late nights should also be avoided or minimized.

To improve the drainage from under the eye, use an under-eye cream made with plant or marine extracts or antioxidants such as vitamin C and soya, which get toxins moving and moisturize the delicate under-eye skin. Apply morning and night with a light tapping motion to stimulate circulation and prevent puffiness.

Herbal Help

Soothing eye pads placed on the eyelids help encourage drainage from this sensitive area. Use cotton make-up remover pads dipped in cooled camomile or green tea. Alternatively, try this mix using diluted euphrasia (eyebright herb) tincture:

    30 ml (2 tbsps) euphrasia (eyebright)
    2 cups of hot water
    2 cotton pads.

Steep the herb in water for three minutes, or until cooled. Strain, dip a cotton pad into the liquid and wipe the eyes.

Diet

Increase your water intake to help your body flush out the toxins. Reduce salt, which can inflate eye bags, and avoid caffeine, a diuretic that will counteract the effect of the water.

JET LAG

The frequency of air travel now means that jet lag is a familiar experience for many of us, but is no less draining. Over-the-counter or prescribed sleeping tablets are often used to force the body to fit in with new night-time schedules, and caffeine tablets to prevent the onset of sleep are also used.

Common Symptoms
- **Disorientation**
- **Exhaustion**
- **Stomach upsets**
- **Nausea**
- **Fatigue**
- **Dehydration**

Aromatherapy
Use 2–3 drops of essential oil, such as cypress or rosemary, in 15 ml (1 tbsp) of grapeseed or soya oil, and massage it into the soles of the feet to promote circulation and prevent leg cramps and swollen ankles.

Massage
If you are trapped in a window seat, try to do foot exercises. Squeeze your toes together, hold for a count of five, and then release. Do this 10–15 times times in each session. If you need to stay awake when you arrive, rub 10 drops of lavender oil onto your torso and immediately follow it with a shower. To sleep, take a bath with three drops of geranium oil added.

Homeopathy
Cocculus (prescription only) will help a headache brought on by travel, especially headaches that feel much worse when you are lying down.

Flower Remedies
Start taking a Bach Flower remedy combination a couple of days before the flight and continue it while you are flying and after, until all the symptoms have gone.

Olive Helps you over the physical exhaustion of travelling and being on the move.

Walnut Helps you to adjust to a new time zone and place.

Impatiens Stops you from getting impatient while sitting in a plane for several hours.

Supplements
Vitamin B complex may help your body cope with the stress of flying and adjust more quickly to the new time zone.

DURING THE FLIGHT, TRY TO EAT ONLY CITRUS FRUITS. INCREASE YOUR INTAKE OF STILL WATER (FIZZY WATER CAN ADD TO THE FEELING OF BEING SWOLLEN AND BLOATED) AND AVOID ALL DEHYDRATING TEA, COFFEE AND ALCOHOL.

7

FAMILY SLEEP HEALTH

AS WITH ALL OTHER ASPECTS OF LIFE, OUR RELATIONSHIP TO AND EXPERIENCE OF SLEEP CHANGES THROUGHOUT OUR LIFETIME, WHICH IS WHY WE MIGHT FIND PREVIOUSLY TRIED-AND-TESTED METHODS FOR RESTORING GOOD SLEEP PATTERNS FAIL US.

Like the frustrated parent who drags a 'slovenly' teenager out of bed, worrying that they are sleeping their life away, we can accidentally work against the body's biological needs through a lack of understanding; teenagers' developing brains and bodies actually need those extra hours, and they are not being lazy, no matter what the parent might think. When we consider that we often ignore our own chronic fatigue by refusing to cut down on work or social commitments, it's easy to see where the misunderstandings come from. Taking time out to examine the patterns and needs of those around us can greatly improve our tolerance, and our effectiveness at achieving satisfying slumber for the whole family.

Every family member may be unique in their sleep requirements, circadian rhythm and the amount of sleep they need for their specific stage in life. When we understand this, our waking hours together with our family members can be less fraught with exhaustion and tension, too – snappy, grumpy breakfasts can be a thing of the past.

NEWBORNS AND BABIES

Our relationship with sleep begins long before we are even aware of its existence (or even our own). A foetus spends a great deal of time asleep, between about 16 to 20 hours out of 24, much of which is thought to be spent in the REM stage. Even our birth is influenced heavily by sleep; sleep expert William C Dement recorded the fact that mothers often go into labour at night, which is thought to be designed to make sure that the birth takes place in a safe home environment.

Once the baby has joined us on the 'outside', it has only two stages of sleep, spending about 50 per cent, or eight hours, in REM and the rest in non-REM. You can usually tell which sleep stage a baby is in. With adults, REM sleep is accompanied by paralysis so we don't imagine we are flying and launch ourselves from the bedroom window, but in newborn infants, this mechanism has yet to develop, so you can observe them twitching and wriggling through their dreams. Their non-REM sleep is entirely passive and still. A smaller baby often needs more sleep than larger babies of the same age.

It takes several weeks for newborns to sleep in any kind of solid patterns or for any length of time. In the initial stages, parents seem summoned at all hours by cries in no obvious pattern, and the parents lose at least two hours of sleep a night for the first five months (after the first year, on average, a parent is losing only an hour a night of sleep). At about eight weeks the child seems to start displaying some sensitivity to day and night, and the sleep periods will begin to be consolidated into longer stretches at night-time.

By 6 months, most infants are sleeping from 12 to 14 hours a day in a solid block with some naps, and the amount of time spent dreaming has dropped to the adult quota of 25 per cent. Even so, many parents can testify that children often still awaken during the night.

Happy Families

Parents should try to create a sleep plan that helps them cope with a newborn. Napping when the baby sleeps (in order to chip away at their own sleep deficit), working out who will take care of which tasks and making sure they support their own wellbeing with good-quality herbal and vitamin supplements (should their attention to their diets prove haphazard) are all essential at easing this initial period of stress. In the current climate, often both parents work and require enough rest to function in their daily tasks, and they'll both want to be in top form to be able to care for their child well. How to best provide for the needs of the whole family is always in constant debate, but research does show some interesting results for finding the best solution for everyone.

Helping Newborns Sleep

Studies have shown that babies who are breastfed spend more time in deep sleep with a lower pulse rate, compared with bottle-fed babies. Of course, many factors are involved when faced with the issue of feeding, so breastfeeding is not always a possible choice for the parent. However, parents can help the development of the circadian rhythm in a child by using light cues; a bright room in the morning and a dim one at night helps, as does a regular feeding schedule (small bellies mean that they need a new feed every four to five hours). Always avoid unnecessary stimulation such as turning on bright overhead lights, playing games or chatting away during the evening hours; it might relieve the tedium for you, but it will drag a baby even further into the waking world and inhibit a swift return to slumber.

If your newborn is having serious problems sleeping, you may want to consult a doctor to see if an allergy to the environment, or even the type of milk you are using, exists. Another major problem is colic. Occurring as frequently as one in every five babies, this condition has definite symptoms, but the cause is still not known, although it is thought to be connected to delayed development in the bowel. As night-time approaches, children with colic often can have recurring agitated crying and screaming attacks, which can last for hours at a time, and they can frequently reawaken during the night and cannot seem to be comforted. Fortunately, most babies outgrow colic by four months (although children who have suffered from colic are more likely to suffer from sleep disturbances later in childhood).

Three to Six Months

A child that falls asleep on its own is more likely to go back to sleep on its own if it wakes during the night. Placing a drowsy child in a cot will also help the child feel comfortable drifting off in that environment, rather than relying on parents' soothing. Your child may also be teething at this age; a good trick is to keep a cloth under your baby's head while it sleeps, to catch the excessive drool caused by this process. That way you can make a swift change during the night, swapping cloths rather than the whole sheet and cutting down on the disturbance.

Six Months to Toddler

A child that is 6 months old should sleep about 11 hours a night, with a substantial nap during the day. This is the time that many parents want to implement a set routine. Don't give a child too many 'conditions' for sleep if you want them to achieve a 'return to rest' more easily; if they associate a certain combination of toys, songs, milk or rocking in the arms of a parent as necessary for achieving slumber, it will become impossible for them to do without these aids.

The most famous and widely used technique is the Ferber Method. This was devised by Richard Ferber of the Boston Children's Hospital in the 1970s. His work was based on the idea that we are not born with the ability to soothe ourselves back to sleep after a night-time awakening, but must learn it as a skill. Parents who concur with Ferber begin the process when a child is roughly six months old, at a stage when they are thought to be physically and emotionally able to cope. (At this age a child should not need a night-time feed.) When a child awakens, the parent is instructed to enter the room and verbally comfort the child, but offer no physical soothing, then leave the room, regardless of whether or not the child is still crying. If the child still cries, the parent returns 5 minutes later and repeats the process. Next time, the parent waits 10, then 15 minutes. On the first night, the longest wait period is 15 minutes for any crying session. The following night, the parents add 5 minutes onto any waiting time; so the periods are 10, 15 and 20 minutes. This continues over a period of several nights, usually two or three, by which time the child should be able to self soothe. Although hard on the heartstrings and ears of the parents, for many families it can be a truly productive exercise. Ferber's theory is expounded in his book *Solve Your Child's Sleep Problems*. Alternatively, some parents choose to keep their child sleeping in bed with them indefinitely; this is called co-sleeping.

At this time, some children can also start to display separation anxiety and they may wake up even more during the night, and do anything to delay bedtime. This can also appear later in their development when a child understands that there is only one of you, and they will do anything to keep you close. Being calm, consistent and saying a loving but clear goodnight, rather than sneaking out of the room, can help the child adjust. A move, new sibling or a change in childcare can all be a trigger, but for some children the cause may never be clear. Despite how upsetting it can be, childcare experts agree that it is usually best not to indulge the child with too much attention, therefore 'rewarding' their tactics.

Bad Dreams and Night Terrors

For some children bad dreams and night terrors can become a problem. A night terror (also known as a parasomnia, Latin for 'near sleep', and associated with deep REM sleep) will find a child waking in the night screaming or shouting as if they are awake, although they will go back to sleep and have no recollection of the experience the following day. Sleepwalking is also part of this category. Although it can be scary to witness, your child is not suffering and is actually sleeping through it. Most children grow out of it by the age of seven.

Nightmares occur mainly during REM sleep. Children suffer from them more than adults, and can be very distressed by them, especially as they may be unable to distinguish between reality and the dream. Many children grow out of them by adolescence, but a recurring nightmare could be a sign of stress or anxiety. Nightmares are commonplace when a house move, divorce or other major change has occurred.

ADVICE FOR NIGHTMARES

- Offer comfort, but do not overstimulate the child, and encourage them to get back to sleep as quickly as possible.
- Younger children who can't understand the concept of dreaming may need a cuddle and soothing voice. Older children should be encouraged to talk it through so you can dispel their fears.
- A night light may help with fear of the dark, allowing children to soothe themselves back to sleep.
- With a recurring nightmare, an older child may benefit from talking the dream through during the day and then being encouraged to change the ending to something more comforting or benign. This can actually help change the sequence of events the next time the dream is revisited.
- Avoid overstimulating television shows and books before bed.

Devising a Bedtime Routine

Establishing a soothing sleep routine as early as possible is essential. The same events, such as bathing and stories, carried out in the same order every night, are a clear signal to a child that bedtime approaches, allowing them to wind down naturally. It is important that children of different ages have different bed times; try not to let the younger child's bedtime drift towards that of an older sibling. Research shows that tired children underperform at school, are more likely to get into trouble and are more temperamental. Winning a battle at this time could save you from several the next day.

This simple routine can be used to easily guide your child from the transition of a fun-packed day to a restful night's sleep. Make sure the room is quiet and at a comfortable temperature – 18°C (65°F) is optimum. A night light will comfort, but also allow you to attend any night-time awakenings without switching on a more powerful light. Make sure you don't allow the child to watch television up until the time you expect them to go to bed; they won't be able to make the transition from stimulation to rest that quickly. And avoid the temptation to put a TV in their room or let them take their phone, Kindle, iPad, laptop, etc with them; this can send them mixed messages about what the bedroom is for – they need to see it as a place to rest.

- Make bedtime the same time every night, alerting your child, or children, 30 minutes and then 10 minutes beforehand.
- Give your child a light snack, avoiding sugar or anything hard to digest. Don't give your baby or toddler a bottle (breast milk, formula, or any sugar-containing drink) to help him or her fall asleep. This can cause 'baby bottle tooth decay' because the fluids tend to pool in the baby's mouth.
- A warm bath will help lower your child's temperature, making them drowsy.
- Put them in warm pyjamas after their bath so they feel cozy and comforted.
- Brush teeth.
- Read a story, but agree a maximum number, such as a two-book limit.
- Anticipate your child's last-minute requests, such as for a drink of water or a night-light, and incorporate them into the routine.
- Tuck your child into their beds, to promote a feeling of security and comfort.
- Say goodnight, tell him or her you'll be back to check on them in five minutes, and leave. They should be asleep by the time you return.

SCHOOL-AGE CHILDREN AND PRETEENS

Children ages 8 to 12 need a little over 9 hours a night. A child at this age shouldn't need a daytime nap; in fact, children of this age should enjoy the ideal mix of total alertness and high energy during the day and a full, deep nourishing sleep at night. If your child does seem drowsy, try the Sleep Latency Test on page 13. Like adults, some children need more rest than others, and identifying this will help you set a relevant bedtime.

Overtired children often exhibit exhaustion by excessive energy, grouchiness and tantrums. Some sleep experts, such as William C Dement, who has created the esteemed Sleep Center at Stanford University, California, and launched the American Sleep Disorders Association, believes that some cases of ADHD (Attention Deficit Hyperactivity Disorder) are misdiagnosed; these children are simply excessively tired, and this manifests itself in a very similar way to ADHD.

Children with ADHD — a common behavioural disorder — act without thinking, find it difficult to focus or pay attention and are hyperactive. Boys are about three times more likely than girls to suffer from it. It can affect a child's family relationships and those with society in general, although improved understanding and treatment can provide great results. Treatment usually takes the form of medication and behavioural therapy. A doctor will need to diagnose the child with having the syndrome, and may make a referral to a neurologist, psychologist or psychiatrist. Many children can be fidgety or lack focus, but a child with ADHD displays these symptoms constantly and has problems controlling their behaviour without professional help. A child who has recently experienced a house move, separation of parents or other emotional disturbance may exhibit similar symptoms, but these should be temporary. Children with ADHD may also suffer from difficulties such as anxiety, and about half of all children with ADHD also have a specific learning disability such as dyslexia, which can add to their frustrations.

There are two main categories of ADHD, although a child may exhibit symptoms from both of them. Those with the 'inattentive' type may find it difficult to pay attention to details or they may produce sloppy schoolwork. They might find it difficult to follow instructions, be forgetful or seem distracted.

A 'hyperactive-impulsive' type can often be found fidgeting, always running or climbing, talking excessively and often interrupting others. It is important that these children are shown understanding and are diagnosed correctly in order to help manage their symptoms. Children who do suffer from ADHD can experience a worsening of their symptoms if they don't get enough sleep.

Bedwetting

The American Academy of Child and Adolescent Psychiatry suggests that 15 per cent of three year olds wet the bed, which is also known as 'nocturnal enuresis'. Boys are more prone to do it than girls, and the problem can be a result of late development in bladder control, constipation or increased urine production. It is often hereditary. One way of controlling the problem is for the child to wear an alarm in their underwear which triggers as soon as the child begins to urinate – this can help train them to wake up. Plastic under the base sheet and on top of the mattress can help contain the mess if an accident occurs.

Limiting fluids, encouraging urination before bed and waking them in the night for a toilet trip will also help curb the problem. The most important thing is to avoid making the child ashamed because the child may become more anxious, which leads to broken sleep. No child wants to wake up in a cold, wet bed, so reassurance is key; almost all kids grow out of it relatively quickly. For persistent cases, seek help from a healthcare professional.

TEENAGERS

When it comes to sleep patterns, teenagers are often the most maligned of family members, with their desire to stay up all night and in bed all day, usually with important exams and commitments looming (which worried parents feel may dictate their whole future). In reality, adolescents need about 8 to 9½ hours of sleep per night, with this amount increasing as they make their way through their teens. But part-time jobs, homework and maintaining their ever-important social network eats into those essential hours. A bad-tempered, argumentative teenager will only become more difficult operating with a sleep deficit. Lack of focus, tolerance and comprehension can all affect their performance at school and a lack of sleep has been linked with increased outbursts of aggression and substance abuse.

Adolescents also experience a change in their sleep patterns in that their bodies want to stay up late, which often leads to them trying to catch up on sleep at the weekend. This is not purely designed to irritate parents; a shift in the circadian rhythm occurs at this time, making them stay up later. Although teenagers tend to be 'owls', by their thirties many become 'larks' (see page 11). Hormones are making radical changes to the teenage body, with the cerebral cortex undergoing development, and are creating sudden sexual interest.

Ideally, a teenager would go to bed at the same time every night and wake up at the same time every morning, allowing for at least 8 to 9 hours of sleep. It may seem impossible to legislate for your teenager's behaviour, but trusting them to be in charge of their own sleep patterns may not be the best solution. Encouraging a consistent waking time, explaining how lack of sleep affects mood and discouraging stimulants such as late-night TV, mobile phones, computer games, caffeine drinks and sugar will all help them see sleep as an essential part of wellbeing. In the same way that removing gadgets and distractions from an adult room helps make it a restful environment, do the same for the teenager, making sure these temptations aren't part of their sleep space (see also page 55). A mind struggling to sleep will be too tempted to switch on the Internet and while away the hours if it is clearly in view. Instilling in them the value of (and respect for) sleep can affect the quality of the rest of their lives.

THE WOMEN IN OUR LIVES: MOTHERS, DAUGHTERS, SISTERS

A woman's hormonal cycle will affect the quality of her sleep and the sleep of those around her throughout her life. The menstruation cycle, as any woman can tell you, can make her incredibly tired, whether before, during or just after her period. The American National Sleep Foundation released a poll that shows women's sleep quality is vastly affected by their cycle, with 71 per cent of women reporting that cramping, bloating, headaches and tender breasts disrupted their sleep during their period. Hormones causing changes in body temperature can also make sleep difficult.

Pregnancy has a huge effect on the way women sleep. In the same poll, 79 per cent reported more sleep disturbances at this time, and had an increased frequency of daytime sleepiness. The inability to get comfortable, the need to urinate more often and a kicking baby with no sense of the circadian rhythm can all add up to a restless night. Scientist Paul Martin records that pregnant women get only 5 per cent slow-wave sleep a night, compared to the average 25 per cent slow-wave sleep in normal adult sleep. Women also experience more dream sleep. A partner may be surprised to find that the woman suddenly becomes a snorer, which can have serious health implications for both mother and child, such as an increased tendency to high blood pressure and pre-eclampsia. A doctor's advice should be sought immediately as help, such as special breathing masks, can relieve symptoms quickly.

Insomnia is often regarded as a key symptom of menopause, which most women begin at around 50 years of age. Hot flashes, increased need to urinate, disordered breathing, mood disorders and other hormone-related changes all diminish good quality sleep. Oestrogen-replacement therapy or hormone-replacement therapy can help relieve symptoms, which tend to last a year but in some cases can last up to five, although there have been health concerns regarding their use (such as increased risk of breast cancer). Oestrogen is very effective for women suffering from menopausal insomnia, reducing the time it takes to fall asleep and decreasing the number of night-time awakenings. Some women prefer to use nutritional supplements such as calcium, vitamin D, soy products (which contain phytoestrogen, a plant compound similar to oestrogen), evening primrose oil, black cohosh and ginseng. Bear in mind, though, that herbal products are now banned by the NHS as a misuse of resources.

When experiencing menopause, or supporting someone who is, it is important to eat healthy meals, avoiding spicy or acidic foods that can trigger hot flashes. Keep the bedroom well ventilated and cool, and get professional help with anxiety or depression, which are treatable symptoms and do not have to be suffered quietly. Relaxation techniques, such as those on pages 60–63, can help reduce tension.

MIDDLE AGE AND PARTNER SLEEP

Although many of us will sleep with a partner at different stages of our lives, it is in middle age that most of us find this particular experience most challenging. The manifold pressures exerted upon us in middle age, from children, elderly parents, work and social responsibilities plus health challenges, all come at a time when we probably need our sleep most. Middle-aged and elderly women suffer the most from insomnia, and it's easy to understand why. Worry, an increase in snoring and sleep apnoea in partners, and the effects of menopause can all erode precious slumber.

Sharing a bed with a partner means that whatever sleep challenges they may be facing,you will, too. You may simply be an owl and your partner a lark (see page 11), which can make your

MIDDLE-AGE
WEIGHT GAIN CAN
ALSO INCREASE THE
NARROWING OF THE THROAT,
WHICH INCREASES THE
CHANCE AND SEVERITY OF
SNORING IN BOTH SEXES.

schedules difficult to reconcile (although with age we all drift towards lark tendencies). Understanding that neither partner is wilfully trying to be difficult, but rather that it is simply a predisposition, can help ease tensions.

Relieving the Tension
The best way to tackle such problems is to set aside fear of offending each other and be frank. Talk through the challenges you may now face: the following is a suggestion of possible solutions.

- Snoring is not a state that needs to be accepted by either party; through exercise, cutting back on alcohol and smoking and adopting a sensible diet, symptoms can be greatly relieved.
- Women (who are not experiencing menopause) tend to get colder at night than men; duvets that are warmer on one half than the other are available, or use separate coverings.

- Explore the possibility of buying a bigger bed with a mattress division (so you effectively each have your own mattress), which will allow you both to move freely without disturbing your partner.
- Illnesses, such as fibromyalgia, or conditions like menopause, can also make sleep difficult, as can the medication that accompanies them. Be prepared to return to your doctor and discuss alternatives. You may have been given a convenient popular medication, but be better suited to an alternative.
- Busy schedules and stress can eat into sleep through worrying. Write down all your concerns and schedule challenges and see what you can practically address, and what are just late-night fears. As well as helping you feel more in control, this will allow you to see if you have real room for practical improvement (such as a redistribution of chores) or have anxiety and relaxation issues.
- Make changes work. Some changes, such as the tendency towards 'larkness' and the reduction of hours needed to sleep, are a natural part of ageing. Perhaps the best way to deal with these changes is through acceptance; changing a schedule to take advantage of the peaceful morning hours to work or do chores can help make the most of your time and alleviate frustration. However, excessive daytime tiredness is not normal and should not be accepted as such. See your doctor if you feel particularly sleepy or fatigued during the day.

OLD AGE

As we know, babies spend at least 50 per cent in REM sleep, normal adults 25 per cent and in this later stage of life, these figures drop to only 15 to 20 per cent in the dreaming state. Older people also sleep less, which is thought to be linked to the drop-off in production of the growth hormone, and in the production of melatonin as we age. The amount of Stage Four deep refreshing sleep (see also pages 10–12), is also reduced drastically. Most of our sleep in later years is shallower, which can also lead to more night-time awakenings.

Despite less REM sleep, senior citizens are much more likely to remember their dreams because they waken more often in the night. Sleep scientist Paul Martin suggests that as we enter old age, we lose roughly half an hour of night-time sleep every 10 years. A study performed by America's Stanford University found that of a sample of adults from 65 to 88, 40 per cent suffered from 'micro-arousals', awakenings lasting seconds, between 200 to 1,000 times a night. This was shown to have a direct relationship to daytime sleepiness. A short afternoon nap, however, has been shown to greatly improve alertness and mental performance; although you should experiment with naps to see what works. A short nap during the early afternoon works best; however, avoid napping altogether for a while to see if the naps could be the cause of poor night-time sleep.

Medication for various illnesses associated with ageing can often cause insomnia as a side effect, so speaking to a doctor should be the first step, in case a simple change in prescription can help. Lavender has been shown to have exceptional results for helping the elderly overcome sleeplessness, and can be applied in drops on a pillow. Other age-related sleep difficulties are Restless Legs Syndrome, sleep apnoea, and Periodic Limb Movements in Sleep, disturbing for a sufferer and their partner, all of which can be treated if diagnosed (see pages 20–21).

Taking control

Do a lifestyle stock take: review coffee, alcohol and nicotine intake because they can all be much more stimulating to an older person than to someone in their twenties. Stick to a rigid waking time, even if you have had a difficult night, and include some exercise early in the day, which will improve your mood, rest and general heath. A partner's illness may have made them a cause of disruption, or a beloved pet could be mouse-chasing in the middle of the night, causing awakenings. Make sure your room temperature is correct; we become more sensitive to temperature as we sleep. Ask yourself if anything has changed recently which could be a cause. A poll carried out by the American National Sleep Foundation found a direct link between good sleep and a positive outlook and life experience in the elderly, and that those lacking in vital rest often suffered from undiagnosed sleep problems. Getting help could transform the quality of your waking hours as well as your slumber.

SLEEP-AID PROGRAMMES

ALTHOUGH THE CAUSES OF INSOMNIA AND SLEEP-RELATED PROBLEMS ARE VARIED, THERE ARE SEVERAL COMMON METHODS TO GETTING YOUR SLEEP BACK ON TRACK.

Here you will find three suggested programmes — one addressing stress and anxiety caused by daytime events, one for relieving persistent night-time awakenings, and one for a weekend catch-up to help put your sleep routine back on track.

You may prefer to devise your own tailor-made pre-sleep regime that includes writing in a journal or performing yoga, breathing or meditation exercises (see pages 60–63). Music is a great relaxer and can be used to supplement meditation and relaxation techniques; try nature sounds, mood music or light classical or jazz, but avoid anything with lyrics or spoken words or that is too loud or disharmonic, which will only serve to keep your mind stimulated.

TOUGH-DAY SLEEPLESSNESS SOLUTION

Some days we all find ourselves at home with a racing mind and an anxious to-do list, with a much-needed restorative slumber an impossibility. This usually means we find ourselves lying awake in the dark, trapped in a cycle of worrying about our inability to sleep. Try this relaxing 90-minute programme to speed the onset of sleep, leaving you refreshed and able to start the next day energized and with a rebalanced outlook.

Step One

At the end of your active day, turn off your phone and switch on low lights around your home, including the bathroom (hard, overhead task lighting will not allow you to relax). Let your body adjust to the new lighting, encouraging melatonin production, and play soothing music. Especially useful are CDs specifically created for inducing sleep or deep relaxation. Have a warm bath and add five drops of mandarin or lavender essential to the water (see pages 57–58 for other excellent options). Leave the doors and windows closed to allow the atmosphere to become fragrant and steamy. Place a soft towel and bathrobe over a radiator to warm, and place a pen and note pad by the tub. While the bath is running, prepare and enjoy a snack, such as a wholemeal sandwich of banana and peanut butter, or turkey and lettuce with a glass of warm milk and honey. (See pages 38–41 for other foods that aid rest.)

Step Two

Return to the bathroom, where you need to soak for at least 30 minutes to allow the relaxing essential oils to work on your system. In the first few minutes in the tub, use the pen and paper to draw a list with three columns; tomorrow, one week, one month. Writing each task under the relevant time frame will help you see what you really have to deal with. Once you have written out your tasks, circle each one that you can delegate or ask for help with (can you have your shopping delivered or ask a colleague to help source information for a report?). Write out your real to-do list for the morning and put it to one side. Enjoy the remaining time in the water. After your bath, dress in comfortable, loose sleepwear that makes you feel relaxed.

Step Three

Your body and mind need 30 to 60 minutes to wind down. Go to a comfortable, warm room and, in low light, try the following breathing method to help the body and mind release tension and worry.

Sit upright in a firm and comfortable chair. Begin to breathe in a slow, regular way (see also pages 61–62 on developing breathing techniques), concentrating on the inhale and exhale sensation. Now think of two words, such as 'calm' and 'relax', which equate 'rest' to you. When you breathe in, say one word in your mind, and as you expel the air, think of the other. Repeat for 5 to 10 minutes. The technique will help banish other, worrisome thoughts that are hard to release with conscious effort. The more you practise and run through these steps, the more readily your body will respond; you are creating your own relaxation 'trigger'.

Step Four

Move to your bedroom and get into bed. Lie on your back in the Corpse position (see page 63) and begin some positive visualization to calm a racing heart and mind. Imagine a scene dear to you in which you were completely relaxed, perhaps on a winter holiday in a rustic ski chalet, lying on an old couch. Imagine the smell of the burning wood on the fire, then the sensation of the threadbare couch fabric, comfy underneath you. Then imagine the drowsy heat from the fire. Focus on different details and sensations in the scene, feeling yourself gradually relax. It may be that your ideal scene draws on a memory such as a picnic or a beach outing – just choose somewhere that you felt safe, happy and rested. This visualization technique should lull you off to sleep.

As another aid, create an 'emergency relaxation kit' consisting of a notepad, pen, essential oils or fragrant candles, self-massage tools and a music CD, which you can pull out after a harassed day for 30 minutes of instant relief. Make sure you maintain the kit so you don't find yourself turning the house upside-down for missing components, and always keep it in the same place so you're not searching for it every time, further adding to your stress.

NIGHT-TIME AWAKENING PROGRAMME

Night-time awakenings can be very distressing and isolating. It is essential to create a system to help manage these jolts, as they can rapidly become a source of great discomfort, resulting in excessive daytime sleepiness. The first thing to appreciate is that everyone has night-time awakenings, several times a night, but usually they are so brief we have no recollection of them.

Step One

First, make sure you go to bed when you are sleepy; we often force ourselves to bed feeling tired, but the fatigued body is kept awake by a mind racing with dramas we have just seen on TV, in a brightly lit environment, not allowing the ourselves the preparation for sleep. Avoid daytime naps – no matter how tempting – if you are having this problem, to ensure you are truly tired. Some night-time awakenings can be caused by hunger and can be easily resolved; try a small meal 30 minutes before bed. It should be easy to digest, such as a glass of warm milk with nutmeg and honey.

Step Two

Some people wake with a jolt of panic or fear, a sudden adrenaline rush that pulls them into consciousness. The relaxation technique here was devised by Michael Krugman, founder of the Sounder Sleep System. After years of studying arts such as yoga, qigong and meditation, Krugman devised a system called 'mini moves™', which is based on breathing and visualization techniques and which helps achieve a state of deep relaxation and deep sleep. This adaptation is ideal for returning to sleep after a late night awakening.

1 **Lie on your back in bed in a comfortable position, with a pillow under your head. Become aware of your breathing; is it anxious and laboured or are you feeling calm? Krugman calls this 'breath surfing'. Keep concentrating on your breathing until you feel completely focused on the sensation.**

2 **Move into the 'home position' by bending your arms at the elbows, still allowing the upper arm to rest comfortably by your side, and then place your hands – palms open, fingers slightly apart, thumbs wherever comfortable – on your**

NIGHT-TIME AWAKENING PROGRAMME CONT

chest, on either side of your sternum, tips of the fingers resting on the sternum. Everything should feel comfortable and loose.

3 Observe the movements of your breath, the rise and fall of your chest, feeling through your fingers.

4 Tune into the area underneath your thumbs. Slowly, begin to lift your thumbs a tiny way from your chest as your chest rises to inhale. Lower them as you exhale.

5 Synchronize your breathing and thumbs so each lift and breath corresponds in duration.

6 Stop, rest and feel. The anxiety should be gone, and your breathing fuller. Krugman says this practice will 'stimulate your body-mind's ability to sleep'. You may drift in a dreamlike state before nodding off.

Step Three

If you are still unable to return to sleep, get up, tidy the sheets and move to another room. You must avoid stimulating activities such as work and watching TV. Reading by lamplight, so that your body still appreciates that it is night, can soothe the mind, but avoid murder mysteries or anything over-stimulating. Repetitive tasks can help lull the mind back to sleep, or looking at a photography book such as rural landscape scenes with quiet music or nature sounds in the background can help. When you feel drowsy, and not before, return to bed. Repeat the 'mini moves'. Your body must associate only sleep with the bedroom. Avoid looking at a clock, but if you are still awake after what feels like 20 minutes, get up again and repeat.

Step Four

Despite a difficult night, get up at the same time. A regular wake time is essential for good rest, and trains the body to return to its natural pattern.

REJUVENATING WEEKEND
REST PROGRAMME

As a matter of mental, physical and emotional health, we should all try to set a day a month aside to catch up on our sleep and neglected needs. This plan will help you enjoy a calm, relaxed day to help you unwind and attain a rejuvenating night's sleep.

Step One: Preparation

Choose a day when you don't work. Make sure to stock up on the recommended foods beforehand to prevent you from grabbing sugar-packed fuel, which will give you energy and mood spikes, and also eliminate the need to enter a busy and stressful supermarket on your 'recharge' day. Let friends and family know you are not available, unplugging the phone and leaving your computer and emails safely switched off. Try taking some gentle exercise such as a long walk or swim, as exercise is shown to improve sleep quality, but make sure you do this in the earlier part of the day (too near bedtime and you become overstimulated and unable to rest). Try booking a treat such as a massage or facial. If you are excessively tired, you may find yourself low at mid afternoon during your daytime circadian dip. Do something enjoyable that you rarely have the chance to do, like watch an old black-and-white film, but try to avoid napping. This is a day of reward and nourishment, so a glass of wine with dinner is fine, but limit it to that; more will destroy sleep quality, as will stimulants such as cigarettes and caffeine. Keep yourself hydrated by drinking at least 2 litres (3¹/2 pints) of water throughout the day.

Step Two: Diet

Choose food that will keep energy levels balanced all through the day, which will help you feel at peace and reduce the risk of an afternoon nap, keeping you awake later.

Breakfast Choose slow-release carbohydrates such as an egg on brown or wholemeal toast or porridge. Try to avoid caffeine, but if you feel unable to start your day without it make this your one cup, in order for it to leave your system by mid afternoon. Change to camomile tea throughout the rest of the day.

Lunch Include lean protein, such as fish, poultry or red meat, or soya, and green leafy vegetables; this will deliver a boost of vitamin B, great for combating the effects of a stressful week.

Dinner This should occur at least two hours before bed and include carbohydrates such as brown pasta, rice or potatoes, pasta and lean protein, with a salad packed with healing antioxidants. A small glass of mandarin or orange juice can also act as a sedative. Avoid spicy foods or excess sugar.

Step Three: Bathtime

Before bed, dissolve two cups of Epsom salts in a warm bath. The salts will help rid you of any of the toxins accumulated from previously eating and drinking excessively, and also relax the muscles. The salts can, however, leave the skin dry, so do moisturize well after your bath. You may like to add a few drops of bath oil to counteract the dehydrating effects of the salt. Those with skin complaints or high blood pressure should check with their doctor first. After your soak, dress in loose, comfortable nightwear.

Step Four: Massage

Move to your bed or a comfortable chair, using only a low light source, and try this self-massage technique for releasing tension from your head, neck and shoulders. The scalp especially can hold a great deal of tension. Think of the sensation in the forehead, when furrowing the brow or raising the eyebrows, which we often do when stressed.

Place the three middle fingers of each hand at the front centre of your hairline. Making firm circular movements, move in a straight line along the scalp down the back of your head to the hairline at the back. Move back towards the front, working your way gradually outwards until your whole scalp has been manipulated. End the massage by kneading the whole scalp rhythmically and softly.

Enjoy a relaxing read or listen to peaceful music, and when you feel tired, make your way to bed. Have a restful sleep that will help prepare you for the week ahead.

KEEPING *a* SLEEP JOURNAL

KEEPING A DAILY JOURNAL DOCUMENTING YOUR SLEEP AND LIFESTYLE HABITS WILL HELP YOU UNDERSTAND YOUR TRIGGERS FOR POOR SLEEP AND IDENTIFY PATTERNS THAT STAND BETWEEN YOU AND GETTING A GOOD NIGHT'S REST.

Answer the questions for the morning chart directly after waking up, and fill in the evening chart before you go to sleep. Getting enough sleep allows you to fight off disease, feel refreshed and able to function well during the day, and helps your powers of concentration and memory. If you continue to have trouble sleeping, take the record of your journal to your doctor for advice.

WEEKLY SLEEP JOURNAL: MORNING

Day	1	2	3	4	5	6	7
What time did you first go to bed last night?							
How long did it take you to fall asleep?							
How many times did you wake during the night?							
How many hours did you sleep?							
At what time did you wake up?							
How did you feel when you woke up? (a) refreshed (b) neutral (c) tired							

WEEKLY SLEEP JOURNAL: EVENING

Day	1	2	3	4	5	6	7
Did you nap during the day?							
Did you consume any coffee or alcohol?							
How would you rate your daytime function? (a) energetic (b) somewhat energetic (c) neutral (d) somewhat tired (e) lethargic							

NOTES

RECOMMENDED
READING
and
RESOURCES

Caldwell, Paul J., *Sleep: The Complete Guide to Sleep Disorders and A Better Night's Sleep*, Firefly, 2003.

Choudry, Bikram with Bonnie Jones Reynolds, *Bikram's Beginning Yoga Class*, Thorsons, 2003.

Clarke, Jane, *Jane Clarke's Body Foods Cookbook*, Cassell, 2000.

Dement, William C., *The Promise of Sleep*, Pan, 2001.

Hillard, Elizabeth, *Brilliant Colour at Home*, Kyle Cathie, 1999.

Holford, Patrick, *Patrick Holford's New Optimum Nutrition Bible*, Piatkus, 2004.

Idzikowski, Chris, *The Expert Guide to Sleeping Well*, Watkins, 2019.

Kryger, Meir H., Thomas Roth Thomas and William C. Dement, *Principles and Practice of Sleep Medicine*, 6th edition, W.B Saunders Company, 2016.

MacEoin, Beth, *The Total De-Stress Plan*, Carlton, 2002.

Martin, Paul, *Counting Sheep*, Harper Collins, 2002.

Ryman, Daniel, *Aromatherapy Bible*, Piatkus, 2002.

Walker, Matthew, *Why We Sleep: The New Science of Sleep and Dreams*, Allen Lane, 2017.

RESOURCES

Worldwide
Sleepio: www.sleepio.com

United Kingdom
Asthma UK
18 Mansell Street
London, E1 8AA
Helpline: 0300 222 5800
Email: info@asthma.org.uk
Website: www.asthma.org.uk

Awake Ltd
14 Paterson Drive
Leicestershire, LE12 8RL
Tel: 01509 891 162
Email: louise.reyner@sleepresearch.co.uk
Website: www.awakeltd.info

Allergy UK
Planwell House
LEFA Business Park
Edgington Way, Sidcup
Kent, DA14 5BH
Allergy Helpline:
01322 619898
Email: info@allergyuk.org
Website: www.allergyuk.org

Association of
Reflexologists,
Victoria House, Victoria
Street, Taunton, Somerset

TA1 3FA
Tel: 01823 351010
Email: info@aor.org.uk
Website: www.aor.org.uk

Association of Traditional Chinese Medicine
Brentano House, Unit 5
The Exchange, Brent Cross
Gardens, London, NW4 3RJ
Tel: 020 8457 2560
Email: info@atcm.co.uk
Website: www.atcm.co.uk

BackCare
69–71 Windmill Road
Sunbury-on-Thames
TW16 7DT
Tel: 020 8977 5474
Email: info@backcare.org.uk
Website:
www.backcare.org.uk

British Acupuncture Council
63 Jeddo Road
London W12 9HQ
Tel: 020 8735 0400
Website:
www.acupuncture.org.uk

British Complementary
Medicine Association
PO Box 5122
Bournemouth, BH8 0WG
Tel: 0845 345 5977
Email: office@bcma.co.uk
Website: www.bcma.co.uk/

British Sleep Society
c/o Executive Business
Support, City Wharf
Davidson, Lichfield
WS14 9DZ
Tel: 01543 442156

Email:
admin@sleepsociety.org.uk
Website:
www.sleepsociety.org.uk

British Snoring and Sleep
Apnoea Association
Precision House
Lamdin Road
Bury St Edmunds
IP32 6NU
Tel: 01284 717688
Email:
info@britishsnoring.co.uk
Website:
www.britishsnoring.co.uk

The British Wheel of Yoga
25 Jermyn Street, Sleaford,
Lincolnshire NG34 7RU
Tel: 01529 306851
Email: office@bwy.org.uk
Website: www.bwy.org.uk

Cry-sis
BM Cry-Sis, London
WC1N 3XX
Helpline: 08451 228669
Email: info@cry-sis.org.uk
Website: www.cry-sis.org.uk
Support for families with
excessively crying, sleepless
and demanding babies.

European Herbal &
Traditional Medicine
Practitioners Assoctiation
Office 3, 47 St Giles Street
Norwich, NR2 1JR
Email: info@ehpa.eu
Website: www.ehtpa.eu

General Osteopathic Council
Osteopathy House

176 Tower Bridge Road
London SE1 3LU
Tel: 020 7357 6655
Email:
info@osteopathy.org.uk
Website:
www.osteopathy.org.uk

The London Sleep Centre
137 Harley Street
London, W1G 6BF
Tel: 020 7725 0523
Email: info@
londonsleepcentre.com
Website:
londonsleepcentre.com

Millpond Children's Sleep
Clinic
Tel: 020 8444 0040
Website:
millpondsleepclinic.com

Mind - Mental Health
Unit 9, Cefn Coed Parc
Nantgarw, Cardiff
CF15 7QQ
Tel: 0300 123 3393
Email: info@mind.org.uk
Website: www.mind.org.uk

Narcolepsy UK
PO Box 701, Huntingdon
Cambridgeshire, PE29 9LR
Tel: 0345 450 0394
Email:
info@narcolepsy.org.uk
Website:
www.narcolepsy.org.uk

The Royal College of
Psychiatrists
21 Prescot Street
London, E1 8BB

Tel: 020 7235 2351
Website: www.rcpsych.ac.uk

The Shiatsu Society
20-22 Wenlock Road
London, N1 7GU
Tel: 01788 547900
Website:
www.shiatsusociety.org

Sleep Apnoea Trust
PO Box 60, Chinnor
OX39 4XE
Tel: 0800 025 3500
Email:
info@sleep-apnoea-trust.org
Website:
www.sleep-apnoea-trust.org

The Sleep Council
High Corn Mill, Chapel Hill
Skipton, North Yorkshire
BD23 1NL
Tel: 01756 791089
Email:
info@sleepcouncil.org.uk
Website:
www.sleepcouncil.org.uk

The Society of Homeopaths
11 Brookfield, Duncan Close
Moulton Park
Northampton, NN3 6WL
Tel: 01604 817890
Email:
info@homeopathy-soh.org
Website:
www.homeopathy-soh.org

Surrey Sleep Research
Centre
University of Surrey
Egerton Road
Guildford, Surrey

GU2 7XP
Tel: 01483 682502
Email: sleep@surrey.ac.uk
Website: www.surrey.ac.uk

North America
Better Sleep Council
501 Wythe Street
Alexandria, VA 22314–1917
Tel: 703-683-5595
Website:
www.bettersleep.org

Canadian Sleep Society
Tel: (416) 483 6260
Email: info@css-scs.ca
Website: www.css-scs.ca

National Association for
Holistic Aromatherapy
6000 S 5th Ave
Pocatello, ID 83204
Tel: 877 232 5255
Email: info@naha.org
Website: www.naha.org

The National Sleep
Foundation
1522 K Street NW, Suite 500
Washington, DC 20005
Tel: 202 347 3471
Email:
nsf@sleepfoundation.org
Website:
www.sleepfoundation.org

Office of Dietary
Supplements, National
Institutes of Health
6100 Executive Blvd,
Room 3B01, MSC 7517
Bethesda, MD 20892–7517
Tel: 301 435 2920
Email: ods@nih.gov

Website:
www.ods.od.nih.gov

Zero Balancing
Health Association
8640 Guilford Road Suite
240, Columbia MD 21046
Tel: 410 381 8956
Email: zbaoffice@
zerobalancing.com
Website:
www. zerobalancing.com

Australia
SomnoMed Australian
Sleep Association
GPO Box 3993
Sydney, NSW 2000
Tel: 1800 445 660
Email: contactaus@
somnomed.com
Website:
www.somnomed.com/au

Australasian Sleep
Association
Tel: +61 2 9920 1968
Email: admin@sleep.org.au
Website: www.sleep.org.au

INDEX